Southern Cross

A NOVEL

by

T. C. Isbell

D1736956

A MYSTERY ALLEY BOOK

First printing
ISBN 978-0-9846610-0-8
ISBN 978-0-9846610-1-5 (Kindle)
ISBN 978-0-9846610-2-2 (Epub)

This fictional work is set within the historical background of events preceding the start of the Second World War. Every attempt has been made to remain true to historical events and the beliefs of the time, however some events and geographical locations may have been fictionalized to enhance and strengthen the plot. All characters appearing in this work are fictitious. Any resemblance to real persons, living or dead, is entirely coincidental. The U-37 was a German U-boat active during the Second World War, however all events in this book referring to the U-37 have been fictionalized.

Cover design by T. C. Isbell

Category: Historical Fiction

For current information about the author, including his next novel, please go to www.MysteryAlley.com.

This book is dedicated to my loving wife, Nancy. Without her support, it would still only be a dream.

ACKNOWLEDGMENTS:

Frank Horton, Mary Clark, Ronnie Way, and Tonia Clark deserve my undying gratitude for their tireless reading and editing of my endless revisions. Thank you for never turning out the porch light.

The magnifying glass of my writers' group can never be replaced. Thanks to Richard Neumann, Clayton King, and Charis Himeda for being honest and supportive.

Many thanks to the following friends for their insightful comments and encouragement: Bob Beecroft, Bill Brown, Mike Lawson, Jan Matheson, and Randy Robinson. If you are not careful, you could find yourself in my next book.

NOTE FROM THE AUTHOR

After reading *Southern Cross*, please take a few moments to write a review and post it with the merchant where you purchased your copy. Written reviews are important to readers and authors alike. A few sentences are all that are needed. Naturally, I hope you will enjoy reading *Southern Cross*, but even if you don't, please provide a review. Thank you, T. C. Isbell

Southern Cross

Chapter One

December 2, 1938
Hamburg, Germany

A rush of apprehension inexplicably shot through Chris Schulte's mind as the key slid past the worn tumblers and the aged brass lock snapped open. Two telegrams lay just beyond the threshold of the darkened studio apartment, but went neglected when the door swept them into an encampment of spiderwebs beneath the rusty cast iron radiator.

Settling into a well-seasoned leather chair, Chris stared into the darkness outside the window as fatigue from a difficult espionage mission in Madrid engulfed the room. The rumblings from the coal furnace in the basement went unnoticed, until a series of loud water hammers shook the steam pipes on the second floor and slammed through the ice-cold radiator. Flinching, Chris turned toward the noise and spotted the half-hidden telegrams.

The first telegram was delivered last Friday and the second two days ago. Drawing in a hesitant breath, Chris carefully tore the edge from the first envelope and fished out the message. It was from Elsa:

WESTERN UNION Nov 23 – New York - Possible unstable business partner. Investigating. E

Elsa wouldn't have made contact except under the gravest of circumstances. Chris rushed over to the floor lamp standing beside the bed and ripped open the second envelope:

WESTERN UNION Nov 29 – New York - Worst fears realized. Trust no one. E

Lighting a cigarette and sloshing the last of the Starka vodka into a water glass, Chris lay back against the bed and studied a picture of Elsa displayed at the rear of the nightstand. Memories of the last night they spent together—her soft touch, the scent of English lavender in her golden hair, and her moist lips—welled up seeming as if they had happened just yesterday.

Damn it. What have you gotten into?

Chris banged the empty glass on the nightstand, and began undressing, but stopped at the thud of hobnailed boots on the stairs and squeaking floorboards in the hallway. The sounds halted abruptly as a heavy fist pounded against the door.

"Telegram for Chris Schulte."

Chapter Two

December 3, 1938
A bar in Germany

The overpowering stench from smoldering cigarette butts and decaying sea life assured no one could mistake the Blue Marlin for a gentlemen's club. The low-life dive in the seediest area of Hamburg's waterfront had a reputation for collecting bodies along with the trash under the pier, keeping all but the most desperate hookers away. The mood in the room was somber and depressed; laughter departed years ago. The Marlin was empty except for the bartender and his solitary customer sitting on a stool in near darkness at the far end of the bar. A row of blood red candles flickered as a cold draft intruded between the worn oaken floorboards. The silence of the night was broken by the roar of waves crashing past the pylons beneath the Marlin.

As if trying to stay as far from his patron as he could, the bartender leaned against the service counter near the front door and watched the sheets of water cascade from the warehouse across the street. Ordinarily he would be seen listening to problems and giving sage advice, but tonight this customer didn't want to talk and did not want counseling.

The lone drinker had sat in the same place for more than two hours without saying a word, holding a crumpled telegram in one hand and a whiskey glass in the other:

> *WESTERN UNION Nov 30 – Baltimore -*
> *Elsa Gable struck by subway train last night*
> *in New York City. Could not claim body.*
> *Condolences, Karl Reinhardt*

It seemed like only yesterday that Chris Schulte and Elsa Gable were children growing up in Hamburg, and now the last link to the past was gone.

Schulte placed the telegram on the bar and pulled out a rosewood and ivory handled stiletto. Studying the intricate inlay pattern, Schulte listened to the pounding waves and felt the pier shudder under their mounting attack. Tonight, nothing was right with the world.

The front door crashed open and a drunk merchant marine staggered in wearing a tattered peacoat and the paint-stained clothes of a deckhand. He stomped his feet and shook the water from his sou'wester as he peered into the dim candlelight.

"I'll serve you over here," the bartender said, gesturing to the sailor while he wiped a spot at the bar near the front door.

The sailor stumbled past the bartender and flopped onto the stool beside Schulte. He reeked of urine and several nights spent sleeping in back alleys. A layer of chewing tobacco encrusted his knotted beard.

"I said . . . I will serve you over here." The bartender wet his lips and motioned toward an empty stool.

"I'll have my drink next to this cute little piss-ant. Gimme a shot a whiskey with a beer chaser and be quick about it," the sailor said in a gravelly voice, revealing rotting black teeth under his untrimmed mustache.

The bartender hesitated and then reluctantly slid a schooner of beer in front of the sailor and started pouring rot-gut whiskey into a shot glass. The sailor snatched the glass from the bartender before he could finish filling it and dropped it into the schooner, causing a rush of beer to spill onto the bar. His hands shook as he swilled the mixture down.

"Hit me again." The sailor slammed his fist on the bar. His lips stayed parted as if he intended to speak, but he remained silent except for the raspy staccato of air oozing through his mouth. He turned toward Schulte and spit a wad of tobacco on the floor.

"Damn Jews are everywhere." He cocked his head and scowled. "You're not a Jew are you?"

Schulte continued to examine the stiletto.

The sailor's nostrils flared and his chest puffed up as he eyed Schulte.

"Effeminate little shitter. No prissy son of a bitch is going to ignore *me*," he mumbled as he wiped his mouth on the sleeve of his peacoat and shifted hard against Schulte. "Say, what have you got there?"

"None of your damn business."

A seven-inch blade snapped out of the stiletto. Schulte shredded the telegram until it was a pile of pulp and snatched a nearby candle from the bar. The flame flickered with the movement and was almost extinguished. Turning the candle sideways, Schulte watched the molten wax drip onto the pile, and then held the burning wick against it, causing the flame to spread.

"Hey, asshole, what the hell ya think you're doing?" the bartender demanded, charging at the flames. Schulte flicked the point of the blade toward the movement.

The bartender stopped cold when the steel blade flashed in the light. Tiny beads of sweat formed and trickled down his brow. His ashen face mirrored a sudden realization of his mortality as he silently withdrew and gazed into the darkness beneath the sink.

Schulte's thoughts returned to Elsa as the symbolic funeral pyre began to char the oaken countertop. The Marlin remained hushed except for the thunder of the waves and a distant ship's bell tolling the hour.

The sailor's gaze shifted to the flames as he continued to gawk with the glazed eyes and dull face of a man who always drank too much and never knew when to shut up.

"Barkeep, set up a beer for my little friend."

"Get out of here and quit staring at me, or I'll cut your eyes out and feed them to the fish," Schulte hissed as the reflection of the last of the yellow-blue flames died out on the silver blade.

Pale smoke from the smoldering embers rose and blended with the smell of stale beer, forming a thin, gray haze that floated listlessly through the room.

The sailor's breath became shallow as he silently pulled back. His hands began to tremble and his eyes darted from side to side, finally focusing on the front door. His fingers groped to pull the change from his pockets and, without counting the coins, he tossed them on the bar.

"Devil damn me for coming in here," he muttered as he lurched toward the front door.

The bartender quickly swept the money into his cashbox. "Hey, you forgot your drink."

"Keep it."

We all make choices, and tonight the sailor made the right one. Some people are killer-crazy; like a coiled snake, they are best left undisturbed. He had been a knife-blade away from his open grave and a second away from eternity. He didn't know it, but he was lucky. Schulte was leaving for America in the morning and didn't feel like killing anyone tonight. Tomorrow might be a different story.

Chapter Three

December 4, 1938
The North Sea

Light from the full moon highlighted the sleek, dark gray shape of a U-boat as it slipped toward the North Sea on a classified mission for the Abwehr, the German intelligence service. The U-37 was commissioned four months earlier under the command of *Korvettenkapitän* Hans Adler. Less than 200 feet long inside, the living conditions onboard were humid and cramped. The smell of diesel fuel covered everything.

Two days ago while on patrol in the North Atlantic, Commander Adler received a message to return to base. As soon as they moored, Chris Schulte boarded with sealed orders from Admiral Dönitz. There would be no shore leave for the crew; their families would not learn of their return to port. There was no time for the crew to shower or change into clean clothes. The U-boat was provisioned and departed within two hours of her arrival. The men knew this mission must be unusual for Abwehr agents rarely traveled by submarine.

As the U-37 entered the North Sea, Commander Adler addressed the watch officer. "You have the con. Continue on the current heading until I return. I intend to learn what this spy wants to do with my boat."

"Aye, I have the con."

As he stepped through the hatch, the commander turned to the executive officer.

"Let's see to our guest."

Lieutenant Klaus Bergman was wearing a standard *Kriegsmarine* grayish-green battle dress uniform and canvas shoes. He was thin with sandy blond hair and tall for someone in the submarine service. He moved through the boat with a permanent kink in his neck, having the uncanny knack of just missing everything protruding from the low overhead. The lieutenant had graduated in the same Neustadt submarine training class as the commander. They had become close friends in school but had served on different submarines until they were reunited as part of the commissioning crew on the U-37.

A crewman braced tightly against the bulkhead as the commander and lieutenant crowded past.

"What do you suppose is so damn important that Dönitz would pull us off patrol?" The commander massaged the back of his neck. "I'll bet we are going to the Americas."

"We might be heading for the Mediterranean, or better yet, we could be going to a Caribbean island where we can enjoy the sun in the daytime and dancing girls at night. I'd love to leave this miserable weather. Anywhere would be better than the North Atlantic in early December."

"Nice dream you have, but I wouldn't sell the farm just yet." The commander stroked his salt-and-pepper beard. "We might end up in Reykjavik where you can forget the sun and the dancing girls. The only place colder would be the Baltic Sea. Please locate and escort our master spy to the radio room." The commander's eyes narrowed. "I want this milk-cow mission finished as soon as possible."

Five minutes later Chris Schulte and Lieutenant Bergman huddled in the cramped passage next to the open radio room door. Schulte handed a sealed envelope to the commander. Removing a code book and cipher key from the safe, the commander began to decode the orders. After several minutes, he put down his pen and cleared his throat.

"We are to proceed at best speed to the East Coast of the United States and transfer you to the beach near Cape May, New Jersey at midnight on the twenty-second of December."

The secrecy surrounding the mission had prevented the commander from learning anything before their departure. The commander paused as he tried to size up Schulte. He had a peculiar feeling about the mission and now he knew why. Their passenger was not what he had expected and was sure to be a problem.

"We'll travel far away from the normal shipping lanes and run on the surface, but at this time of year the boat will pitch and roll. If the sea state becomes too great, we'll dive below the turbulence and run submerged. In that event, our speed will be cut in two, placing the rendezvous at risk."

The commander clasped his hands behind his head and leaned back. "Since I don't expect you have ever been on a submarine before, do you have any questions?"

"No . . ." Schulte hesitated and took a deep breath. "I have no questions."

A week ago the trip seemed like it would be a grand adventure, but now the reality of the last week's events closed in as the U-37 forced her way through an endless onslaught of whitecaps and deep swells. Schulte was isolated, yet at the same time completely surrounded, and acutely aware of each sound the U-37 made as she punched farther into the North Atlantic. The thrashing of the twin props and the roar of the ocean pounding against the hull had become relentless.

The prospect of being covered by tons of seawater in an icy grave made Chris Schulte increasingly uneasy. The close quarters rekindled childhood memories of being trapped in a basement surrounded by death. In the closing months of the Great War Chris' family had sought shelter at an abandoned farm; one night while they slept a mortar round leveled the house. Chris, barely ten years old, had been pinned under a fallen floor beam in the basement and was forced to listen as each family member fought against death—and lost. By the end of the first day the basement had become tomb-quiet and only Chris remained alive. Three days passed before Elsa's father happened upon the devastation.

The incident left Chris with a slight, but noticeable, limp. However, the wounds had cut deeper than skin and bone. They had slashed through the young child's soul leaving nothing but a void where the purity of youth once thrived. Chris Schulte no longer believed in the innate goodness of a world mastered by men.

"Did you hear me?" The commander interrupted Schulte's daydream. "I said . . . you will be using a bunk belonging to the Chief Diesel Officer when he is on watch. I have ordered the men to provide you with as much privacy as possible, but under the circumstances, understand this is the best we can do. As you can see, we don't have personal space; everyone shares living quarters. I have fifty-four men divided into two duty sections in my crew. We live on top of each other twenty-four hours a day, and sometimes it can get annoying. Try to develop a thick skin quickly; if you have any problems, contact Lieutenant Bergman. The section watch officer in the control room can locate him for you."

Schulte leaned through the radio room door. "I do have one question. Does it always smell of diesel fuel on this ship?"

"This is a *submarine* not a *ship*—we *sink* ships." The commander winked. "Sometimes the odors are worse, but you soon won't notice. Fresh water is at a premium when we are deployed. We take cold saltwater showers and, I am sure, the men will not wash as often as you may be used to at home. I hope you brought a good supply of talcum powder and scent. Mister Bergman, escort our guest to meet Chief Bower. Have the chief fill in the details of our daily routine."

The Lieutenant used the intercom and quickly located the chief.

"Please follow me. Watch your head as we move through the spaces. Some equipment hangs low in the overhead, the passages are narrow, and the hatch openings are small, but you'll become used to the interferences and soon be moving through the boat as fast as one of the crew."

As Schulte and the lieutenant started to leave the commander said, "Lieutenant, I want to speak with you after you have delivered our guest."

"Aye, sir."

Rumors and Schulte's demeanor increased the mystery surrounding this agent. No one was ever alone on the U-37. No one. Curious eyes constantly probed every movement.

The crew's surreptitious glances didn't go unnoticed. They only served to deepen the sense of being surrounded by a crush of doomed men beneath a boundless ocean with no escape. While submerged, there was no distant horizon, no sunlight in the day, no stars at night; only the constant procession of watchstanders would signal the passage of time as the U-37 pressed farther into the cold Atlantic.

A layer of pipes, valves, and cables wove through each stark white compartment, binding them and Schulte as securely as a straightjacket. Everything pieced together as tightly as a jigsaw puzzle with no open space, no room to breathe. The atmosphere was heavy and stale like the deepest, darkest bat cave.

Leaking valves were everywhere; moisture covered the overhead and formed drops that randomly tumbled to the deck. Each drop brought Schulte closer to the belief that the ocean would soon crush the U-37. The possibility of being entombed under ten thousand feet of water made the perception of time slow to a crawl. The passing of each minute gave way to another minute longer than the last, making the shores of America and Cape May seem farther away then ever.

"Watch your head when we enter the control room," the lieutenant cautioned. "It is filled with valves and levers that maintain the boat's stability. Do not touch anything."

Just then the U-37 hit a swell and pitched upward causing several drops of condensation to plummet to the deck. Schulte flinched and gazed into the mass of pipes pressing down from above. *Damn it! I hate this place!*

The lieutenant watched the anxiety escalate as they approached the control room. When they stepped through the hatch, Schulte stumbled and reached out for support, seizing the large, red painted handwheel of a valve protruding from the overhead. A shrill siren cut through the sounds in the control room as the boat lurched and shuddered downward.

"*Scheisse!*" The watchstander closest to the valve swore as he ripped Schulte's hand from the handwheel and, spinning it clockwise, shut the valve.

"VB-119C checked shut," the watchstander said, returning to his station.

"Aye, VB-119C checked shut," the watch officer repeated.

The alarm silenced, but the men continued to stare.

"Please be more careful," the lieutenant said. "We were lucky this time. In a few more seconds we would have been in real trouble. I must caution you again to never touch the equipment."

Schulte glowered at the lieutenant. In another time and place the reaction to the reprimand would have been more direct and final.

The lieutenant ignored the intense stare as they exited the control room and made their way aft through the petty officers' berthing and the galley to the engine room. He undogged and swung the engine room hatch open. A torrent of heat and noise rushed past them as they stepped through the opening and stood, compressed between two thundering diesel engines. It was like walking into an oven. The atmosphere in the compartment was laden with a thick oily haze and the piping and deckplates resonated with the pounding of the diesel engines.

The chief glanced up from his work and smiled at the visitors when he heard the heavy hatch slam shut.

"Chief Bower, this is Chris Schulte," the lieutenant yelled over the roar of the engines.

Schulte stood without saying a word looking at the chief and lieutenant, as if in a trance, until a water droplet fell from the overhead. *Will this incessant dripping never quit?* Schulte's muscles tensed, but there was no safe place to hide—no way to elude the ocean's ever tightening grip.

"Chief, I'll leave you to brief our guest about the boat's daily routine," the lieutenant said as he turned to leave. "I have some pressing business."

The commander was still sitting in the radio room when the lieutenant returned.

"Request permission to speak, Sir."

"Permission granted, what is it?" The commander knew the lieutenant must have something important to say for he always spoke formally when he felt what he had to discuss would not sit well.

"I wish we could return to Kiel and leave this Abwehr agent back on the pier. We are not configured to transport civilians. We have been underway for only a short time, and the agent is already edgy."

"That's precisely why I wanted to speak with you. I want someone near our guest at all times. Quietly pass the word to the senior men to be prepared to intervene. The safety of the boat and crew comes first. If need be, we'll use chemical restraints."

"What do you think the mission is?"

"I wouldn't want to guess. After we deposit this spy on the beach in New Jersey, I plan to forget we ever met and you should do the same. The less you know the better. We have value only as long as we contribute to the success of the mission. A word of advice: Don't appear overly interested in this business. It wouldn't be good for your health. These people don't think like us. Their world is black or white consisting of missions and enemies; if you aren't careful, you could become the latter. Do not underestimate this agent—appearances can be deceiving."

"I have already had an unnerving encounter."

"Yes, I am aware of the incident in the control room. Tread lightly. Let's see how uneventful we can make this trip."

The commander and lieutenant exited the radio room and returned to the con to plot the course to Cape May. Winter weather and the distance to New Jersey troubled the commander.

"We will not conduct operational drills during our transit."

"Request permission to speak frankly."

"Permission granted and stop being so damned formal. Klaus, you sound like a midshipman on his first patrol."

"Even though the crew has completed a year of classroom and simulator instruction, I am concerned they have been operating the boat for less than four months. The drills sharpen their response to real emergencies and help relieve the monotony of our daily routine."

"Our guest worries me more. Drills might have an adverse effect by emphasizing the potential for disaster. I trust your instincts, but I have noticed our guest shows signs of claustrophobia. I can't take any chances with our safety or slow the boat's progress. No, we will not conduct drills."

Despite Schulte's presence, the crew settled into a familiar routine as days blended into nights in an unbroken chain of four-hour watches. The arrangement with Chief Bower didn't work, and the chief was forced to find another, less comfortable, place to sleep.

In spite of the closeness of the chief's bunk, Schulte remained behind a makeshift curtain, except for brief excursions to eat and to use the head. The prying eyes of the crew were more intrusive and confining than the solitude of the bunk. Just as Commander Adler had predicted, Schulte did not like traveling in a submarine. If there was a hell, it must be on a diesel submarine in the North Atlantic in December.

Chris Schulte couldn't escape the physical bondage of the submarine. The only choice was to block out the U-37 and its crew and retreat to thoughts of more pleasant times spent growing up with Elsa.

Elsa's family took in Chris after the accident. The two children were the same age and soon became inseparable. However hard Elsa's mother tried, she couldn't break through the emotional barrier. It was obvious Elsa was the only person Chris trusted. Times were difficult, forcing the children to grow up quickly, never experiencing the joys of childhood. Perhaps they became adults much too soon.

Most nights Chris read the classics to Elsa while she wrote in her diary using the secret code they had invented as children. The scent of English lavender from Elsa's perfume always filled the air. Elsa's bright smile and infectious laugh made the darkest days pass without notice. She had a habit of twisting a lock of her long blond hair around a finger as she talked; then suddenly, she would blush as she became self-conscious. Her blue eyes would twinkle as she laughed at herself. Their bond became unbreakable and as they matured they became more than family, more than friends.

After Elsa's parents died, Chris and Elsa shed their secret life and lived in a studio apartment in Hamburg until earlier this year when Elsa was assigned, along with two other Abwehr agents, August Kruger and Anna Hoffmann, to gather intelligence from the Philadelphia Navy Yard. Chris remained in Europe and continued to work with Messerschmitt and Luftwaffe agents as they covertly monitored developing British and French fighter aircraft designs.

Chris stared into the glow from a red light in the passage just outside the chief's bunk and tried to close out the noise—the constant drone that filled every compartment since the U-37 had left Kiel. *August and Anna must have known of your death. Why did this stranger, Karl Reinhardt, contact me?*

Chapter Four

December 22, 1938
Near the Coast of New Jersey

The penetrating yellow beacon from a lighthouse on the point of Cape May tirelessly searched the midnight sky as a melodic foghorn sounded over the roar of waves crashing against the sandy beach. The U-37 edged ever closer to land, shrouded by the darkness of the new moon and a thick marine fog. The surfaced U-boat remained concealed from shore; yet there was the constant danger of passing ships recognizing its dark silhouette against the coastal lights. Tensions ran high; the tide was going out, and the U-37 needed to offload its cargo before getting caught in shallow water with no room to maneuver.

Preparations were nearly complete as three figures dressed in black watch clothes worked on the narrow weather-deck loading a small rubber raft. Flashlight signals from the beach farthest away from the lighthouse indicated it was safe for the raft to come ashore.

"Be quick about it, I don't have time to waste while you three fumble with these damn boxes." Schulte pushed past the working party and stood, scowling down at the raft.

A number of wooden boxes containing radio transmitters destined for agents on the East Coast had already been stowed. A metal case was passed through the hatch from below deck and tossed to the crewman who was packing the raft. He was distracted by Schulte's movement and was caught off-guard. The case struck the back of his hands. It dropped to the deck and careened over the side.

"Damn it!" Schulte glared at the crewman and lunged, just missing the case as it fell into the water.

"Scheisse! Herman, get that case before it sinks," the crewman yelled at the deck watch. Their eyes met in panic. The color drained from the crewman's face as he scrambled from the raft and pointed his flashlight toward the case.

"Turn that light off before someone spots us. What the hell happened?" The deck watch raced to the side with a gaff. He grappled for one of the handles, but only succeeded in bumping the case and pushing it farther away.

"You almost lost it. Give me that damn gaff and hold my hand." The crewman grabbed the pole from the deck watch and stretched precariously over the water. "Just a bit farther."

He moved off the upper deck and onto the curved outer surface of a ballast tank. His leading foot slipped on the damp surface causing him to lose balance and almost pull the deck watch into the frigid water. The gaff bumped the case as they struggled to regain their balance.

"*Macht schnell!*" The deck watch's muscles tightened as beads of sweat formed and dripped from his forehead.

A third crewman linked arms with the deck watch, making a chain. The three men strained to extend toward the case as it was hit by a swell and rolled over.

Schulte's eyes flared in disbelief. "Quick, it's sinking!"

The men extended one last time, fighting to snag the case as it bobbed just out of reach.

"Damn, almost had it." The crewman gripped the end of the pole with one hand and maneuvered forward. The case continued to drift farther away until a second, larger swell rolled past and raised the case toward the submarine enabling the crewman to hook one of its handles.

The crewman hoisted the case onto the deck and, turning toward Schulte, smiled with relief. He picked up the case and held it out.

"Morons, I didn't travel six thousand kilometers to lose my equipment. Save me from incompetent people." Schulte jerked the case from the crewman's grasp and, unlocking the lid, inspected the cameras and lenses for damage. "You're damn lucky this time. No water got past the seal."

The crewmen revealed studied smiles that slipped away just as quickly as they had appeared. For sixteen days they had been forced to listen to Schulte's demeaning barrages in resolute silence, but this time was different— their guest was leaving, and like an unwelcome visitor who had stayed too long, would never be missed. More than enough time had passed to develop a mutual dislike. Most sailors make friends as a way to live together. On the other hand, Schulte cultivated enemies instead and displayed an ability to get along with no one.

Schulte paused and ravenously inhaled the rich night air. The scent of White Pine coalesced with beached seaweed and errant chimney smoke from distant fireplaces. Each breath was almost too pleasurable, too intense—in stark contrast with the stale, dead atmosphere on the U-37. It was like being newly born and experiencing these pleasures for the first time.

A crewman picked up the oars and motioned it was time to leave. Moisture from the fog sprinkled cold against Schulte's face as the raft hastened into the darkness.

The roar of the waves became louder as the crewman guided the raft through the boiling surf.

In the distance a sharp yip followed by a quick succession of howls proclaimed that another act of the timeless dance between the hunter and the hunted was over—a coyote had just captured dinner.

Schulte smiled and glanced toward the New Jersey shoreline as the anguished squeals of a dying rabbit fell silent. *And now to meet Reinhardt.*

Chapter Five

December 31, 1938
Baltimore, Maryland

Multicolored Christmas lights sparkled from the majestic blue spruce outside the living-room window as large, powdery snowflakes floated past the streetlights. The muffled quietness of the evening belied the ferocity of the approaching storm. Snow began to blanket the ground, forming drifts as the wind swirled between the Craftsman style houses and parked cars on East Plymouth Lane.

The brown house on the corner looked like all the homes in the working class neighborhood. By all outward appearances, its occupants were celebrating the beginning of a new year; however, 1261 East Plymouth Lane was not typical.

A yellow and black Checker Cab pulled to the curb, its wipers slapping loudly from side to side, barely able to keep up with the increasing snowfall. Its lone occupant jumped out and rushed up the steps to the front door, pausing for a moment and listening before waving the cab away. A dark green and red holly wreath hung from a hook in the dark oak door, framing a large brass lion's head door knocker. Two resounding raps from the striker rudely intruded on a tranquil passage of Beethoven's Seventh and announced the visitor's presence. No one came to the door. The hour was late, perhaps too late for visitors.

After a second series of raps, Karl Reinhardt cracked open the door viewer just above the lion's head and stood in silence for a moment as he tried to place the figure standing under the glaring porch light. He slipped his right hand into his tan cardigan pocket and clutched his small Mauser WPT II pistol.

"Yes, what do you want?" Reinhardt spoke in cautious tones from behind the wrought iron grill.

"Karl, I'm Chris Schulte. I should have called before I came. I hope this visit isn't inconvenient, but I wanted to wish you a happy New Year."

Reinhardt continued to stare and clutch the Mauser. *Schulte? Chris Schulte. Damn. I never should have sent that telegram.* Reinhardt cleared his throat.

"I . . . I thought you were in Hamburg." Reinhardt glanced around the porch and then at his pocket watch. "When did you arrive?"

"Aren't you going to ask me in before I freeze to death?"

"Yes, of course, I just didn't expect to see you." Reinhardt unhooked the safety chain and swung the door open. "I don't see any suitcases. Where are you staying?"

Schulte stepped into the foyer as Reinhardt closed the door and replaced the chain.

Once inside, it was obvious from the furnishings and lack of personal items the house was not a home. It was more like an office or hotel room with everything in its place, but no character, no personality.

They moved through the living room to an overstuffed, brown leather couch placed beside a crackling fire. Schulte took a seat farthest away from the fireplace and lit a cigarette. A wispy column of smoke rose and drifted across the ceiling. Reinhardt filled two glasses with ice and vodka.

"You didn't say how you got here."

"Submarine." Schulte swigged the vodka and set the empty glass on the coffee table.

In his late forties, Reinhardt was short with rounded shoulders. Dark bags under his eyes and balding brown hair made him look every bit his age. During the Great War a grenade blew the finger tips off his left hand. He was self-conscious and always wore gloves and a toupee in public. If he had known he was going to have company, he would have put his gloves and hairpiece on. The thought of being exposed in front of a stranger made him feel uncomfortable and, somehow, naked.

Before Reinhardt could say anything, Schulte jumped up and placed a large log on the fire. A loud pop echoed across the hearth and sparks jumped against the brass fire screen as Schulte sat down.

"I have always wanted to see the inside of a submarine, but not travel in one." Reinhardt pulled at his bushy eyebrows and studied Schulte's face for any sign of emotion. He knew of Schulte from conversations with Elsa, but never expected they would meet.

"Was the trip exciting?" Reinhardt removed his tie and unbuttoned his collar. Perspiration began to show through his shirt.

"It was an endless descent into hell. I don't want to talk about it."

"More vodka?" Reinhardt pointed to their empty glasses.

"Yes, quality vodka has been hard to find in Germany since Göring introduced the Four Year Plan."

"It was unfortunate about Elsa." Reinhardt filled the glass and watched for a response. "Her death came as a shock, especially coming so close after August Kruger's murder. Losing two agents within a week's time was a tragedy."

Reinhardt's words were distant. Schulte stared through the living room window at the drifting snow remembering Elsa and the last Christmas they had spent together in Hamburg. Elsa had sat in the audience while Chris performed as Viola in a sold-out production of Shakespeare's Twelfth Night.

Reinhardt lit a cigarette and, placing it in the ashtray, casually sat back.

"Did you know I was with her that night?"

"No."

"We were returning from a Bund rally in Brooklyn. It had rained hard all day and the hour was late. We ducked into the subway station at Prospect Park. The platform was crowded, but at least it was dry. I started to browse the newspaper when I heard the train approach. As I looked down the tunnel, Elsa screamed. To my horror she was sprawled on the track. For a brief moment our eyes met and I felt her terror as the train drew past me and screeched to a stop. The scene was beyond all description."

Reinhardt rattled the ice in his empty glass and positioned the glass squarely in the center of the coffee table. He pulled out a cigarette and lit it, forgetting he already had one burning in the ashtray.

"One minute she was standing safely beside me and the next she was gone." He released a dense column of smoke from pursed lips and drew it in through his nose. "It all happened too quickly; there was nothing anyone could do."

"An accident?"

"Perhaps." Reinhardt took a deep breath. "I don't know. I noticed a woman wearing a dark tan trench coat and brown hat rushing up the stairs, but it could have been a coincidence, nothing more. As people jammed to the platform edge I faded into the crowd and disappeared into the darkness of the park before the police arrived. I am sorry we couldn't claim Elsa's body."

"What happened to her belongings?"

"We weren't concerned about recovering her things. She never carried identification or any items of a personal nature."

"Except the knife."

"Well, yes." Reinhardt hesitated and turned away. "She never was without it. How did you know?"

"Her knife was from a matching set of two custom knives. I have the other one. We couldn't marry so we exchanged knives and vows in private before Elsa sailed from Germany. Did anyone collect her things from her apartment?"

Reinhardt shifted in his seat.

"Did anyone collect her things? The police, um . . . would have recovered everything at the scene. I called Anna Hoffmann and asked her to search Elsa's apartment in Trenton. The apartment was completely empty. It was as if Elsa had moved without a trace. We were at a loss."

"I had hoped you would have her knife and diary."

Reinhardt leaned forward and nervously twisted one corner of his collar. "Diary? She kept a diary?"

"It was written in code. I always feared someone might find it. Elsa said no one would know what it was even if they did and I suppose, after all, she was right."

Reinhardt eyed Schulte as the grandfather clock in the hall struck the quarter hour. Schulte's expression remained unchanged. A wave of relief eased into Reinhardt's mind as he hung his sweater on the coat rack in the foyer and returned to the couch.

"Only a few minutes until the new year and we'll say good-bye to the sorrows of 1938 and await the achievements of 1939. It promises to be a year of extraordinary change."

"Heil Hitler," Schulte said as their glasses touched.

Reinhardt grinned and made another toast. "To the success of your mission in Brazil."

Schulte's gaze snapped around, locking on Reinhardt.

"What are you talking about?"

"Come on Chris. It's our trade to uncover secrets. Elsa and I often talked before she moved to Trenton. I know you took Portuguese in Hamburg last year and Brazil is the only Portuguese speaking country in the Americas. You came here to have a meeting with someone special or pick up something important. Admiral Canaris wouldn't have sent you here by submarine if you were just joining a ring in the States. No, your mission has something to do with the United States and Brazil and the home office wanted to ensure no one knew you were here."

"Seems you know more about my mission than I do."

Schulte drained the last of the vodka into Reinhardt's glass and waited for his tongue to loosen with the added lubrication.

"I have always wanted to travel in South America, but what's Brazil have to do with the United States?"

"I'm not sure." Reinhardt emptied his glass and opened a cabinet beside the couch. He removed two small goblets and a bottle of Sekt sparkling wine. "Maybe it's not the United States, but Britain. Our submarines could operate from a base in Brazil and cripple British shipping in the region."

"Brazil has nothing to do with me. I'm traveling to Southern California next week to investigate rumors about a top-secret fighter Lockheed is developing. It sounds a little like the Dutch Fokker G-1. I'm not sure what I'll find, but I have always been intrigued by airplanes."

Rubbing his hands together, Reinhardt smiled and touched Schulte on the shoulder.

"Well, I'm glad you stopped by tonight. I was alone and am fortunate to have someone from home to help celebrate the New Year."

Reinhardt filled the two goblets with Sekt and handed one to Schulte as the grandfather clock struck twelve.

"It is time to embrace tradition. Let's salute the new year and the memory of old friends. May the Reich live for a thousand years. *Frohes Neues Jahr.*"

"Frohes Neues Jahr," Schulte said, ". . . and here's to the memory of August and Elsa."

Reinhardt took Schulte's goblet. "I have another bottle of vodka in the kitchen. Can I interest you in a fresh drink and maybe some crackers and cheese? A friend sent me some nice Gouda from Holland last week for Christmas."

"Just straight vodka, no ice." Schulte stood and walked toward the picture window. The lights on the Spruce in the yard twinkled through the frost on the glass. Schulte glanced back at Reinhardt. "You never mentioned how August died."

Reinhardt gestured with his cigarette as he exhaled a billowing cloud of smoke.

"He was discovered in a third-rate hotel with his throat slit. We suspect a prostitute killed him for his money. During the last two years he developed the unsavory habit of frequenting the fringe areas of the city and picking up young streetwalkers. I talked with him several times about the choices he was making, but he wouldn't listen. We could have safely provided whatever he wanted."

"Like a flickering candle about to extinguish, an old man sometimes does strange things in an attempt to recapture the flame of his youth." Schulte glanced around the room. "Karl, do you mind if I play something else on the phonograph?"

Reinhardt picked up the empty goblets. "Help yourself. I store my records in the cabinet beside you." His voice trailed off as he moved into the kitchen, but he could still be heard enthusiastically humming a melody from Beethoven's Seventh.

After replacing the record stack, Schulte crowded another log on the fire and was poking the embers when Reinhardt returned with a newly opened bottle of vodka and a plate of sliced cheese. Reinhardt stopped and stared at the fire as he wiped his forearm across his brow. At nearly ninety degrees, the room had become uncomfortably hot. He glanced toward the side windows and thought of opening them, but remembered they were painted shut.

"Aren't you warm?"

"Have you ever noticed how quickly the tip of a poker changes color when it's heated in a fire?" Schulte turned up the phonograph until the room thundered with Beethoven and moved back toward the couch. "I find the allegro in the Fifth Symphony particularly moving. Don't you?"

After a momentary hesitation, Reinhardt sat down and started to fill Schulte's glass. "Say when."

"Karl, I sense there's more to Elsa's death than you are telling me."

Reinhardt froze when he noticed that Schulte still held the red-hot poker and had moved menacingly close.

"What do you mean?" He stared at the glasses and no longer felt like drinking. It was late and he suddenly wanted the night to end. The conversation had become personal and was heading to a place he feared most. He thought of the Mauser and wished he hadn't hung his sweater in the foyer.

"Come on Karl, finish filling the glasses and drink up. We have much to talk about."

Reinhardt glanced toward the door and considered making a dash for the coatrack; however, Schulte's cold stare impaled him. As their eyes met, a wave of fear surged through his body. He wanted to look away, but was drawn inescapably into Schulte's steel-gray eyes. His hands began to tremble as he topped their glasses.

Schulte reached over to steady the bottle as vodka spilled onto the table. "You know, Karl, good vodka is a lot like blood; they're both precious and when spilled, they're lost forever."

Chapter Six

Wind-blown trash pirouetted in the front alcove of a two storey red brick building located near the Baltimore waterfront. A "Closed" sign was sandwiched between the venetian blinds and the glass in the front door. Pigeon feathers danced as wind gusts scoured the sidewalk. All outward signs indicated the offices of Royal Imports had been closed for some time, but in reality they were never open. No one ever used the front door. Only the office on the second floor at the rear of the building was occupied. The rest of the building was empty except for spiders and field mice.

Royal Imports was a front for a special British MI6 operation, code named Colonial Watch. Clive Smith, the station head, had served in the British Army during the Great War until being wounded and interned in a German prisoner of war camp. After the war ended, he joined MI6. He looked average and could pass for a mill worker, banker, or priest—depending on how he was dressed. He spoke without an accent and was the kind of guy that fifteen minutes after you met him, you wouldn't remember his name.

Colonial Watch was investigating German Abwehr and Spanish Falangist activity on the East Coast. Europe would soon be at war, and the United States was isolationist. They knew if the activities of these foreign agents were exposed, politics in the United States would shift to favor Britain. Colonial Watch was not attached to an embassy. They walked a cautious line. Without diplomatic cover, they were on their own and subject to criminal prosecution as foreign agents if they attracted the attention of the authorities.

Thin slivers of light from the closed venetian blinds in the upstairs office pierced the dark alley as a drifter dug through the trash barrels looking for anything of value. He didn't have time to pay attention to the late-night activity in the building. He lived day to day by selling what he found and tonight there was nothing to show for his efforts.

Five MI6 agents had been sitting around a massive boardroom table in spartan surroundings for more than three hours without a break. An industrial gray time-clock next to the door showed it was past midnight. Smoke filled the air, and the bouquet of burned coffee grew stale as the large pot in the corner continued to smolder. The thick haze did little to shroud the single 100 watt light bulb that glared above the table. The amber light revealed nicotine stained walls and a legion of spiders' eyes sparking from the dark corners searching for their next meal.

The meeting had gone on for far too long, but Clive still had several items to cover. He ran his fingers through

43

his gray hair and drained the thickened remains of this afternoon's brew into a cup. The coffee always smelled like burned rubber and tasted even worse after midnight.

"Let's take a ten-minute piss break and then wrap this up."

"Can't we just finish now?" Gwen Wells said. "I have been up for over twenty-four hours and want to go home."

Gwen was single, in her early thirties with long auburn hair pulled into a bun. She wore little make up, but was still stunning, with a figure that didn't often go unnoticed.

"Hey, I'm out of tobacco," Mick Jenkins said. "Ten minutes sounds good."

Mick sat beside Gwen. At five feet six he was taller than Gwen, even when she wore high heels. He always tried to look down her blouse but usually got caught. Mick looked like a refugee from a B gangster movie. His jet black hair was slicked back, and he sported a pencil thin mustache. He proudly displayed a small scar over his left eyebrow from a bar fight in Algeria five years ago. Mick enjoyed cultivating his gangster appearance.

Clive hated it.

"I thought you quit smoking," Jacob Bonner said, but he already knew the answer. Mick had been trying to quit for as long as Jacob had known him. Mick even switched to rolling his own cigarettes to make smoking less convenient. The switch hadn't worked. Now he just had more crap to carry around.

"Quittin' is easy." Alec Bonner pulled out a fresh pack of Old Golds and carefully removed the cellophane wrapper. "See these? I can quit anytime I want—anytime."

Alec removed a cigarette and slid the pack across the table to Jacob.

Jacob looked at Mick as he flipped a match into the ashtray and blew a smoke ring that encircled the overhead light. "Yeah, didn't you make your annual New Year's resolution just last week?"

"Bugger off." Mick's chair squealed against the battleship gray linoleum tile as he abruptly pushed away from the table.

Jacob and Alec were half-brothers on Clive's MI6 team. They had grown up in Whitecastle in East London and spoke with decided Cockney accents. Jacob was good with explosives. Ever since he was a young boy, he enjoyed blowing things up. His father had been an explosives specialist during the Great War. Jacob thought of his hobby as carrying on the family trade, like a cobbler or a butcher. Alec, on the other hand, was good with numbers and at deciphering code but couldn't catch a ball even if it landed at his feet. He was more suited to working in the office than in the field.

The agents stepped out of the room and headed for the toilets. After a few minutes Mick returned carrying a fresh pouch of Bugler tobacco and a new package of rolling papers. He sat down at the table and began hand rolling a cigarette when he heard a noise in the alley. Spinning around, he forced his hand between the metal slats in the venetian blinds and cracked open the window.

"Oi, piss off and don't come back," he yelled using his best mobster impression as the drifter fled from the alley.

"What was that?" Jacob rushed to the window and peered into the darkness.

"Nothing, just a wharf rat."

"You should-a drilled the son of a bitch." Jacob withdrew his hand and let the slats pop back into shape.

"I would have; except my gun was empty, and he scampered away before I could reload." Mick's gold tooth sparkled in the light as he burst out laughing.

"You two are deplorable," Gwen said as she finished filling the coffee pot with water and opened a new can of Maxwell House.

"Thank you, it's good to be recognized." Mick touched his right hand to his chest and bowed his head.

Clive ambled into the room and paced back and forth in front of the table as he stared at the floor. After a long silence he abruptly stopped and faced the others.

"Let's quit pissin' around, people." He pressed his fingers against the table and leaned in. "Do we have any new information on Falangist activities?"

"Nothing since last month, but I know they are up to something," Jacob said. "Several of their agents have flown in and out of Baltimore Municipal on Pan Am this last month. They flew to Miami and then on to Georgetown in Guyana where they met with Brazilian nationals, but we can't determine what they are working on and haven't been able to locate their hideout. They always lose us in the warehouse district."

"I believe there is a connection between what the Germans and Spanish are doing," Clive said. "Yesterday I received a message from Bletchley addressing rumors about German interest in building an airfield in the jungles of Brazil. As preposterous as it sounds, I don't have to tell you what the establishment of a German airfield in South America would mean."

"Brazil isn't aligned with Germany and, besides, the United States will not tolerate their encroachment into the Americas," Jacob said. "Monroe Doctrine and all that."

"Washington has already dismissed the idea as impractical," Clive said. "They believe the Americas are safe from Nazi intrusion because of the distance across the Atlantic and Hitler's preoccupation with Austria and Poland. They're leaving the matter up to the Brazilian authorities."

"Blimey, they still don't get it." Alec shook his head as he approached the coffee pot. "Anybody else want a refill?"

Clive shifted his gaze toward Mick. "What about the German Abwehr agent, Otto Vogt? He arrived here a month ago. How come you don't know more about him? What's he been up to? Needless to say, if this guy gets away and the FBI finds out we knew about him, all our careers will be in the crapper."

"Don't worry, two of my operatives have Vogt under surveillance," Mick said. "So far he hasn't changed his routine. Every afternoon at exactly four he goes to the Horn and Hardart on Eighth Avenue in Manhattan, has a plate of mac and cheese, a cup of black coffee, and reads the newspaper for an hour. Then he leaves precisely at five, everyday like clockwork. He eats alone and never talks to anyone. I can't figure him out."

"Must be waitin' for a contact," Jacob said.

"Maybe he just likes mac and cheese and the *New York Times*." Alec adjusted his Coke-bottle glasses and crushed out his cigarette.

"When he changes his routine, we'll be all over him." Mick stood and maneuvered to a perfect position behind Gwen, but retreated to his chair when she slid forward and fastened the top button on her blouse.

"Are you sure you have enough manpower on this?" Clive glanced up at Mick. "Blackwell and Bechet arrive from Europe next week. I plan to move them to Cuba in August, but you can use them temporarily. We can't afford to let this Nazi slip away."

"We already have the German's movements locked up tighter than the Crown Jewels," Mick said. "More people would just get in the way. Maybe Blackwell and Bechet can work the Brazilian airfield angle."

"Alec, have you been able to confirm the rumor about a German agent transferring from a U-boat to the coast of New Jersey? It's been over two weeks."

"No, so far it's still unsubstantiated. My sources keep coming up empty."

"It's time to notify the FBI about Vogt," Clive said. "I only wish they were more competent. They're not proficient at this counter intelligence business yet and don't believe they have a problem. I think Hoover is more concerned with making headlines about gangsters and gun molls than catching spies."

"Damned isolationists are so busy looking the other way, hoping Europe's problems will stay in Europe," Jacob said.

"They got their heads up their proverbial arses." Alec removed his glasses and drummed his fingers on the table. "What's it going to take to wake them up?"

Jacob opened his penknife and started cleaning his fingernails.

"A bomb, . . . a very big bomb."

"Anything else before we quit for the night?" Clive asked as he glanced at his watch.

Gwen sat forward and clasped her hands. "I hesitate to bring this up, but what I saw two months ago in Brooklyn still troubles me."

"Crap, not that again." Mick tilted his head toward the ceiling. "I thought you wanted to go home *tonight*."

"Yes, that again." Gwen's eyes tightened to slits like a cobra about to strike as she glared at Mick. "When I followed the two German agents into the subway station at Prospect Park I'm positive I saw the man push the woman into the path of the oncoming train. I still hear her chilling cries for help. Yesterday there was a story in *The Guardian Post* about a man's mutilated body being discovered in a house in Baltimore. I recognized the victim's picture as the man who committed the Brooklyn murder last November."

"Cor . . . I read that story." Jacob's eyes widened as he turned toward Gwen. "Apparently the bloke was tortured with a knife for days while being hung naked from a meat hook in the basement. The sorry bastard had crystal Drano repeatedly rubbed into his wounds. I'm surprised the neighbors didn't hear the screams."

"What a way to go." Mick looked squarely at Gwen as he poured tobacco onto a fresh cigarette paper and suggestively licked its edge. "Do you think the guy was a masochist? Maybe it was just a kinky sex game, like autoerotic asphyxiation, that went south. You know, there are some enchantingly perverted people in the world."

"Auto what?" Alec said.

"Never mind." Gwen's jaw muscles tightened as she continued to glare at Mick.

"I think the killer was a sadist, and the game went exactly where it was intended," Alec said.

Clive looked up from the table and his gaze locked squarely onto Alec and then shifted to Gwen. He opened his mouth as if he was going to speak, but then looked away and shook his head.

"Mum won't be happy when she finds out what you've learned in the big city," Jacob said. "Since when does my little brother know about stuff like that?"

"Since I learned where Mick hides his magazines." Alec looked at Mick and winked.

"I'm serious," Gwen snapped, "and you degenerates sit here cracking jokes about wharf rats and perverts. The Baltimore murder was obviously not a random act. It was retribution for the killing in Brooklyn. They knew each other; the killer was, in all likelihood, a rogue Abwehr agent."

"They?" Jacob said.

"The woman in Brooklyn and whoever left the stiff on the hook in the basement."

"You may be right," Clive said, "but we have live German and Spanish agents to catch. Let the Devil dance with the dead ones."

Chapter Seven

Saturday, January 28, 1939
Burbank, California

The Totem Motor Lodge, on the outskirts of town, had lost its luster years ago and now was just a greasy truck stop kept alive by its twenty-four hour, Flying A gas station. A green neon Indian in full war bonnet danced tirelessly up and down on a pole in front of the office as a bright red vacancy sign flashed in the window. The cabins of the Totem were tacky sun-bleached stucco buildings resembling twenty foot high teepees, but not so much that any real Indian would admit the similarity.

At six-thirty in the morning there was no need for the Indian to dance or the vacancy sign to flash; there wasn't much traffic on San Fernando Road. The bars down the street had closed at two this morning and the shift change at the Lockheed assembly plant had passed by hours ago. The only sounds on the highway came from the occasional whine of a big rig making its way up the long grade toward Bakersfield.

The Totem was empty except for Cabin 4. Gunter Klein and Chris Schulte, sat opposite each other next to the writing desk. Gunter leaned his chair back on two legs and pulled out a pipe and tobacco pouch. He had worked for Lockheed in their Burbank plant as a machinist since 1934 when he immigrated from Germany.

"The test flight proved interesting," Schulte said. "I wish I could have gotten closer, but I suppose I'm lucky no one spotted me in the brush."

"Considering the distance you were from the runway, these photographs turned out quite well. They reveal surprising detail of the wings, props, and turbocharged engines." Gunter placed the prints on the desk and lit his pipe. "This is the first time I have seen the plane assembled. Rumor at the plant says it will be flying to Wright Field near Dayton, Ohio within the next two weeks."

"I just arrived. Why are they moving it?" Schulte's jaw clinched. "Damn it."

"More testing by the Army's Materiel Command. The prototype plane for every new Army contract undergoes lengthy evaluation at Wright Field. That's why I was surprised when you came here instead of going directly to Dayton."

"No one told me about Wright Field." Schulte suddenly stood and paced next to the bed. "I presumed the testing would take place in Southern California near Lockheed."

"Well in any event, they will move the plane to Wright Field for acceptance and to be closer to Washington DC. The Army will use every opportunity to sell the plane to

Congress before the vote for funding. Americans have such a strange way. No wonder it takes them so long to get anything done."

"They will be easily defeated."

"Don't mark them so casually." Gunter relit his pipe and glanced out the window at the sunrise. "I have learned much about these Americans in the last five years. They may surprise you."

"I'll leave for Dayton tomorrow. I need to be at Wright Field when the plane arrives."

Schulte reviewed the coded message one last time before sealing the envelope:

TOP SECRET – Witnessed initial test flight of Lockheed XP-38 at March Field near Riverside, California yesterday morning.

Reports appear correct. XP-38 similar in design to the Fokker G-1, utilizing twin tail booms, a central fuselage, and turbocharged, twin V-12 engines with counter rotating, three-bladed props. Tricycle landing gear configuration worked well with this large plane. Estimated wingspan near fifty feet.

Plane ran off end of runway during ground testing with what seemed to be a braking problem.

Following lengthy delay the XP-38 flew for approximately thirty minutes before landing. The test pilot was conservative and did not reveal the plane's potential. However, it appeared somewhat sluggish when entering into right and left hand rolls. This may indicate diminished capability in close aerial combat.

After placing the photographs in a second envelope, Schulte handed both envelopes to Gunter. "Deliver these to the drop point in Los Angeles before eight this morning."

"I'll return and drive you to Union Air Terminal this afternoon," Gunter said as he opened the door to his rusty Dodge pickup and climbed in. He pulled the choke handle out and started the engine. A cloud of blue smoke erupted from the tailpipe as the engine clattered to life. He started to pull away, but stopped and glanced back. "You can arrange your flight to Dayton at the airport this afternoon."

Schulte leaned against the cabin doorway and lit a cigarette as the last of the night stars gave way to the orange glow of a new day. A warm Santa Ana breeze carried the scent of mesquite and sage brush down from the dark canyons of the Verdugo Mountains.

It is obvious the American government is preparing for war despite the isolationist feelings of the people.

Schulte took a deep breath and let it out slowly.

Maybe some day I'll live in this San Fernando Valley and grow oranges.

Chapter Eight

The XP-38 raced in from the west and maneuvered into a high bank turn, speeding around the field twice before landing on runway three. The ground crew guided the pilot to a spot in front of the control tower. He shut off the powerful engines, bringing the gleaming three-bladed props to a stop for the first time in hours. The only markings on the plane's polished aluminum skin were the red, white, and blue rudder stripes and the Army Air Corps' star roundels painted on the wings.

A swarm of Army officers gathered on the tarmac near the left wing and cheered as the pilot unstrapped and opened the canopy. As soon as he reached the ground, the group disappeared into a large hanger standing next to the air control tower.

A church bell in the distance struck two as Schulte put down the binoculars and stepped away from the window. *That was near record time from California. He must have flown at almost 600 kilometers per hour. Impressive.*

A fuel truck pulled up to the plane as a team of mechanics emerged from the hanger and removed the engine cowlings. A short time later the cowlings had been replaced and the pilot and officers reappeared and stood beside the plane as the pilot climbed back into the cockpit.

What are they doing?

Everyone stood back as the props hesitated and then sprang to life. After a brief series of operational checks, the pilot taxied back to the runway using the rudders to maneuver. The twin V-12 engines rumbled as exhaust gasses passed through the turbochargers and the props came up to speed.

He's taking off!

Schulte quickly focused the binoculars on the airfield. Seconds later the XP-38 sped down the runway and pulled into a steep climb. It banked and flew east, disappearing from sight.

Where in hell is he going?

In less than twenty-four hours the answer came on the front page of the morning paper:

DAYTON DAILY LEDGER

*MYSTERY PLANE CRASHES INTO LONG
ISLAND GOLF COURSE*

NEW YORK Feb. 11 (1939) – Late this afternoon the wreckage of the United States Army's newest experimental twin-engine pursuit plane lay crumpled in a sand trap just short of Mitchel Field on Long Island.

The XP-38, designed and built by Lockheed in Burbank, California, was attempting to break the speed record for transcontinental flight set by Howard Hughes in 1937 when it crashed.

No weapons were onboard the aircraft. The pilot was slightly injured with minor cuts. However, the plane was damaged beyond repair. The Army and Lockheed refused comment.

Schulte closed the paper and picked up the phone.

"Operator, please connect me with Murray Hill 5-9975. I'll hold."

The phone rang several times at the other end as Schulte lit a cigarette.

"Hello Rick, I called to express my condolences on the loss of your new business partner. His death was an unexpected tragedy for all of us. He had so much promise and will be greatly missed. Please let me know if there is anything I can do to help. I am between assignments and will have some free time."

Schulte paused to listen and poured some vodka into a glass.

"I understand. I have a few loose ends to tie up, but should be in Baltimore by the end of next week and will contact you."

Chapter Nine

Saturday, May 27, 1939
Baltimore

Schulte awoke at four in the morning to a series of sharp raps on the door, but the hallway was empty. The intruder had disappeared down the stairs. Closing the door and turning on the light, Schulte found a sealed envelope sitting on the rug. The light blue note paper carried the sweet fragrance of jasmine and the penmanship was ornately feminine:

> *Come alone to the Cairo Theater at nine*
> *tonight. Sit in the balcony near the back. I*
> *have something of great interest for you. A*
> *friend.*

Schulte's gut reaction was to dismiss the note as a ploy; however as the day wore on, curiosity eventually won out. Temperatures for over a week had reached well into the nineties with humidity to match. The air conditioned theater would provide a welcome break from the stifling

May weather and besides the meeting might prove to be an interesting diversion from an otherwise dull week.

The sun had long since set, but waves of heat continued to radiate from the sidewalks and tall masonry buildings along Sixth Avenue. It had been one of those memorable fry-an-egg-on-the-sidewalk days cab drivers refer to with pride when talking to tourists.

A red and white flashing marquee came into view as Schulte rounded the corner and approached the Cairo. *Wuthering Heights* starring Laurence Oliver and Merle Oberon was the main feature. With its Egyptian facade and tall columns the Cairo looked like it should be located on the banks of the Nile, not in downtown Baltimore next to a bookstore. After ducking in and out of several buildings along the way, Schulte noted it had taken longer to walk from the hotel than expected.

The smell of hot butter and the sounds of popping kernels spilled through the entrance and enveloped the sidewalk under the marquee. The lobby was empty except for the usher and a snack bar attendant, who were idly passing time leaning against the candy display. Schulte ascended to the balcony and glanced back toward the lobby. No one else entered. The newsreel had already started and the low flickering light made it hard to distinguish faces. No one appeared to pay attention as the usher led the way to the back of the balcony to a row just in front of the projection booth.

The newsreel reported a dramatic recovery effort underway off the coast of Portsmouth, New Hampshire for an ill-fated US Navy submarine. The acrid smells and sounds flooded back as vivid memories of the weeks of confinement in the North Atlantic aboard the U-37 returned without warning.

It was a little past eleven when the feature ended. The Cairo was air-conditioned, but otherwise the trip had been a complete waste of time. No one made contact, approached, or so much as looked in Schulte's direction.

The theater emptied quickly. Most movie-goers had already made their way through the lobby and into the humid night air.

Schulte lit a cigarette and descended the stairs toward the exit. The usher called out from the balcony and hurried down. "Excuse me, a woman handed me this package saying you left it behind."

"What?"

"You forgot your package."

"Oh yes . . . thank you."

Schulte grabbed the plainly wrapped package and raced back to the balcony but found it empty except for a piece of light blue note paper fastened to the back of one of the seats. The faint fragrance of jasmine and distinct aroma of Haus Bergmann Privat cigarettes still lingered in the air:

> *I share your sorrow. Do not attempt to find me. We will meet again. A friend.*

It took nearly half an hour of dodging through the crowded streets to return to the hotel room. Alone at last, Schulte downed a shot of vodka and ripped open the package. Its contents fell on the bed.

Schulte's lips parted with a gasp. *Damn, I thought this was gone forever.*

Reading the pages of the diary was like sitting in a corner cafe and talking with Elsa again. It spoke of their last year together in Hamburg and Elsa's time in America. The entries flowed as easily as reading the morning paper. Schulte finally reached the last two entries:

> *November 27 – Crescent moon, clear and cold. Identified August Kruger as an MI6 double agent. Followed him to his drop point and recovered the envelope he left. Hard to believe. It contained the names of our operatives. It is inconceivable that British gold could buy the loyalty of such a highly decorated agent. The mere thought of what might have happened turns my stomach. I wish Chris were here. I need to move.*
>
> *November 29 – Windy and rainy. August is dead. It was easier than I expected, just got him drunk and played to his ego. It may have been a mistake to tell Karl about August. He became agitated and asked if I had told anyone else. Tonight we are going*

to attend a Bund rally in Brooklyn. I'm looking forward to hearing Fritz Kuhn speak. Maybe it will take my mind off what has happened. Sent Chris a telegram this morning, but will wait to talk about August.

Schulte lay the diary on the bed and thought back to the interrogation in the basement of the safe house. Karl Reinhardt had confessed to being a double agent. Schulte was furious when Reinhardt prematurely died from a heart attack before divulging all he knew. Perhaps the last cuts had been too deep, the questioning too intense.

Elsa's diary brought everything into perspective. August Kruger and Karl Reinhardt were collaborators. MI6 was responsible for Elsa's death.

Schulte moved to the dresser and, pulling out the top drawer, removed a tarnished silver box. Seeing Elsa's face suddenly became more important than anything else.

Returning to the bed, Schulte undid the hasp and opened the engraved lid. A small black and white picture of Elsa lay comfortably cradled in the blue velvet lining with the other mementos—the dried rose from their first date, a lock of Elsa's blonde hair, and a small heart-shaped stone they had found on a beach as teenagers. Schulte held Elsa's picture under the light and gazed at her smile, trying to hear her laugh and see the light sparkle in her eyes, but it was no use. The picture was an empty, lifeless reflection of the past, a memory and nothing more. Even the scent of English lavender had faded from the lock of hair. Elsa was gone.

Schulte tore the picture in half and threw the silver box and its contents into the trash can under the sink.

They'll pay, Elsa. I swear, every one of them . . . will pay.

Chapter Ten

THE GUARDIAN POST

BODY FOUND IN ALLEY

BALTIMORE July 30 (1939) – An unidentified man's mutilated body was found wedged into a trash can in the alley behind the Melody Room on Pratt Avenue. The grisly discovery was made a little after four this morning when a beer truck driver stopped for his normal delivery.

Chief of Detectives John Cavendish from the Baltimore Police Department Homicide Unit stated the murder took place late last night. Cavendish refused to confirm or deny if this latest murder is connected with two similar murders that have occurred in the infamous waterfront neighborhood within the last two months. He stated the cases are currently under investigation. Robbery did not appear to be a motive.

The morning edition of the Guardian sailed past Mick's head and exploded into a shower of pages, flying in all directions, as Clive stomped behind Gwen. He suddenly turned and slammed his fist against the table; his bulging eyes challenged everyone in the room.

"Boswell is the third agent to meet this bastard's knife since May. Someone's killing MI6 agents faster than we can import them."

"Simpson in May and Potter in June, and now Boswell in July." Mick grabbed the coffee pot and started to fill his cup. "Gives me the heebie jeebies."

Alec picked up the paper and put the pages back in order. He glanced at the article again. "Why always on the 29th of the month? What's the connection?" He tightened his lips and shook his head as he placed the paper face down on the table.

Returning from the coffee pot, Mick took out a pouch of Bugler and rolled a cigarette. "Do you think the cops have figured out what's really happening?"

"Nice job, mate," Jacob said.

"What?" Mick said, pulling out his Zippo.

"Nice job of rolling. You're getting better at rolling your own."

"Thanks." Mick snapped his lighter shut and admired his handiwork. "It did turn out rather well."

Clive drummed his fingers on the table and scowled as he looked at Jacob and then back at Mick. "Quit pissin' around. No, they don't know who the victims were. If they did, the waterfront would be crawling with cops looking for us. My informant in the department said the victims were stabbed in the same manner before being mutilated. I'm sure the police have deduced by now that the murders were not random and they're dealing with a serial killer."

"Bloody hell, it's going on three months now and they're only dealing with a six block area. Maybe solving the murders isn't all that important to them," Mick said. "The Melody Room is a gay bar. The cops might think they're dealing with a bunch of dead closet queens."

"That's a terrible thing to say." Gwen crossed her arms and turned away from the table.

"Well, just think of how they were mutilated."

Clive flipped the paper over and looked at Boswell's picture one more time. "Only MI6 agents are being targeted. It's plainly connected to something involving MI6 that occurred on the twenty-ninth day of the month. This bastard is sending a message directly to us and we have to figure out what it is and who is sending it. We can't go to the cops and he knows it."

"Maybe the killer is one of our Spanish Falangist friends from the warehouse district?" Alec adjusted his glasses and glanced at the headline again.

"No, he's definitely German," Gwen said.

Clive leaned forward and interlaced his fingers. "What makes you say that? The killer could be any nationality, even British."

"I'm sure the killer isn't a Falangist. They're too damned preoccupied with organizing cells in Latin America. The Japanese are focused on China and the Pacific and, except for their embassy in Washington DC, they are practically nonexistent on the East Coast. The Americans wouldn't be killing MI6 agents and the Italians are busy working over Ethiopia. That leaves the Germans."

Mick took a sip of coffee and leaned back. "Perhaps the killer is your *rogue* Abwehr agent? You know, the meat hook guy."

Chapter Eleven

Wednesday, August 2, 1939
Baltimore

The Devil's Due was a quiet neighborhood bar where an "open" sign hung in the window twenty hours a day, and the bartender knew more about his patrons' lives than their confessional priest. Most customers came to the Due because they had nowhere else to go. It was their life, their family. They had reached the end of the rainbow, but someone else had already taken the gold.

Today, the regulars sat perched on their normal stools and were only interested in their next beer and the one after that. Their daily entertainment was purchased one nickel at a time; no one cared what hour it was or even what day it was. Most had been at the bar since it opened at six this morning. They were celebrating the new day by skipping breakfast and jumping right into happy hour.

One lone patron sat at a table near the door to the toilets reading a newspaper. He would periodically glance around the bar and stare at the front door before rustling the paper in the air and folding to the next page.

Two olive-skinned men were seated at a dimly lit table in the farthest corner from the front door sharing a pitcher of Schlitz. One leafed through the August copy of *Baseball Magazine* while the other worked the crossword puzzle from Wednesday's newspaper. Victor Barjas and Bernardo Roca were Spanish Falangists who had been working as riggers at Bethlehem Sparrows Point Shipyard since 1936. They were covertly organizing groups of Falangist sympathizers on the East Coast of the United States. The Spanish Falangist party and the German Nazi party had a special relationship. The Nazis understood the key to Central and South America was the common language and religion shared with Spain.

Bernardo was dark-complected with pockmarked cheeks and much shorter than Victor. There was an intensity in Bernardo's eyes that reflected his ardent belief in world change at any cost. Victor, on the other hand, was a follower not a leader and couldn't care less who was in power as long as he wasn't inconvenienced. Victor was rotund and not the least bit athletic. He perspired with the slightest effort, habitually wiping his face with a large white handkerchief despite the two ceiling fans maintaining a constant flow of air through the room.

The two Falangists were at the Devil's Due to meet with a German Abwehr agent. They had been seated at their table for about ten minutes when Schulte, disguised as a hunchbacked old man, stood up from a bar stool and hobbled over to their table.

"I hope you don't mind my asking, but I noticed you're a baseball fan," Schulte said. "Isn't that Lou Gehrig on your magazine cover?"

"Yes," Victor said. "I have finished reading the articles and was just about to throw it away. Would you like it?"

"Thank you, I'm a Gehrig fan."

"I'm partial to Bucky Walters myself. Won't you join us for a beer?"

Satisfied by the exchange, Schulte sat down, but really didn't give a damn about baseball or even care who Lou Gehrig was. The whole discussion was an orchestrated greeting between spies who had never met before and would never meet again.

Schulte scrutinized the man reading the newspaper and whispered, "Do you recognize the guy by the toilets?"

"He looks harmless to me." Bernardo closed his magazine and set it on the floor.

"Were you two tailed?"

"No, he was in here when we arrived. No one followed us and no one knows about this meeting. Relax."

"He's up to something. He's nervous. He keeps looking over here and hasn't turned a page in his paper in the last five minutes."

"Perhaps he's a slow reader."

"Maybe not," Schulte said. "Maybe he's something else." The unmistakable, mechanical sound of a blade snapping out of a stiletto pierced the conversation at the table.

Bernardo glanced to the front of the bar as a young woman bubbled through the door carrying an armload of packages. The man smiled, set down the newspaper, and stood up as she hurried across the room toward him. They embraced and left the bar arm-in-arm.

"See, just a couple, nothing to worry about," Bernardo said. "Put your knife away before you cut yourself."

"What?"

Schulte's expressionless gaze fixed on Bernardo.

"I said put your knife away before you cut yourself."

"You never know who might end up being cut." Schulte stared coldly into Bernardo's eyes as the blade of the stiletto slammed into the wooden table between the index and middle finger of Bernardo's outstretched left hand.

"What the hell?" Victor nervously wiped his face and crossed himself. It appeared Bernardo's hand had been skewered to the table. Victor stared at the knife, Bernardo's face, and back at the knife again. He held his breath as his right foot and leg vibrated up and down causing the floor and the table to resonate.

Neither Schulte nor Bernardo moved. They sat in silence, glaring at each other until one of the regulars stumbled from his stool and made his way toward the bathroom. Schulte wrenched the stiletto from the table top and retired it as the drunk staggered past.

Bernardo slipped his hand from the table. "We need to finish this business. There are still some things to go over before you leave for New York."

"I understand my mission." Schulte moved closer to Bernardo. "Just give me what I came for, so I can leave. I don't have time to waste."

"Look, it's my job to brief you. We don't need to play this game." Bernardo's demeanor was cool but defiant, as he removed a brown envelope from his jacket pocket and slid it across the table. "Here are your instructions, a train ticket to New York, and a key to a room at the New Amsterdam Hotel in Manhattan. A middle-aged man will come to your room this Friday night after ten o'clock with a package."

Victor sponged the perspiration from his face as his foot continued to uncontrollably tap the floor. Schulte scooped up the envelope and stood.

"The Americans are asleep and the British are lost. Soon it won't matter what *they* do." Schulte's open hand slammed loudly on the table in front of Victor causing him to flinch and perspire even more profusely.

The bar fell silent, but no one looked up.

Victor's eyes jumped from side to side as Schulte slowly leaned to within inches of his nose.

"Boo!"

Victor's lower lip quivered as the color fled from his face.

Schulte smiled and sauntered out the front door without saying another word.

Victor and Bernardo remained sitting at the table in silence for a few minutes. At last Bernardo spoke.

"What an asshole. 'The Americans are asleep and the British are lost,'" he mocked. "Maybe the Americans are asleep, but the British are most certainly aware something is going on. I saw a British agent on the docks near the warehouse yesterday. I am glad we are finished here. Drink your beer; let's go. The plane to Miami leaves in less than two hours and we still have to make our report."

"Are all Germans like that?" Victor stared at the front door and mopped his brow. "I thought we were just going to have a quiet meeting and a few beers, not a confrontation with a maniac. What was all that about?"

Bernardo downed his beer and turned the empty glass upside down on the table. "Let's go."

Chapter Twelve

Friday, August 4, 1939
New York City

At eight o'clock in the evening Grand Central Terminal pulsed fresh with life. Commuters rushed, suitcases in hand, through the main concourse and down ramps to trains or up the magnificent, polished marble staircase to the street. A sense of urgency charged the air. After almost a decade of depression, the world was beginning to awaken and regain lost confidence.

Otto Vogt sat on a bench in shadows at the far end of the concourse pretending to read a book. The slightly overweight, middle-aged man with gray hair and a long beard, wearing a dark suit and yarmulke, observed the crowd flowing through the concourse. He watched for anyone who didn't belong, anyone who, like himself, was more than just a traveler.

The terminal dwarfed the bustling masses and pulsed with life. The grandeur of the space, Roman architecture, sandstone block facades, sweeping stairways, and huge stained glass windows helped people forget the turmoil and uncertainty of the world outside. Grand Central enveloped them in the optimistic promise that was New York in 1939.

Individuals blended into the teeming flow with ease and mirrored the unique cultural patchwork found in New York City. Most were ordinary people with nothing to hide, but a few were more. They hid everything in shadows, never appearing to be who they were while they burrowed deeper and deeper into the heart of America.

All of the ticket booths were busy this evening. Otto noticed a small group of Coast Guard sailors standing in one of the lines joking with each other as they watched the girls promenade. Like birds on a wire, their heads turned in unison, drinking in the fluid curves of a young, platinum blond bombshell as she swayed across the main concourse.

She paused at the bottom of the stairs and pretended to powder her nose as she looked back at her admirers through the mirror in her compact and winked.

Otto smiled for a moment as he remembered his carefree days as a sailor on liberty in Hong Kong and Singapore. Sailors all over the world are good at girl watching, and Otto was one of the best.

The coasties were attached to the lighthouse tender *Arbutus* and were returning to the Coast Guard Yard at Curtis Bay. Their main mission was buoy tending, but soon they would be patrolling for German submarines and looking for saboteurs on the Atlantic coast of the United States. All they had to do was look across the concourse to find Otto sitting right there amongst them.

Otto's attention was drawn to the central information booth. Two nuns with heavy French accents were trying to ask directions. Short and petite, wearing wire-rim reading glasses low on their noses, they didn't speak English well, and the young booth attendant was having trouble understanding them. Otto knew exactly what they were asking and was amazed the booth attendant couldn't understand French.

At last one of the nuns pulled out a picture postcard showing the passenger liner they were taking to Panama.

Finally the attendant understood. He marked Pier 64 on a map of Manhattan and handed it to the nuns. Grinning from ear to ear, he spoke the only French he knew, "*Bon Voyage.*"

He made a point to know how to say something cordial in as many foreign languages as possible and beamed with pride when he could work a few words into a conversation. Born in New Jersey, New York was the farthest he had been away from home.

"*Merci,*" the nuns said in unison, nodding and returning his warm smile. They were on their way, postcard in hand, excitedly talking to each other in a-mile-a-minute French. They flew up the stairs and disappeared into the streets of Manhattan.

Otto listened to the announcements of arrivals and departures as they echoed through the main concourse.

"All aboard for Boston at Track 23. Last call for boarding. The train leaves in five minutes."

"Broadway Limited to Philadelphia and Chicago boarding at Track 36. Empire State Express from Cleveland and Buffalo arriving at Track 11."

Announcements flowed without end, documenting the passage of people in and out of New York. There was no pause in the pace, rushing, rushing, always rushing.

Travelers leaving for a new life or returning to an old home, mothers caring for their children, lovers dreaming of their future, and grandparents amused by it all.

Otto was not interested in travelers who passed through the concourse. He was watching for someone who didn't appear to be meeting anyone or catching a train themselves. Someone who had remained in the concourse longer than would be expected. An individual could be part of the crowd without much effort, but anyone loitering stood out against the backdrop of constant motion.

Periodically Otto looked at a train schedule and strolled over to the departure board, as if he were waiting for an outbound train. He was an experienced agent who had worked in espionage since 1930 and knew how to blend into a crowd.

He observed the concourse for almost an hour; content with his surroundings, he placed his book under one arm, picked up a tattered, brown suitcase, and descended to the locker area. The keyed baggage lockers on the lower level concealed many secrets. Otto walked past several rows of metal lockers and headed toward a shoeshine booth facing the stairs. He sat down and handed the attendant a nickel.

"Just a quick shine, please."

"Yes sir." The attendant rubbed brown polish onto Otto's shoes and began brushing them to a luster. The attendant whistled as he popped his buffing rag in the air and brought each shoe to a mirror shine. The rich fragrance of warm Kiwi wax filled the air.

"What's that tune?"

"*Deep Purple.*"

"It's quite catchy."

"Yes sir."

Otto watched the locker area while the attendant finished his shoes. No one came down the stairs. He and the attendant remained alone.

"Thank you." Otto handed the attendant a tip and moved to the back row of lockers and located Locker 39. He inserted a key and tried to open the door, but the key wouldn't turn. Perspiration trickled down his face as he adjusted his glasses. Otto took a deep breath and pulled the key from the lock.

He had received the key and instructions at Horn and Hardart last night when he removed the plate holding his dinner from the automat. He inspected the key and reinserted it into the lock. Otto wiggled it up and down and rattled the handle. The door clicked and swung open revealing a plainly wrapped package and sealed envelope. He glanced around. His palms were sweaty and his throat was dry.

Otto withdrew the contents from the locker and placed them into his suitcase. He noticed the package was unexpectedly heavy for its size. He checked the locker. Ensuring it was empty, he shut the door. He looked at his watch for the third time in twenty minutes as he picked up the suitcase and moved toward the stairs.

He disappeared into the churning river of people in the main concourse. As he hurried past the central information booth he glanced at the ornate, four-faced clock on its roof. He had only a few hours to complete the delivery. He needed to travel halfway across Manhattan to deliver the package and return uptown to Penn Station to catch the 11:25 for Richmond.

Otto rushed up the stairs toward the exit, pausing at the doorway just long enough to allow a gentleman in his sixties and his young female companion to pass.

Mick Jenkins and Gwen Wells stepped from shadows in the main terminal. They had been watching Otto ever since he had picked up the contents of Locker 39. Gwen and Mick waited a moment, then moved up the stairs as Otto opened the door to the street. They hoped he would lead them to his accomplice. He couldn't be crowded or he would know he was being tailed.

When they reached the sidewalk, Mick paused and adjusted his hat, signaling associates across the street that Otto was the person they were following. The agents covertly began to observe Otto as he traveled down 45th Street.

As Otto threaded his way through the commuters a refreshing mist began to wet his face, unusual New York weather for August. He hurried to a twenty storey high-rise a few blocks north of Grand Central Terminal where without hesitation he entered the lobby and glanced back to make sure he hadn't been followed. He sighed with relief when no one else came through the revolving doors.

The elegance of his surroundings caused him to pause and momentarily look toward the ceiling. The Italian marble walls and bronze detail belonged in a palace. There was no elevator operator on duty at this time of night. Otto slid his hand along the smooth white marble slab adjacent to the elevator and pressed the call button.

An arched ceiling soared thirty feet above his head and rich multi-colored oriental tapestries and finely patterned Persian carpets adorned the walls and floors. He wondered how there could be so much opulence, when so many were struggling just to survive.

He watched the white indicator lights turn on and off as the elevator descended and thought of Germany and his wife at home. A stark contrast existed between the New York Otto saw and the Germany he knew. There was a dreamlike aspect to life in New York where people had time to party. In Germany the party had never started. He closed his eyes for a second as he rubbed the bridge of his nose and felt tension building in the back of his neck.

The call bell startled Otto from his distant thoughts. He stepped into the open elevator.

Alone, at last. His ears rang in the silence as the constant noise of downtown Manhattan was shut out, if only for a moment. He pressed random buttons for several floors.

The agents watched from the sidewalk while Otto boarded the elevator. They entered the lobby as the Chinese-red doors were closing.

"Gwen, take the next elevator to the top floor and work your way down, one floor at a time," Mick said. "I'll use the stairs and work my way up. Alec, you and Jacob stay here."

The agents had to proceed with caution. Otto might be going to an office in the building, or he could be using the building to lose anyone tailing him. They didn't want to apprehend him, only to follow him.

Gwen pressed the call button and waited. Mick rushed to the stairwell and ran up, pausing at each floor long enough to determine the elevator was still going up and he was losing the race.

Less than five minutes after Mick and Gwen had left, a uniformed security guard approached Alec and Jacob. They weren't hard to notice, they stood out like a pair of house-dicks in the lingerie department at Macy's.

"Looks like we're in a spot," Jacob said under his breath. "Now what?"

Alec looked up and couldn't believe their luck. They must be in the only building in Manhattan with a security guard who took his job seriously.

"Let me handle this," Alec said as he turned toward the approaching guard.

"Here now, what you two blokes up to?"

"We're waitin' for an associate, so we can go to dinner," Alec said.

"I saw you and your mates enter the lobby and you didn't look like you were looking for a supper club. Where did your mates go?"

"They're meetin' a friend at her office."

"And which office might that be?" The security guard knew each office in the building and most of them were already closed at this hour on a Friday night.

"I don't know the number, but it's on the thirteenth floor."

The security guard stepped back and unclipped the black leather strap restraining his pistol.

"Thirteenth floor, my arse. We don't have no thirteenth floor. We're superstitious. What you tryin' to pull? I need to see some identification before I call the cops."

The situation was deteriorating rapidly. Jacob had heard enough. Alec wasn't handling the security guard well, and they were about to be thrown out of the building or, much worse, arrested.

"Right, you got us." Jacob wrung his hands. "We're detectives working on a dicey divorce case. Our client believes his wife is slipping around on him with his boss. We followed the gent to this building and are just waitin' until they come down so we can find their love nest."

"Say, where you blokes from?" The guard rubbed his chin and cocked his head as he scrutinized the agents.

"We're from Netley, near Southampton. My name is Jacob and this is my mate Alec."

"Cor blimey, I'm from Totton," the guard said. His whole demeanor changed to someone who had just met some old school chums.

"Hey, I used to go with a bird from Eling," Jacob said. "Small world, ain't it?"

"Anyone from Southampton is all right in my book. I hope you find the goods on 'em. Gotta get back to my rounds. Imagine, meeting blokes from Southampton all the way over here," the guard said as he turned and moved toward the elevators.

After the guard disappeared, Jacob looked at Alec and said, "Thirteenth floor? What were you thinkin'?"

"Well, we don't even know anyone from Eling, and how the hell did you know he was from Southampton?"

"I could tell from his accent."

"That was a stroke of luck," Alec said.

"You're telling me. It's about the only lucky thing that has happened to us all night."

Jacob didn't know it yet, but his words would prove to be prophetic. The chase was still on as Mick and Gwen continued to look for Otto.

The elevator stopped on the seventh floor. A well dressed woman in her twenties stepped into the elevator wearing a dark blue evening dress, high heeled shoes, long sleeved gloves, a fur wrap, and a wide brimmed hat. She looked like a model in one of the fashion magazines Otto's wife read when she could afford them. The woman's perfume embraced the air with the light scent of jasmine, and for a moment his thoughts returned to his wife and home. He longed for his wife's soft touch. He wanted to experience the warmth of her smile, to hear the music of her laugh. Otto closed his eyes and shut the world out.

"Eleven please," the woman said.

Otto's blank look faded as he glanced toward the woman and cleared his throat.

"Excuse me, could you press the button for the eleventh floor please."

"Oh, sorry. My mind was miles away."

Out-of-breath and drenched in sweat, Mick reached the seventh floor and cracked open the stairwell door just as the elevator doors closed.

"Strike a light, he's still going up," Mick muttered to himself. "I should be a gaffer behind a desk, not running up these damn stairs. I need a smoke."

But there wasn't time, and besides, he had forgotten he was trying to quit. Mick spun around and ran up the stairs toward the next floor, although not so quickly as the last seven floors.

Otto worried the young woman might think it was strange so many call buttons were lit up this late on a Friday night.

"I'm not used to riding in elevators and pressed too many buttons when I got on."

"I've made the same mistake. It takes a little longer, but I'm not in a hurry."

The brief ride provided Otto with a pleasant interlude. When they reached the tenth floor he wished her good evening and stepped through the open doors.

Otto rushed to the end of the hall and entered the stairwell. He could hear someone moving up the stairs a number of floors below. He ascended to the twelfth floor two steps at a time and stopped in the stairwell. His heart was racing. He needed to change disguises. The sounds of shoes crashing on steps and heavy breathing echoed louder in the stairwell as Mick drew closer.

Opening the suitcase, Otto hurriedly removed the package, the envelope, a change of clothes, and a businessman's tan leather briefcase. He stripped off his disguise.

Otto was clean-shaven with dark brown, graying hair. He changed from his gray jacket and sturdy brown cap-toed shoes to a finely tailored black flannel jacket with a charcoal gray fedora, black slip-on shoes, and a gray chesterfield overcoat.

The new clothes made him look taller and twenty pounds lighter. He slid the envelope into his overcoat pocket and quickly placed the package in the briefcase. He stuffed the old disguise into the suitcase and abandoned them in the stairwell. In less than a minute Otto was a new man. He looked like he had been working late in the office and was on his way home, another New York executive with more work than time.

Opening the hallway door, he rushed to the middle elevator and pressed the call button. Otto rode the elevator to the second floor. He raced out the door and down the stairwell to the lobby.

Gwen checked each floor as she descended in the elevator from the twentieth floor. When the doors opened on twelve Mick was standing there, bedraggled and exhausted. He stumbled into the elevator, barely able to catch his breath, and sank against the back wall.

"What happened to you?"

"I lost him. He left this behind in the stairwell." Mick held out the tattered brown suitcase. "There's nothing in it, except a bunch of sweaty clothes, nothing useful."

"He could be anywhere," Gwen said. "Who knows what he looks like now?"

"We know he no longer looks like a New York diamond merchant. We better call this in. Clive won't be happy this guy gave us the slip. I need a cigarette and a stiff drink. I bet our next assignment will be in some humid shit-hole filled with mosquitoes and head-lice where you can't drink the water."

Several minutes passed as the elevator stopped to pick up passengers on the way down. By now the elevator smelled like a steamy locker room after a rugby match. When it reached the lobby and the doors opened, the lobby was empty except for Alec and Jacob relaxing on a sofa in the waiting area. They were nonchalantly smoking and looking at the paper like two tourists on holiday.

Mick turned to Gwen. "How the hell could this Nazi bastard have slipped past all four of us? Shit."

Mick's temples were throbbing as he and Gwen approached Alec and Jacob.

When they noticed Mick, they dropped their newspapers on the floor and abruptly jumped up looking like five-year olds who had just been caught stealing cookies.

"Did you two spot anyone?"

"No one out of the ordinary, just a group of businessmen and secretaries leaving for the weekend," Jacob said as he glanced down at his shoes. "We've been here the whole time and I can guarantee you the Nazi didn't come through here." He glanced at Alec and shifted away from Mick.

"What about the stairwells?"

"A . . . no one special," Alec said. "One bloke came out from the stairwell and stepped through the side door leading to the street, but—"

"Bloody hell, that was our man." Mick gestured toward 46th Street. "What were you two here for? I don't care if he looked like Neville Chamberlain, one of you should have followed him. Clive will go stark ravers about this. We're screwed." Mick's jaw clinched as he shook his head and stormed across the lobby.

The chase was over. The agents exited the building and plodded to the corner. They had underestimated Otto and needed to face Clive. Mick threw his rolling papers and pouch of tobacco into a trash can and bought a pack of Camels from a street vendor.

"And you were doing so well at rolling your own," Jacob said as Mick fished out his Zippo and lit a cigarette.

"Bugger off," Mick said under his breath as he exhaled a large cloud of smoke. For the first time in over a year, he didn't have to spit out bits of tobacco from a hand rolled cigarette. *Shit . . . how am I going to explain losing the damned German?*

Chapter Thirteen

"Where to, Mac?" the cabby asked as he pulled into traffic with Otto safely in the back.

"Christopher Street Station, please."

"Sure, be there in no time. My name is Mario de Luca, but everyone calls me Champ, 'cause I used to box a little. That's why my nose is so crooked." Mario touched his nose and winked in the mirror. A red rose rested in a bud vase on the dashboard as a crucifix on a chain swayed below the mirror.

Otto watched the street while they drove away. Mario's cab was the only one that pulled out and it soon disappeared into the rain and traffic—just another cab in New York City. Otto glanced at his watch and folded his hands on his lap.

"First time in the city?" Mario asked.

"Pardon me?"

"Is this your first time in New York?"

"No. My business often brings me here." Otto lied. Mario was probably a nice fellow, but Otto didn't feel like making cabby-cheap-talk. He knew Mario didn't really care if it was his first, or last, visit to New York City. He was just passing time and trying to be pleasant.

"Turn right at the next corner and drive around the block before you continue."

Otto watched as they rounded each corner. A Checker Cab made the first two turns, then pulled to a stop in the middle of the block and let its passenger out. Otto smiled as Mario cleared the next corner with no traffic in sight.

"Tryin' to shake someone? Say the word and I can even lose your shadow."

"No, I have a meeting tomorrow morning and wanted to find out what the building looks like." Otto yawned and looked out the side window. He didn't care what Mario thought. He was worried about making the delivery tonight and had a premonition that wouldn't go away.

"Here ya go, Mac." Mario handed Otto a card with his name and number. "Call for me in the morning, if you need a ride to your meeting. I'll give you a good rate."

The cab drove past the Sixth Precinct and pulled to the curb in front of the Christopher Street Station. The entrance to the small brick building in the middle of the block was sandwiched between mom-and-pop stores and cramped apartments. Otto thought it was a strange location for the entrance to a train station as he jumped out and descended the dingy, soot-covered stairs to the ticket booth. The attendant put down his magazine and turned to face the counter window when he heard Otto approach.

"One to Hoboken." Otto raised his voice. "When does the train leave?" He wanted anyone within earshot to hear where he was going.

The attendant made change as he chewed on a well-worn cigar stub. He peered up at Otto from under his green eyeshade and momentarily pulled the stub from the corner of his mouth and took a deep breath.

"You don't have to yell. I ain't hard a hearing, bub. Like the schedule on the wall says, the train to Hoboken leaves at 9:30." The attendant picked up his magazine. Otto noticed it was a copy of Time from January 1939. The cover proclaimed Hitler as Man of the Year. Otto shook his head as he walked away.

Moving to a dark corner, he sat alone until the train pulled in and stopped. He descended the stairs to the narrow boarding platform and waited for the doors to open. Two other passengers, a man and woman, were talking and laughing as they moved down the stairs. He paused until they passed by. The woman stumbled in her high-heels as the couple boarded the forward car; they were three sheets to the wind and felt no pain. Otto waited until they sat down and then moved to the last car in line, becoming the car's only occupant. It was almost time to make the delivery, but he had one more card to play. He looked at the boarding platform. It was empty.

As the doors started to close Otto jumped back onto the platform and stood alone while the train pulled out. Taking a deep breath, he rushed up the stairs and disappeared down the empty street.

The sign for the New Amsterdam swayed precariously over the sidewalk several blocks away. He could barely make out the lettering. Most of the lights were burned out; those that still worked protested by blinking unpredictably as the sign was buffeted in the wind. When Otto approached closer, he noticed the rust-stained paint was peeling from years of neglect and the top of the sign was caked with pigeon droppings, which fell in clumps to the sidewalk in the rain. A bolt of lightning lit up the skyline across the river, followed by a resounding crack of thunder that echoed off the nearby red-brick buildings. In the flash, he spotted a side door hidden in the alley running between the hotel and an empty store. He ducked into the darkness.

Almost immediately, Otto felt someone's presence. He surveyed the alley, but his eyes weren't adjusted to the darkness and he couldn't make anything out. He stood still and pressed his eyelids closed, hoping to force his pupils to adapt more quickly to their surroundings.

"Who's there?" Otto shifted nervously on the balls of his feet, ready to run. He spotted a razor-thin line of light coming from under the side door. He started toward it, but shrank back as someone spoke.

"Any spare change?" A low, almost inaudible voice drifted from the shadows just ahead.

Otto stared into the darkness, barely recognizing the crouched figure of a man wearing the threadbare clothes of someone who had lived on the street for far too long. The man was wedged between two large crates as a shield from the weather. Otto hurried past without stopping; but after a few steps, paused and returned. He reached into his pocket and handed the man a dollar.

"Here, get some food and a warm place for the night."

"Thanks, buddy. You're a pal." The man smiled at Otto as he tossed his small canvas rucksack over his shoulder and turned the brim of his fedora down against the weather. The sound of his cane echoed in the alley as he hobbled from the darkness.

Otto wanted to say something more, but remained silent as the man disappeared around the corner. *There but for the grace of God, go I. Where will I be when this Nazi business is finished?* Otto felt a chill course down his spine as all of the warmth drained from his body. He pressed his overcoat collar tightly around his neck and reached for the doorknob.

Chapter Fourteen

A mixture of stale cigar smoke and garlic from the Italian cafe next door greeted Otto when he entered the lobby. No one looked up or paid attention as he quietly closed the door. Otto glanced around and located the stairs leading to the next floor.

The hotel should have been called the Old Amsterdam and condemned years ago. It catered to lonely down-and-outers whose world was encompassed by their cheap rooms, free soup lines, and the beer joints down the street.

The night clerk sat in his cage leaning perilously back against the wall in a rickety, old wooden chair reading the remnants from yesterday's newspaper.

A few old men sat in the drab lobby, reflecting on the life that had passed them by during the Depression. Their routine didn't change much from night to night. Some nights they would play checkers, other nights they would listen to the radio, but tonight there was an air of impending doom defining the mood in the lobby as world events seemed to point down an all too familiar path. No one felt like doing much of anything for they hoped tomorrow would feel different, but tonight all the energy had drained from the room. Their lot was not much different from many Americans who still wondered where the good times had gone. The lobby was full of victims. Some were veterans and victims of the Great War. Some were victims of the Depression and the auctioneer's gavel.

Today the rich could envision a bright future, but the Depression still pressed heavily on the spirits of many, and for them a bright future seemed only possible in the hereafter. Politics, religion, greed, and past mistakes spiraled the world toward another war.

Otto moved, unnoticed, past the night clerk's cage and up the steep, narrow stairs to a dimly lit corridor on the second floor filled with the musty smell of a sealed tomb. A frayed carpet runner led past a row of wooden doors to a room at the end of the dingy hall. The ceiling was discolored with years of water spots and thriving black mold. Specks of ceiling plaster peppered the carpet.

The floor creaked with each step as Otto approached the last door. He paused for a moment. Exhaling slowly through tightly pressed lips, he knocked on the door three times and then counted to four and knocked two more times. There was no response.

Otto had grown tired of the intrigue and his shadowy life. He yearned for something different. He had seen his ideology melt in the heat of reality and wanted to return to a saner time, a time in the past when he didn't have to worry about being shot as a spy. He had become just another nameless actor in the never-ending drama of world espionage.

As Otto turned to leave the door cracked open. He felt a cold, piercing gaze. His heart jumped into his throat when the door fully opened to reveal a figure silhouetted against the light from the window at the back of the smoke filled room. Unexplainable insecurity overwhelmed him.

He stepped into the room. The door closed and locked behind him. There was no greeting, no handshake, only silence and the overpowering presence of evil. What little energy Otto had left raced from his body. His face became ashen as beads of sweat began to show through his shirt. He clinched his fist and placed the tan briefcase on the bed while trying to observe his host.

The periodic flashing of the small red neon "Vacancy" sign hanging just outside the window and the occasional glow from a cigarette illuminated the depressingly small space. Otto's eyes adjusted to the low light revealing a pedestal sink faucet dripping in the corner next to the bed.

One, two, three . . .

He instinctively counted the drips as they fell, wishing he were anywhere other than where he was. The room was so quiet he could almost hear the rats gnawing in the walls.

The dark figure turned away and moved to the window. The hair on the back of Otto's neck stood up; for a moment, his life froze as he held his breath. A distant crack of thunder punctuated the chorus of rain drumming on the window panes. The ozone in the air produced an unmistakable metallic taste in his dry mouth as static electricity surged through the room. This was an ideal night for espionage, but not an ideal night for Otto. He placed his right hand on the back of his neck and dug the nails against the bone.

Damn it, say something.

Chris Schulte and Otto Vogt had business to conclude, but no one spoke. They were from different worlds, different generations, and had never met.

Schulte had graduated with top honors from the Abwehr spy school in Hamburg and had received a private audience with Admiral Canaris, the head of Abwehr, before leaving for the United States. Schulte had always been a deceiver and a sneak and never answered a direct question with a direct answer. Schulte was born to be a spy.

On the other hand, Otto was recruited into espionage from the maritime docks in Hamburg by youthful patriotism. Otto's experience had been gained through nearly ten years of field work. He couldn't endure the silence any longer. He cleared his throat and swallowed.

"You have been looking out the window for the last five minutes. I still need to catch a train to Richmond, Virginia and drive to Newport News."

"Newport News?" Schulte turned from the window and glanced at Otto and then at the briefcase. "Isn't Newport News where the SS *America* is being built?"

Otto disregarded Schulte's question as he fumbled with the envelope in his raincoat pocket. "Here are your boarding passes and passports. You depart from pier 64 tomorrow morning at ten. A Japanese agent, code named *Inazuma*, will contact you before you reach Havana. The meeting details are in the envelope."

"And the briefcase?"

"The briefcase contains a claim check for a trunk held by Panama Shipping and Export Limited in Rio de Janeiro and a package with the coded maps and initial funds for your mission in Brazil. You have passage to Los Angeles, but you will change ships and identities in Havana. The SS *Orion* leaves Havana for Rio the same day you arrive from New York. In Rio you claim the trunk and proceed to Recife."

Otto wondered why Berlin had chosen this young agent for such an important mission. He could not figure out Schulte's personality, for the agent did not fit into any of the classic personality types—rather was none of them, yet all of them. If Schulte hadn't become an Abwehr agent, one could imagine a politician or even an actor—definitely a chameleon—changeable, yet one who inspired trust. Maybe that was what made a good espionage agent: the ability to cultivate trust, like a priest, while stealing souls in the night.

Schulte struck a match and lit a cigarette. In the flash Otto saw steel gray eyes intently staring right through him. His discomfort with Schulte increased. Otto looked away. He wanted to leave but hadn't been dismissed.

"The package—its contents—must not fall into enemy hands," Otto said as he alternately massaged one forearm and then the other.

Schulte yawned and turned toward the window.

Otto edged closer to the door. "Be extremely careful. Exposure of our plans will galvanize the United States into openly siding with England before we can secure Europe." Otto glanced at his watch and then at the floor as Schulte brushed by. "I have to catch the train. Do you have any questions?"

"No." Schulte opened the door, indicating it was time for Otto to leave.

The cold finality of death was reflected in Schulte's piercing gaze. Berlin had made the right choice. Schulte was a psychopath who would kill, or die, to complete the mission. Otto was sure either prospect would suit Schulte's sadistic nature equally well.

Otto's heart pounded as he rushed toward the Christopher Street Station. His mouth opened taking in giant gasps of air. He didn't want to miss the next train to Penn Station. He leaned into the wind as his left hand pressed his hat against his head and his right arm pumped wildly back and forth keeping time with his legs. His movements were not fluid like a young stallion, but jerky and hitched like a tired old hack. Otto stumbled on the threshold and almost fell when he reached the station entrance. He stopped to catch his breath in the light and then dashed down the stairs.

Schulte watched with icy contempt from the second floor window as Otto disappeared.

"That doddering, old man is nothing but a liability," Schulte whispered. "Elsa, did you see how he avoided direct eye contact? He's another double agent. I should have killed him while I had the chance."

Chapter Fifteen

Schulte moved away from the window and hurried down the stairs, reaching the street just as a Yellow Cab stopped at the curb in front of the Italian cafe next to the New Amsterdam. A young couple jumped out and the cab started to drive away, but stopped when Schulte ran up and knocked on the passenger's side window.

"West 31st Street and 8th Avenue in midtown. There's five dollars in it for you if you make it in less than five minutes. I'm in a hurry."

"A five spot? You're on, pally. But you gotta pay my ticket if we're stopped." The cabby spun the steering wheel, making a U-turn in the middle of the block. The rear tires squealed as the Plymouth sedan flashed down Christopher Street and turned left onto Greenwich without slowing for the stop sign.

"You're lucky it's late," the driver said, pulling the shift lever into third. "There is no way I could do this in normal traffic. Need to catch a train?"

"No, just a friend."

The cab screeched around corners and slipped through the light traffic passing on the right, the left, and then the right again.

Schulte held tightly to the hand-strap to keep from sliding across the seat as the driver made a hard right turn. Normally it would have taken at least seven minutes, but the cabby made it in under five.

"Here you go," the cabby said as he pulled to an abrupt stop at the corner.

Schulte handed the cabby a five dollar bill and disappeared into an open service doorway.

While the Yellow Cab raced through Manhattan, Otto approached the Christopher Street ticket booth. "One ticket to the 33rd Street Station." His chest heaved as he tried to catch his breath.

"Five cents. Back up, bub, you're dripping water all over my counter. Say, didn't you buy a ticket to Hoboken about an hour ago?" The booth operator's eyebrows raised as he eyed Otto through his green eyeshade. He moved his cigar stub to the other side of his mouth and tilted his head upwards as if questioning Otto's sanity.

"I decided not to go tonight."

Otto descended to the dimly lit waiting platform and nervously checked the time on his watch. *The express to Richmond leaves Penn at 11:25.* He wound his watch and shook it. *Maybe I don't have the correct time? Damned, old watch needs cleaning.*

Otto was alone as he paced back and forth on the platform, only looking up as the sound of the approaching train became louder. The cars clanked to a stop. He took a seat in the first car, still shaken by his meeting with Schulte, and massaged the back of his neck.

God help us.

He looked past his reflection in the window and into the darkness of the tunnel as the train sped down the track.

I've been in this wretched business for almost a decade and all that has happened is that I am ten years older.

He hadn't seen his wife for over two years. She didn't know where he was, or if he were dead or alive. If he died tonight, she would never find out. He rubbed his tired eyes and sighed.

How did it all become such a mess? Now I'm on my way to Newport News to play another role. What for? I've no true friends. I can never let anyone know who I am.

He gazed at his reflection and brushed his hand across his face. Looking down, he turned his palms up and studied the lines and scars.

Just exactly who am I?

Otto's thoughts were abruptly interrupted by the squeal of brakes as the train pulled to a stop at 33rd Street. He stepped from the car and slipped past several people who were waiting on the boarding platform. He hurried up the stairs and made his way down the street toward Penn Station.

He couldn't shake his unexplained apprehension. Maybe the rat-infested hotel and Schulte's dismal personality had affected him more than he first thought. Otto realized Schulte, a child of the Great War, had died inside, losing all humanity and compassion. All that remained was a cold, empty shell the Abwehr had honed for their own purpose. The prospect of more children of the Great War, like Schulte, made Otto sad and frightened at the same time.

As he neared Penn Station, the entrance reminded him of the Brandenburg Gate near the Reichstag. The first time he had seen his wife she was standing by the gate with two of her girlfriends. He had returned every weekend hoping to meet her and had often observed her from a distance. Margaret had seen him too and had wondered if he would ever overcome his shyness and talk to her. It took another month watching and waiting for her to be alone before he summoned enough courage to speak and finally to ask her out. They exchanged vows a year later in Berlin and had been married eleven years the fifteenth of last month. He had missed their last nine anniversaries.

It was 11 p.m. when Otto passed under a large hanging clock in the concourse. He made his way to a ticket booth and bought a ticket on the express to Richmond.

"Is the train running on time?"

The booth attendant slid the ticket toward Otto. "Our trains always run on schedule. You can set your watch by them. Ever hear of railway time?"

Otto pocketed his change as he hastened away. *Twenty-five minutes, just enough time to use the restroom and buy a paper.*

The concourse was immense but not as majestic as the main concourse at Grand Central Terminal. The stonework and the exposed steel beams contrasted with the glass ceiling high overhead. As he moved through the concourse, he thought Penn Station felt rather industrial compared with Grand Central Terminal.

Otto spotted a sign for a men's room. He had been on the move since early in the evening and was by now acutely aware of the pressure in his bladder. He entered the men's room and rushed into one of the alcoves containing urinals. He took a deep breath, glad to be finally alone. His solitude lasted only for a moment.

A custodian placed an "Out of Service" sign on the door and ducked in, pushing a mop bucket.

"Take your time, buddy," the custodian said with a Scottish accent. "I got a lot of work. You're not in the way."

Otto finished at the urinal. As he turned to leave the alcove a hand covered his mouth from behind. He heard a blade snap from a spring-loaded knife and felt the cold steel surgically plunge deep into his back.

"Sleep tight, old man," the custodian whispered pulling the knife from Otto's back.

The pain was excruciating as Otto collapsed onto the cold, wet floor. He tried to cry out but couldn't. His mind was racing, but his body wouldn't react. *You little Abwehr bastard, I knew something was wrong. I shouldn't have let my guard down.*

Each breath became harder as his chest cavity filled with his own blood, and his lungs collapsed. *So this is how it ends? Bleeding to death next to a urinal in a public restroom. If I could just make it to the door, I could find help. I can't die, not here, not now.*

Death's finality, like sinking into quicksand, rapidly enveloped his mind and body. His vision narrowed and the light in the room seemed to dim as he heard two men approaching the restroom.

"Glad that's over. I can't believe that fat turd camped in the restroom all the way from New Rochelle. He didn't open the door until we pulled into the station. It smelled like he left a dead cat in there. Made my eyes water. I'll be right back."

"Bill, this restroom is out of service. There'll be another in the main concourse."

Reacting to the sound of the approaching men, the custodian threw the knife into the trash can and just as quickly thought to recover it—but it was too late. The men were outside the door.

"Fred, I really need to pee," Bill muttered as he pushed on the door.

The custodian stood inside the entrance blocking Bill's path.

"Can't you read? This restroom is secured. You'll have to use one in the main concourse."

"But I just need to use a urinal."

"I told you this restroom is secured. Go to the main concourse."

The sounds of hurried footsteps echoed in the corridor as a wave of passengers approached.

The custodian pushed past Bill and Fred and rushed through the crowd.

Bill turned away from the restroom but stopped as the custodian rounded the corner and disappeared.

"Wait here. I'll be right back." Bill hurried past a row of sinks and darted into one of the alcoves. As he relieved himself he glanced to his right and saw Otto sprawled in a pool of blood in the adjacent alcove next to the last urinal. Otto's dark red blood contrasted starkly with the bone-white tile floor and walls.

"Fred, someone's been attacked in here. I'll do what I can. Get help!" Bill knelt next to Otto and rolled him onto his back. Otto's face was pallid and covered with sweat. His lips moved, trying to form words, but no sound came out. Bill leaned in, placing his right ear just above Otto's quivering mouth.

Fred raced into the main concourse where he saw a uniformed policeman drinking coffee and chatting with the snack bar attendant. He ran up to the snack bar.

"A man's been mugged in the restroom." Fred blurted out in a shaky voice as he gasped for air. "Quick, follow me."

"Call for an ambulance and backup," the policeman said to the attendant as he ran after Fred.

The policeman grabbed Fred by the arm, spinning him around and stopping him before he could enter the restroom. "Do you know who is in there?"

"As far as I know just Bill and the victim."

"Who is Bill?"

"My friend, Bill Jackson. We're traveling together. I thought I told you."

"Remain here, and don't let anyone in unless they show a badge.

106

The policeman drew his gun and cautiously entered the restroom hoping to find nothing more than a bloody nose and a bruised ego.

"Police," he said, turning toward the alcove. Otto was sprawled on the floor with Bill still kneeling beside him.

"I'm Patrolman Brown." The patrolman felt Otto's neck and looked into his eyes.

"Are you Bill?"

"He's going to be all right isn't he?"

"No. He's dead."

"I tried to help but . . ." Bill's voice choked with tears as he glanced at his hands, not knowing how to hold them nor what to do about Otto's blood. "I've never watched someone die." Bill sat back against the wall.

Patrolman Brown moistened his handkerchief.

"Here, wipe the blood from your hands. When you're done just place the handkerchief next to you, against the wall. Don't touch anything else. I'd like to ask you some questions for my report while events are still fresh in your mind. How do you feel?"

"I . . . I'll be all right . . . ask anything you want." Bill stopped and closed his eyes for a moment. "Did I tell you, no one ever died in front of me?"

"I'm sorry, but I have to ask some questions now. Have you ever seen this man before?"

"No."

"Approximately what time did you discover his body?"

"He wasn't dead, he was alive when I found him. Fred and I had just gotten off the train from Boston. Guess it was around quarter after eleven."

"Was anyone else near the restroom?"

"A custodian."

"Can you describe him?"

"Sure, near as I can recall, he was a slightly built Joe, about five and a half feet tall. He spoke in a Scottish accent and had red hair and a full beard. As he walked away, I noticed he had a slight limp on his left side."

"Is there anything else?"

Bill paused and then said, "Yes, his eyes."

Patrolman Brown looked puzzled. "His eyes?"

"The custodian's gray eyes were icy cold and intense. They looked right through me, like I wasn't there."

"Do you mean he appeared to be mentally disturbed?"

"Not at all. Intense."

"Did the victim say anything after you found him?"

"Yes, but it didn't make any sense. He whispered 'southern cross' several times. What does it mean?"

"Your guess is as good as mine."

"Can I finish cleaning up?" Bill glanced at his hands again.

"When we're done, I'll ask someone escort you to a restroom in the main concourse."

Two detectives and a uniformed policeman entered the alcove. One detective was wearing a gray suit, and the other was wearing a dark tan, pinstriped suit. Bill strained to hear their conversation with patrolman Brown, but they were too far away.

The detective in the gray suit raised his voice and addressed the uniformed patrolmen, "As soon as Doc shows up, let him view the body; when he makes it official, call the Medical Examiner's Office at Bellevue and inform them we have a murder investigation and a stiff at Penn Station."

Turning toward Bill he said, "I'm Lieutenant Paul Watson, and the guy in the fancy tan suit is Detective Doug Marshall. Sorry for the inconvenience, but you and your friend will have to come to the station for questioning."

Things were happening around Bill, and he felt like an impartial observer looking at a scene in a movie. He was beginning to feel cold and confused.

"I should call my wife." Bill began to slowly rock back and forth against the wall.

"We'll give you a chance to use the phone at the station. I must ask you to step into the hall and wait with your friend until I am finished in here. It won't take long and then we'll drive you downtown. Thanks for your help."

Visibly shaken, Bill stood and moved to the exit. His features were pale and expressionless as he pushed open the door and joined Fred in the hallway.

"Please have Nelson accompany Mister Jackson to another restroom where he can wash his hands. Also get some coffee for the witnesses," Lieutenant Watson said to a patrolman standing guard at the door. "I'll be done shortly."

Detective Marshall checked Otto's pockets for identification as Lieutenant Watson returned from talking to the patrolman.

"This guy has a ticket for tonight's Express to Richmond. He has several passports and enough names to fill the New York City phone book. The name on this passport is John Williams, but it doesn't appear to match any other identification. In fact, nothing matches. He was up to something."

Detective Marshall paused and looked at Otto's pale face as a pool of dark red blood spread and trickled down the floor drain.

"What do you make of this case?"

"I don't know. First I thought this was just another dead queer, but now I don't think so."

Patrolman Brown had been searching the restroom while Detective Marshall combed through Otto's pockets and wallet. Patrolman Brown noticed small blood drops on the floor leading to a trash can near the door.

"Lieutenant, I think I located the murder weapon."

The lieutenant stopped and looked into the trash can as he opened the door to the hall.

"Let the lab boys remove it. Marshall and I are going to run the witnesses down to Central. Call me when the medical examiner leaves for the morgue." The lieutenant glanced back at Patrolman Brown and shook his head. "Geez, I hate crime scenes in public places."

Chapter Sixteen

Lieutenant Watson should have gone home when Detective Marshall did, but for some inexplicable reason he felt driven to work past his normal shift. Maybe it was the brutality of Otto's murder or perhaps it was the lieutenant's gut-feeling that there was something more important lying just under the surface. Watson had finished interviewing Bill and Fred hours ago. No one else questioned at Penn Station remembered seeing the custodian; the custodial staff didn't have a swing shift. Every lead from Penn had quickly played out. If the Medical Examiner came up empty this murder would become yet another cold-case forgotten under a pile of boxes in the evidence room.

The desk sergeant opened the door to Watson's office and leaned in. "Lieutenant, I made a fresh pot of mud, if you want a cup."

"Thanks, but I think I'll head home. I'm exhausted. I'll pick this up on Monday, when I can think."

Watson gathered the papers covering his desk and put them into his file cabinet. The clock on the wall showed it was almost two as he turned out the lights. He shuffled down the hall past the shift board and the desk sergeant in the lobby.

"See you Monday, enjoy what's left of your weekend," the sergeant said as he tilted his newspaper down and looked over the top of his reading glasses.

"Yep, you too. Have a good night. Say 'hi' to Irene for me." Watson barely glanced up as he plodded through the lobby with his head down and his hands buried in his overcoat pockets.

Pausing on the sidewalk in front of the station, he lit a cigarette. *Southern Cross? Why a constellation? There has to be something more. What am I missing?*

He looked up, but the night sky was shrouded by a layer of fog. Embarrassed, he quickly glanced around to see if anyone had seen him. *Geez, what an idiot. I couldn't see the Southern Cross from New York even if the sky was clear.*

Watson turned and watched a street sweeper while it rounded the corner and labored toward the Hudson. He tossed his cigarette into the gutter and reached for his car keys as a fog horn sounded in the distance. Watson stopped abruptly and looked toward the waterfront. The fog horn pierced the haze for a second time.

Damn . . ., it's not a constellation.

He spun around and dashed up the stairs on the balls of his feet.

"How could I have missed it? It's not a constellation!" Watson said as he burst into the lobby and hurried toward his office.

"What?" The desk sergeant sat straight up and almost fell out of his chair as Watson charged by.

"It's the SS *Southern Cross*—sailing this morning from Pier 64." Watson glanced at his watch. "We don't have much time. Get me a sailing schedule."

He rushed to his desk and picked up the phone receiver. It was time to call Bob Steel, head of the FBI field office in New York.

Steel and Watson had been friends ever since their days at the academy in 1922. They had worked their way up from rookies to detectives in the NYPD before Steel left the department to work for the FBI.

Watson dialed the last number. He drummed his fingers and counted the rings, waiting for Steel to answer. "Six, seven . . . come on Bob, pick up . . . eight, nine, ten." He was about to give up when a groggy voice spoke. Tonight luck was on Watson's side. Steel was single and could have been anywhere in Manhattan on a Friday night.

"What?" Steel said. "This had better be good."

"Sorry to wake you, but we have an unusual murder case I think you need to look at."

"Damn it Paul, it's two in the morning. Can't it wait until Monday?"

"No, it can't," Watson said, lighting a cigarette and drawing in a long breath.

"All right, what's this about?" Steel half-heartedly suppressed a yawn.

The sergeant handed Watson a current sailing schedule for the SS *Southern Cross* and pointed to the time of departure. Watson nodded in appreciation.

"The Department is investigating a stabbing at Penn Station that occurred late last night. We recovered the murder weapon but have no concrete leads on the killer or the motive. It doesn't appear to be a robbery."

"So what's that have to do with me?"

"The victim had several passports and identification cards under different names and was wearing a money belt containing a large sum of money. We have no idea who he was. He said 'southern cross' several times before he died. I have a theory he may have been referring to the SS *Southern Cross,* a passenger liner departing from Pier 64 at ten this morning."

"Where do you want to meet?"

"At the Bellevue Morgue. I'll start the coffee."

"Mind if I bring a British friend of mine?"

"It's your party."

Shortly after four in the morning Steel arrived at the morgue accompanied by his "friend." The lieutenant signed them in and handed them visitor badges.

"Paul, this is Clive Smith. He's over here on vacation from London. Clive is a police detective with Scotland Yard and is interested in observing police procedures in the States. Where's the stiff?"

"Pleased to meet you. You may hang your coats and hats over there in the corner."

Clive Smith? Sure, who do you think you're kidding? What's your real name? These cloak-and-dagger types are all the same. It wouldn't surprise me a bit if the dead guy's last name is also Smith. This is going to look good on my report.

They hurried down the hall and stopped at the entrance to the autopsy room.

Watson handed them a jar of Vicks. "Smear some under your nose before we go in. It will help to cover the smell. You're not squeamish are you, Clive? Sometimes it can be pretty graphic in there."

Even with the Vicks the room reeked of old blood, urine, stomach acid, formaldehyde and the unmistakable smell of decaying flesh. The walls and floor were white tile and the equipment was brightly polished stainless steel. The room looked like an operating room in a hospital; however, there was one major difference: none of the patients ever came out alive.

On some nights the parade of bodies through the morgue was like the passage of travelers through a great terminal. Everyone was on a journey; most didn't pick their final destination or how they arrived. Watson had never gotten used to the sounds, smells, and sights of an autopsy room.

The Medical Examiner and an assistant were concentrating on Otto. A second assistant was cleaning a bloody autopsy table in the far corner. Two fresh customers lay, untouched, in body bags at the back of the cooler. The night's work was already beginning to stack up.

The examiner's saw filled the room with the smell and shrill sound of cutting bone. A thin spray of bone and tissue covered the stainless steel autopsy table next to Otto's head. The examiner and his assistant were dissecting Otto like carving a Christmas goose, only no one was enjoying the feast. They removed, inspected, and weighed internal organs as Otto became less of a person and more a collection of jars and bags on a shelf.

Watson led Steel and Smith to the far side of the room.

"The case file is over there in the corner on the desk. That's all the information we have. The photographs and diagram show the placement of the body in the restroom at Penn Station."

"What about the murder weapon?" Steel said.

"There are several photographs of the suspected weapon, a fancy stiletto with distinctive ivory inlays on its handle."

"Anyone figure out who the victim was?" Smith said as he looked at pictures of the tattoos on Otto's arms.

"No, not yet," Watson said. "The passports, a First Mate Certificate of Competency issued by the British Board of Trade, and his wallet with all the different identification cards are in the evidence box next to the case file."

"I understand he was wearing a money belt with three thousand dollars?" Steel said.

"Yes, but so far, we don't know why. Anybody want some coffee?"

"Funny, Paul, very funny," Steel swore under his breath as the lieutenant walked off.

Steel and Smith browsed through the case file and the evidence box. They looked for labels in Otto's clothes, but they had all been removed.

Smith opened Otto's wallet and in a side pocket found a business card with "Panama Shipping and Export Limited, Rio de Janeiro" written on the back and underlined twice.

"What do you make of this?" Smith handed Steel the card.

"I don't know. Maybe he was expecting a package from Brazil?"

"You boys need to see this," the examiner said.

Steel and Smith crossed over to the autopsy table. The examiner's gloves were bloody and his apron was spattered with bits of tissue and bone. Otto's body had been split open and gutted like a tuna at the Fulton Fish Market.

Steel stared at Otto's pale, expressionless face. "I wonder if this guy had a family?"

Smith's heart raced when he recalled similar scenes as a prisoner in a German hospital during the Great War.

"The person who executed this man was an expert at his craft. He must be a highly skilled government agent with commando training. There is no sign of a struggle, only a single knife wound in his back. Here, let me show you."

The examiner snapped off his gloves and spun Steel around backwards.

"It couldn't have been more precise if I had done it myself." He thrust a finger at Steel's back. "The knife entered here on the right flank and severed the inferior vena cava causing the victim to bleed out internally, filling the chest cavity with blood and collapsing the lungs. The killer was not a street thug or gangster."

"Why didn't he just slit the victim's throat?" Steel asked as he twisted and escaped the examiner's clutches.

"That would have been too messy and uncontrolled in this situation." Smith picked up the jar containing Otto's heart and held it up to the light.

"Could the victim have been saved?" Steel asked.

"Not a chance." The examiner snatched the jar away from Smith and placed it securely back on the shelf. "There was nothing anyone could have done. He lost consciousness quickly and died in a matter of minutes."

Steel thumbed through the crime scene photographs. "This is a fancy knife."

"It is very unique, but strangely, I saw an identical one last year," the examiner said. "It was in the personal effects of a woman who died in a gruesome accident when a subway train struck her. I remember the case well because her body and personal effects were not claimed. We never determined her identity."

Smith leaned over and looked at Otto's wound. "Do you recall when the young woman died?"

"Yes sir, precisely. It was November 29. I missed my daughter's thirteenth birthday party."

Smith's brow furrowed as he glanced at Steel. "Thank you."

"Besides their obvious quality, what's so unique about the knives?" Steel asked as he looked at a closeup of the knife.

"Didn't you see the fuller?" The examiner pointed to a groove on the knife blade.

"Sure, I noticed it. Lots of knifes have them. They allow the blood to flow more freely from the wound. The killer should have left the knife in the victim so he would have died faster."

"That's what most people think. Sometimes fullers are referred to as 'blood grooves', but fullers are used to strengthen and lighten a knife. They are not common on a stiletto. This was a special knife. I am sure the killer regrets having to leave it behind."

Smith had seen and heard enough. "Is there somewhere agent Steel and I can talk in private?"

"You can use my office," the examiner said, pointing to the door.

One wall of the dimly lit office was lined with shelves filled with medical reference books and jars of pickled body parts. A mound of folders was sprawled under a reading lamp on the desk. Smith wasn't sure how the examiner could find anything in the stacks of paper cluttering the room. He checked to ensure no one was near before closing the blinds in the window between the office and the autopsy room.

"This man was a Nazi agent. He came to New York in April under a false British passport as John Williams from London, but his real name is Otto Vogt. He worked as a merchant marine prior to joining the Abwehr."

"He doesn't look like a sailor, his hands aren't calloused."

"Did you notice the elaborate nautical star tattoo on his left forearm and entwined rope tattoos around his wrists? They are typical tattoos for a merchant marine. MI6 has been tracking his movements for the last year and a half."

"Damn it. Was the FBI told about Williams, I mean Vogt?" Steel's face reddened as he clinched his fists and scowled at Smith.

"We informed your people in Washington about him three months ago. When no one got back to us, we thought the FBI was not interested."

"Damn bureaucrats. Your report is probably still drowning on some one-dimensional pin-head's desk on Pennsylvania Avenue under a mound of coffee cups and a copy of last week's *Post*. If I'm lucky, I'll get the report before Christmas. I swear all those desk jockeys do is work the daily crossword puzzle, drink coffee, and go to lunch. When you aren't any good at field work, they just promote you to a management position with an office, a secretary, and a subscription to the *Post*."

"Sorry about the mix up. We were following Vogt in hopes of uncovering his mission and contacts. However, he gave us the slip last night after he picked up a package at Grand Central Terminal. Was there a package with the body?"

"You just looked at everything recovered from the murder scene."

"Then we can assume the package reached its destination. That's a bit of bad luck."

"The victim said 'southern cross' several times before he died. Watson believes he was referring to a passenger liner currently docked in Manhattan."

"Yes, I am aware of the SS *Southern Cross*," Smith said.

"If a red-haired Scot is traveling on the *Southern Cross*, he won't be hard to spot. The police have a fair description from the witnesses at Penn Station."

"The description is useless. The killer isn't Scottish. He's a German agent who disguised himself as the custodian, and by now he could look like Quasimodo."

"Scottish or German, it makes no difference. I'll have FBI agents booked as passengers."

"No need, it's MI6's lead anyway." Smith knew if he allowed the FBI to take control of the case, he would need a Ouija board and a séance to find out what day of the week it was—let alone how the investigation was going.

"I don't agree," Steel replied. "The murder occurred in the United States and is under FBI jurisdiction."

"I think it would be more *prudent* if we don't have an army of people bumping around the ship on this. MI6 can handle it; besides I already have two agents traveling to Havana on the *Southern Cross* to investigate the Falangistas and Nazi underground operations in Cuba. All of your FBI agents look like Kansas City Bible salesmen. They won't blend in."

Steel paced back and forth and clinched his jaw. He ran his hands through his dark brown hair and faced Smith.

"Fine, we don't have time to wrestle over rice bowls, but keep me directly informed. Don't go through Washington." His eyes tightened into a squint. "Why is MI6 so interested in Cuba?"

"Italy has its Black Shirts and Cuba now has Gray Shirts. This Nazi-Fascist-Falangistas thing is getting out of control. They're trying to take over Central and South America. Someone should shoot the lot of them before they screw up the whole damned world."

"Can you tell me why one German spy would kill another?"

"That's a good question. I don't know, but there is something more about the killer. I suspect a connection exists between the woman who died in the subway last year and our killer. I believe this German is responsible for murdering three MI6 agents in Baltimore earlier this year. The dates and manner of their deaths are no coincidence. We are dealing with a German Abwehr agent who has become a serial killer. He has moved from Baltimore to New York, and is now about to board a passenger liner with over five-hundred unsuspecting tourists. As an Abwehr agent, he is schooled in the art of disguise and will not be easy to spot."

"Then shouldn't we have more people on the ship?"

"No. They would just get in the way. We have three days before the ship's first port of call in Havana and would spend more time trying to coordinate agents than looking for this German."

Smith opened the office door. He and Steel stepped back into the autopsy room.

There they found Watson drinking a cup of coffee and chatting with one of the assistants.

"Paul, I have no idea who the dead guy was. Probably he was some small-time hood from out of town who got stabbed for moving in on someone else's turf. You know how possessive and territorial these small-time gangsters are, like a pack of wild dogs pissin' on a tree. I would list this guy as a John Doe on the death certificate and in your report, since his identification and passports are fake."

"Very well."

"Don't mention the passports or the money in the report and anonymously contribute the money to the Policemen's Benevolent Fund. I would like to review your report before you file it. As far as this 'southern cross' business, it could mean anything or nothing at all. There doesn't seem to be any connection. Wish I could have been more help."

Watson could read between the lines; he understood exactly what Steel had said. "Thanks for coming down. Sorry to drag you out of bed for nothing."

If you think I believe that line of bullshit, my name is Peaches O'Day and I've got a bridge in Brooklyn for sale.

Watson knew when the official death certificate listed the dead guy as a "John Doe," the final stop would be in an unmarked grave in Potter's Field on Hart Island and he would suffer the last indignity. There would be no graveside service; no one to pay their last respects, and no family to mark his passing. He never existed, only as a number in a ledger. The lieutenant's thoughts turned to his own wife and family as he gave a fleeting thought to how and when his end would come.

Steel and Smith stepped out of the Bellevue Morgue and into the damp morning air. First light was beginning to silhouette the horizon in a scarlet glow. Occasional wind gusts played tag with the trash in the gutter as pigeons huddled on the window ledges across the street.

"I wish Vogt hadn't eluded my agents last night," Smith said as he braced against the morning air. "From now on life is going to be hell until we pick up the pieces."

Steel lit a cigarette and dropped the match to the sidewalk. "Damn, I hate trips to the morgue. Have you ever wondered when it will be your turn?"

"My turn?"

"You know, to meet the examiner's knife."

The streets began bustling with traffic as the city awoke to greet a new day. There were less than five hours until the *Southern Cross* sailed. Steel and Smith didn't know what or who they were looking for. They didn't have all the answers. Answers? Hell, they still didn't know all the questions.

Chapter Seventeen

Saturday, August 5, 1939
New York City

The SS *Southern Cross* was docked at Pier 64 in Manhattan ready to take on passengers. Her red, black, and white paint and polished brass rails glistened in the morning sun, beckoning travelers to come aboard and experience unsurpassed luxury. Colorful pennants and flags hung the length of the ship's superstructure and snapped in the breeze. Crew members stood at the top of the gangway in their impeccably cleaned, starched, and pressed white uniforms, waiting to welcome passengers as they boarded. The ambiance on the *Southern Cross* was one of a grand, five-star hotel. In 1939 there was no more luxurious way to travel.

The dance of river traffic on the Hudson was a well-choreographed ballet as freighters pulled in and out of cargo terminals. In the distance a freshly painted tug pulled a large garbage barge downriver to dump the city's waste at sea. The barge was populated by hundreds of diving, squawking seagulls who bubbled skyward only to plummet and fight over the next available morsel. By any other name they were just rats with wings.

Last night's rain had flushed the sewers into the river and whenever the wind shifted direction, the pier would be alternately enveloped in the mixed smell of raw sewage and industrial waste in the Hudson or smog from the city.

A large crowd gathered on the pier waiting to board the *Southern Cross*. Porters transported luggage from the pier to each designated cabin as the passengers checked in. A free-lance photographer took souvenir pictures of passengers and well-wishers while a newsboy stood halfway down the pier selling the Saturday morning paper.

"Read all about it. Yankees defeat Indians 5 to 4 at Yankee Stadium. Hildebrand starts as pitcher."

"Son, I will take a paper, here is a nickel," a middle-aged man said as he fished for loose change in his pants pocket.

A shabbily dressed boy, not much older than ten, wearing a ragged black bowler maneuvered through the crowd until he stood beside the man. He bit his lip while watching the man indirectly. The boy moved closer, hesitated and then skillfully slipped his hand into the man's coat pocket as the man accepted the paper.

A moment later the scene erupted into chaos as the man grabbed for the boy's arm, but came up empty. The pickpocket spun away and dashed down the packed pier toward the street.

"Stop, thief!"

The man's nostrils flared and his muscles tensed as he gave chase.

"You little tramp!"

The pickpocket darted through the crowd with the red-faced passenger fast on his heels. The boy was quicker and more agile than his pursuer and rapidly gained distance. When the boy looked backward to the turmoil in his wake, he crashed into an elderly woman knocking her to the pier. Her packages flew skyward and landed in a heap. He stopped for an instant and then, without a word, jumped up and disappeared into the stunned crowd.

"Come back here and pick up these packages," the woman shouted after the boy.

Two French-speaking nuns hurried over and helped the woman to her feet while a middle-aged Japanese gentleman picked up her jumbled packages. She searched the faces of the gathering crowd as if looking for answers to what had just happened. The woman opened her mouth briefly and started to speak, timidly at first.

"What . . . what's this world coming to? My land. Someone should box that ruffian's ears." She brandished her index finger like a saber at the crowd, punctuating every word.

The nuns smiled politely, not understanding a word she had said.

"Yes, madam," the Japanese gentleman responded. "I trust your packages are not damaged?"

"There's nothing breakable, just some last minute gifts for my grandchildren. Thank you for your kindness, sir."

The nuns carried her packages and escorted the woman up the gangway as the drama continued to unfold on the pier.

The street and freedom were just ahead. The thief had made it, but at the last moment a cane was thrust from the crowd, skillfully tripping the pickpocket in his tracks. He tumbled through the air and sprawled, face first, on the pier. He was fortunate not to have broken any bones. With no time to think, he bounced to his feet and resumed his flight through the crowd. This time luck was on the victim's side. In his haste to escape, the boy dropped his ill-gotten prize.

The winded man picked up his wallet and checked its contents.

"Thank you for your help. My name is Doctor Phillip Lansing. That little thief almost got the best of me."

Phillip was short and portly in his mid-fifties. He was clean-shaven with well-trimmed blond hair. He would have been more comfortable standing behind a podium in a lecture hall than chasing a thief down the pier.

"You are quite welcome. We travelers need to look out for each other. My name is James Amherst and this is my daughter, Olivia Howell."

James had a thick gray mustache, silver-gray hair, and wore a brown snap brim fedora. He was dressed to the nines in a sharply tailored brown pinstriped suit and sported an ebony walking cane with a distinctive silver lion's head. Olivia was in her late twenties, petite and strikingly attractive with shoulder length, coal black hair. Her bright green eyes sparkled when she talked. She was the kind of woman who took your breath away when you first saw her, and would never forget when she was gone.

"Pleased to meet you," Phillip said. "You not only saved my wallet but also saved me from my wife's wrath. She is always saying I should pay attention to my surroundings when we travel."

"Doctor Lansing," Olivia asked, "are you sailing on the *Southern Cross*?"

"Yes, my wife and I are traveling to California, but also wanted to see the Panama Canal. This year is the twenty-fifth anniversary of the opening of the Canal."

"Are you traveling on business?"

"No, we are returning to Los Angeles where I am a professor in the drama department at the University of California specializing in Shakespearean and contemporary German drama. This summer Helen and I were lucky enough to attend six wonderful plays in Germany. I just completed my book about the Third Reich's control of German theater, but I am having trouble finding an agent. So far, all I have is a pile of rejection letters. Next summer I want to start work on a sequel. Unfortunately, if the political situation in Europe becomes any worse, we may only be able to attend plays at the Pasadena Playhouse next year."

A flurry of excitement swept through the crowd as the public address system echoed the news everyone had been waiting for.

"Attention, all visitors are requested to leave the ship. The SS *Southern Cross* will be sailing in thirty minutes."

"We should be embarking now," James said. "I am glad you have your wallet back."

"Yes, I had better find Helen. She has been watching our carry-on luggage and I have the boarding passes."

The pace quickened as the last trickle of passengers made their way onboard. Excited travelers lined the deck rails, waving and bidding farewell to the crowd on the pier.

A solitary figure hid in the shadows at the back of the crowd and intently studied everyone as they boarded. Schulte wanted to ensure there were no surprises during the trip. So far no one had stood out from the parade of travelers moving up the gangway, not even Tanaka Yashiro.

With average height and build for a Japanese man in his thirties, Yashiro wore a white panama hat, gold rimmed glasses, and a well-tailored royal blue suit. He appeared to be one of the many successful Japanese businessmen who was traveling on the *Southern Cross*, but he was more—much more. Yashiro was an agent of the Japanese Black Hand Society. The German and Japanese agents' paths had never crossed, and for now Yashiro blended into the mass of travelers and disappeared below deck.

As the crowd on the pier dwindled, Schulte recognized two people standing in line. They boarded several minutes apart and didn't appear to be traveling together, but they were British MI6 agents.

What the hell are they doing here? The old man at Penn Station couldn't have lived. I hate loose ends.

Schulte remembered tailing the female agent three years ago for a week in France. Unfortunately, she disappeared into a crowded Paris street one night, and never resurfaced. The other agent's dossier and picture had been circulated in the home office last year. Robert Blackwell fit his description to a "T." It was obvious he still drank too much. He looked positively green as he stepped tentatively up the bobbing gangway; the smell of the diesel fumes coming from the trucks and equipment on the pier compounded his misery. Satisfied there were no more surprises Schulte joined the last passengers to climb the gangway. Traveling with two MI6 agents onboard presented an interesting challenge.

The gangway was lifted and the hawsers cast off from the mooring bollards. Two tugboats edged the *Southern Cross* away from the pier. Passengers waved and threw confetti as a band on the pier played Count Basie's *One O'clock Jump*. The adventure was beginning.

Chapter Eighteen

Unsettled clouds crowded the sky to the south as the *Southern Cross* pulled into the main channel and made its way down the Hudson past the towering Manhattan skyline toward a white-cap filled bay. A young couple and a middle-aged woman stood near each other at the railing on the weather deck watching the pageant unfold as the liner headed into the wind.

The youthful figure of the middle aged woman belied her age. Frustrated, she periodically reached up and brushed the flaming red hair from her eyes as it buffeted about wildly in the breeze.

The young man's right arm enveloped his companion's shoulders. He gently caressed her cheek while her left arm playfully clutched at his waist like an entwining vine. He was tall, over six feet, with the chiseled features and athletic build suitable for a soccer player. His companion was slender and much shorter, with hazel eyes and medium length brown hair set in finger waves. Not conventionally pretty, she had an animated face with beautiful bones that would age well.

The woman turned toward the couple as a strong gust tore her hat free from its hairpins and sent it careening across the deck. The young man jumped and captured the hat just before it disappeared over the edge.

"Thank you. Good catch." The woman tucked her hat into her bag and grinned.

"You're welcome," the young man said with a slight French accent. "My name is Vincent Bedeau and this is my wife, Marie. We are on our honeymoon." The broad smile that erupted beneath his trim black mustache matched the warmth in his eyes.

Marie quickly held out her left hand, displaying her wedding ring.

"Congratulations, you make a handsome couple. My name is Briana Jeffery. My husband, Charles, is somewhere on deck. He always loses his way. He's the typical preoccupied doctor." Briana spotted Charles in the crowd and waved. "Charles, I'm over here. Where have you been?"

"Oh . . . there you are. I was watching the tugboats move the ship away from the pier, and the next thing I knew, you had disappeared." Charles stopped and looked back at the last tugboat as it pulled away. "It's unbelievable how much tension those hawsers between the tugs and the ship can take."

He always had to analyze everything. If he hadn't become a doctor he would have made a fine engineer. Charles was in his late fifties, clean-shaven, with thinning curly gray hair. He was medium height, but a little stoop-shouldered and looked much like a college professor, somewhat absentminded and prone to daydreaming about things most people didn't care about. The picture was complete when Vincent saw Charles wore a pocket watch with a Masonic fob and held a carved Turkish meerschaum pipe in his right hand while a dog-eared copy of *Scientific American* rested under his left arm.

"This is Vincent and Marie Bedeau." Briana brushed the hair from her eyes. "They are newlyweds."

"Pleased to meet you Vincent and Marie or should I say Monsieur and Madame Bedeau?" Charles shifted his pipe and magazine to shake Vincent's hand.

The sweet vanilla aroma from Charles' pipe reminded Vincent of childhood summer evenings spent with his grandfather tending the garden. Charles was not at all what Vincent expected based on his appearance. He was genuinely warm and friendly. His amber eyes radiated a passion for life. This would be an interesting voyage. Vincent was looking forward to learning more about the doctor and his wife.

"This is the trip of a lifetime for us. We have read so much about the Panama Canal, Los Angeles, and San Francisco. Marie's father and mother gave us this trip as a wedding present."

"May we wish you a pleasant journey on the *Southern Cross* and through life as a married couple," Charles said.

"Come on Charles," Briana said as she winked, "I'm sure the newlyweds have better things to do than talk to us old folks. Besides, we have been up since four. We need to unpack and rest before lunch."

Most passengers retreated from the weather decks to settle in for the sea voyage, but Vincent and Marie stayed at the rail watching the panoramic view of the changing shoreline. It would be three days before the *Southern Cross* reached Havana, and they would soon lose sight of land.

In less than an hour the liner was in the Atlantic heading south. The weather was changing for the worse, the seas no longer smooth, and a steady wind blew from the southwest. A tropical depression had formed near the west coast of Panama and was tracking in an unusual north-easterly direction through the warm Caribbean Sea toward the Atlantic coast of the United States.

The *Southern Cross* was on a collision course with a storm that would become the third hurricane of the season. The ship and the hurricane would meet in the Atlantic off South Carolina, but for now the increased pitching and rolling deck was a minor inconvenience for most passengers.

Robert Blackwell was not one of them. He was hung-over and had remained in his cabin ever since managing to climb the gangway. He had consumed one drink, well maybe three or four, more than he should have last night. He had lost count as he worked his way through the Lower East Side, making his way back to the hotel just in time to shower and leave for Pier 64.

Cor, I feel like the coins just fell off my eyes. I'm such a piss-head. Why did I drink like a fish and stay out all night? Gawd, please grant me absolution.

Feeling sick and disoriented the next day after a night on the town was nothing new to Robert, but trying to regain his composure on a rolling ship at sea was. Robert always swore he would never ever drink too much again, but given half a chance, he always did.

Overcome by another rush of nausea, Robert made a dash for the bathroom in his cabin. He didn't know it was possible to be this sick and still be alive. His muscles contracted, but it was another round of dry-heaves. All the bile had left his stomach hours ago. Drinking water did no good, as the water only served to shorten the time between trips to the commode.

There was a knock on Robert's cabin door just as he crawled from the bathroom on all fours. "Who is it?" he weakly asked.

"Mister Blackwell, I'm the cabin steward. One of the passengers told me you're seasick. I brought some Dramamine for you from sickbay."

Blackwell pulled himself up from the floor by the door knob and opened the door. The steward entered and set a brown bottle on the dresser as he glanced at Blackwell.

"Some passengers have difficulty the first day at sea adjusting to life on a ship. You are just seasick. It's nothing to worry about."

Just seasick. No need to worry? I didn't need you to tell me that.

The steward walked into the bathroom and returned carrying a glass of water. He stirred the contents of the brown bottle into the glass and handed it to Blackwell. "Take this. You will feel much better soon."

Blackwell did as the steward directed. However, he wasn't sure what tasted worse, the bile he had been throwing up or the crap he had just taken.

"From the looks of your bathroom you need to drink more fluids. I'll bring you some juice and crackers later and have someone from housekeeping clean your bathroom. I'll sit with you until the medicine takes effect. Your vertigo and nausea should subside soon."

Blackwell groaned and gave a hesitating nod. *I hope so, 'cause right now I feel like shit.*

"Don't worry about participating in the lifeboat drill. You can remain in your cabin. The ship's nurse will check in on you later."

Blackwell lay back on the bed. The room began to spin faster. *Sod.*

He felt worse than ever. *Why am I such a jackass?*

The steward sat next to the bed and read the theater section from the newspaper as Blackwell gradually quieted down and no longer needed to make spontaneous visits to the commode.

"I'll check in on you later."

The steward switched off the light and hung a "Do Not Disturb" sign on the doorknob as he exited the cabin.

Chapter Nineteen

The irresistible aromas of poached Alaskan king salmon, glazed tenderloin of pork, roast prime rib, and duck blended together and spilled forth past the entrance to the dining salon. This would be the first time for most passengers to meet and become acquainted. Some would develop lasting relationships, yet other relationships would end before the *Southern Cross* made its next port of call.

The rolling and pitching of the ship had increased during the day as the ship sailed farther south, but the weather outside did not keep many away from the celebration.

The ship's orchestra played *Shanghai Shuffle* in the background as excited passengers were led to their assigned tables and seats. The first dinner at sea was always a grand affair meant to welcome the passengers aboard. All meals on the *Southern Cross* were social and gourmet masterpieces, but tonight the dinner was extra special. Tonight introduced the passengers to a level of service, culinary preparation, and presentation which rivaled the best five-star restaurants in New York or Paris.

The festive mood onboard was reflected in the crystal, bone china, and silver tableware. Place settings included decorative name cards indicating seating assignments. Large murals, ornate mirrors, and black walnut paneling wrapped the dining salon in an air of luxury making any thoughts of world affairs disappear, at least for the evening.

Dress for dinner was formal. Men wore black tuxedos with a colorful cummerbund and matching carnation attached tastefully to their lapel. Women dressed in their finest jewelry and best evening gowns accented by precisely arranged orchid corsages. Tonight the passengers were the picture of opulence.

James Amherst and Olivia Howell stood at the dining salon entrance talking and waiting for the eight o'clock seating. Some men always looked like they wore a rented tuxedo, for it would hang on them like an old army tent. You would notice the tuxedo long before you saw the man. They would be more comfortable in bib-overalls with a red bandanna hanging from a back pocket and cow manure on their boots. James was not one of those. He always stood out, no matter what he wore. Olivia was wearing a flowing black silk evening gown with an emerald necklace and matching earrings. The sparkle of the emeralds complemented her green eyes. It was obvious she and her father were comfortable with money. A second couple joined them at the entrance to the dining salon.

"Good evening, may I have your names please," the maitre d' said.

"Doctor Charles and Briana Jeffery."

The maitre d' looked at his seating chart. "Yes, Doctor Jeffery, you and your wife will be sitting at the table with Mr. Amherst, Mrs. Howell, and Miss Nancy Bechet. We will seat you shortly."

The couples introduced themselves to each other while they waited for their table. After a few minutes of cordial conversation, a steward approached. "We are ready to seat you. Please, if you will, follow me."

The steward led them past a life-sized ice carving of three jumping dolphins displayed at the center of the dining salon to a round table on the port side of the room, near a large tropical mural painted following the style of Paul Gauguin. The earth-tone mural beckoned the excited travelers to dream of adventure in foreign lands as it depicted a care-free village scene next to a white sandy beach and a blue-green bay.

The couples were soon seated with Miss Bechet. Charles and James noticed that despite her modest attire, she was stunningly beautiful. She was in her late-thirties with light auburn hair in a French braid. Her pastel blue silk evening gown was well tailored, but plain. A simple white pearl necklace hung from her neck and she wore a pair of small pearl earrings. The couples introduced themselves and learned Miss Bechet was traveling alone.

Shortly after the couples were seated with Miss Bechet, a woman in her fifties approached the maitre d' at the entrance to the dining salon. She was wearing a dark green velvet evening dress. It was Victorian in style with long sleeves and a high, closed collar. A finely carved cameo hung from a silver chain around her neck.

"Good evening, may I have your name please?"

"Mary Channing, Miss Mary Channing," she replied glancing around the room.

"We have you seated at a cozy table with an elderly couple, Mr. and Mrs. Brown." The maitre d' looked at the seating chart and pointed out the Browns.

"If it wouldn't be too much trouble, I believe an old acquaintance of mine is sitting at another table." Miss Channing gestured toward the table where Briana and the others were seated. "Would it be possible to be placed over there?"

"The table normally holds six; I see no problem, we will seat you immediately." The maitre d' motioned a steward over.

"Thank you for being so accommodating. You don't know how much this means to me."

The steward escorted Miss Channing to the table. After the introductions were complete, everyone agreed to use first names since they would be table-mates throughout the voyage.

"We'll be glad to return home to San Francisco," Charles said. "In the past few years traveling has become more stressful as the world's political situation has changed for the worse. We are increasingly more concerned about where we feel safe."

"I hope to travel the world someday," Olivia said.

Briana's voice softened as she leaned in. "Nancy, are you on vacation?"

"I am traveling to Havana for my first vacation in five years. I work as a secretary in a brokerage house in New York City. My boss packed me up and sent me off for two weeks and said not to come back without a tan."

"You're traveling alone?" Briana touched Nancy's hand "Aren't you afraid?"

"One of my girlfriends was going to join me, but she became sick at the last moment and had to cancel. There wasn't enough time to find someone else so I have the cabin to myself. It won't be as much fun seeing the sights alone, but so far the trip has been fascinating."

"I'm impressed, but concerned that you are traveling by yourself. Please consider joining Charles and me on Monday. We have a tour guide and a car lined up for the day. There will be plenty of room and we would love to have your company."

"Thank you for the kind invitation. I'll consider it and let you know at breakfast tomorrow."

"Mary, where are you from?" Charles asked.

"I work as a housekeeper in Geneva and am traveling to visit my sister and her husband in Monterey. We haven't seen each other since they emigrated from Switzerland to the United States eight years ago. I have a five year old nephew I have yet to meet. This is all so exotic. I don't have many adventures as a housekeeper."

"Charles, what were you and Briana doing in New York?" James asked.

"Bree and I grew up in New York. My family has since moved to San Francisco, but Bree's mother and father still live in the same brownstone in Brooklyn. Bree spent time catching up on family news while I attended a four day medical conference at the New York University School of Medicine where I presented one of the papers. When the conference ended, we spent two days touring the New York World's Fair."

"Just before we left San Francisco Charles and I attended the Golden Gate Fair at Treasure Island."

"There were a number of interesting exhibits."

"Not now, Charles." Briana covered her mouth and lowered her voice as she kicked him softly on the shin.

But he persisted.

"I found the Sally Rand Nude Ranch particularly spellbinding."

"It wasn't *spellbinding*, it was embarrassing. The women wore nothing but cowboy hats, gun belts, and boots. Can you believe it? Nothing but hats, belts, and boots. What's this world coming to? I'm glad no one we know saw us. I don't think a nude ranch has much to do with the future."

"Well maybe not, but it sure made for some interesting research in the present," Charles replied with a noticeable, but coy smile.

Everyone laughed, amused by Charles' quick wit. Briana blushed as she gave Charles a look that would burn a hole through a nickel at twenty feet and kicked him harder this time.

By his grimace, it was obvious that Charles knew it was time to drop the subject.

"What was the topic of your paper?" James asked.

"I conduct research in virology and immunology at San Francisco General Hospital. My paper was on the use of the new electron microscope in viral pathogenic research. Until the invention of the electron microscope a few years ago, we could not observe viruses. They are so small, a normal microscope is useless. My specific area of study is viruses in the Orthopoxvirus family."

Mary's eyebrows raised as she turned toward Charles and blotted her mouth with her napkin.

"Isn't smallpox part of that family?" Mary shifted in her chair and leaned in.

"Why, yes it is. How did you know?"

"A long time ago, when I was in school, we studied world history. One lesson I still vividly remember is how the British gave the Indians blankets infected with smallpox during the French and Indian War in North America. It was devastating. The Indians were decimated. It was a brilliant tactic."

Nancy had been observing Mary ever since she came to the table.

There is something familiar about Mary, but I am sure we have never met. She looks a little like my Aunt Ruth. Perhaps I'm just homesick.

The table fell silent until Olivia spoke. "Briana, what did you think about the World's Fair?"

"We only had two days. We could have spent a week going through all the exhibit halls. I found the General Motors Futurama exhibit predicting what life would be like in the future most fascinating, but 1960 seems so far away."

"My favorite was the RCA exhibit," Charles said.

"It sure was. Something called a television captured Charles' attention for over a half an hour."

"Who knows what television will be used for fifty years from now. Maybe someone like Sally Rand will have a program," Charles said with an impish twinkle in his eye.

Briana gave him the look again.

"My brother, John, says by 1950 we will all own small airplanes instead of cars," Olivia said. "When we need to travel somewhere, we will just jump into our private airplane and fly there. Imagine, a sky full of little multi-colored airplanes darting all over, to the market, to school, and to work. Fascinating."

"Scary, but John may be right," James said. "Pan American Airways just started regular passenger air service between Long Island and Lisbon, Portugal."

"Mary, since you are traveling alone, we would be pleased if you would join us on Monday along with Nancy," Charles said.

"Thank you, I wish I could, but I have a commitment Monday in Havana to meet a family friend for an early lunch."

"Well then, I'm sure you'll enjoy your day."

The conversation flowed effortlessly, binding the dinner courses together; by the time the main course was finished, the six travelers were chatting as if they had known each other for years. The dinner plates were cleared and a rich chocolate cake was served for dessert.

"I, for one, would like coffee to go with dessert," Mary said. "Coffee is one indulgence I have allowed myself to keep." The others agreed and the waiter filled their cups.

"There is something primal about dark coffee and chocolate. They were made to be enjoyed together," Briana said.

"I enjoy coffee, but I can't drink it black or my stomach becomes upset," Nancy said. "I must use cream and sugar."

"I know exactly what you mean." Mary pulled a small bottle from her purse and dropped two tablets into her coffee. "I use saccharin instead of sugar. It is much healthier for you. Here, try some."

Mary handed Nancy two tablets. Nancy thanked her and mixed the tablets and some cream into her coffee.

"I have read about saccharin but never tried it. Can you spare some?" James asked.

"I'm sorry, but those were my last tablets. I should have checked and bought another bottle in New York before we sailed. I hope I can find some in Havana."

Nancy sipped on her coffee.

"You're right, the coffee tastes sweet. It's amazing what modern science has come up with."

"Yes, it is, my dear." Mary smiled across the table at Nancy. "Science is full of wonderful surprises."

Optimistic conversation about the future continued over dessert and coffee for another twenty minutes. The effect of the waves on the *Southern Cross* became more noticeable as the storm grew closer. The color drained from Nancy's face and she began to perspire. She placed her napkin on the table beside her cup and stood up.

"You must excuse me. I'm sorry to leave, but the movement of the ship and my overindulgence at dinner have combined to make me feel a little nauseous. I need to turn in for the night."

"Would you like some help to your cabin?" Briana asked.

"Thank you, but I'll be all right by morning. I just need to lie down and rest. I guess I've had too much excitement today."

"This storm will pass by morning," Charles said.

After Nancy departed, the topic of conversation changed to Havana and everyone's expectations for the sunny days and fair weather of Cuba. Gradually the dining salon emptied as most travelers returned to their cabins and turned in for the night.

Briana noticed Mary hadn't touched her cake or coffee.

"Aren't you feeling well, dear?"

"I'm also a little queasy," Mary said. "You must excuse me. I am fatigued from today's activities and should retire to my cabin. I'll join you in the morning for breakfast."

The others finished and the steward cleared the plates.

"Anyone up for an after-dinner drink in the lounge?" James asked. "I understand they have a wonderfully aged bottle of *Delamain* cognac at the bar."

"Dad, I'll meet you in the lounge in a little while."

"Is anything wrong?" James' face reflected his concern.

"I just need to visit the cabin."

"I'll walk with you."

"No, I'll join you in the lounge." Olivia smiled and touched her father on his shoulder as she stood up.

"Very well." James glanced back at Charles. "What about that cognac?"

"Sounds good to me," Charles replied. "What do you think Bree? How about spending a little time in the lounge?"

"Well, just for a while. It's almost ten." Briana turned and glanced around at the other tables as they emptied. "Oh look, Vincent and Marie are sitting in the corner."

"Vincent and Marie?"

"Remember, the young couple we met this morning? Let's invite them to join us."

Charles was looking in the direction Nancy had gone and hadn't been listening. He drummed his fingers on the table and glanced at Nancy's empty chair.

"Certainly, that would be fine, dear."

Chapter Twenty

Between pausing to control the roiling nausea in her stomach and turning down the wrong passage, it took Nancy fifteen agonizing minutes to reach her cabin. She leaned against the bulkhead next to her door while she searched for her key. An elderly couple turned the corner and approached as she struggled to push the key into the lock. She reversed the key several times, before dropping it to the carpet and almost kicking it under the door.

"Ma'am, may I help?"

Nancy bent over and ran her hand along the carpet until she felt the key. "Thank you, but I can manage. I'm just a little under the weather." However, Nancy bobbled the key and dropped it as she stood up.

"Damn it, what a botcher," Nancy whispered under her breath as she braced herself against the bulkhead.

The man retrieved the key.

"Ma'am, at least allow me to open your door," he said as he inserted the key in the lock. "May I call the ship's doctor for you?"

"No, really, I'll be all right. The movement of the ship has affected my equilibrium—that's all." Nancy turned away and entered her cabin.

"Well, if you need anything, my wife and I are staying in the cabin directly across from you. Don't hesitate to knock, Margaret and I are light sleepers."

"Thank you, but I'm sure this will pass by morning." Nancy's lips tightened into a forced, wooden smile as she closed the door. She had already been overly social during dinner.

She steadied herself on a corner of the bed struggling to gather her unmarshaled thoughts. She needed to concentrate. Her mind was racing. Her random thoughts had no meaning. They might become clear in the morning after she recovered, or they could prove to be nonsense. Nancy noticed ship's stationery and a pen on the desk and scrawled down a few words. She folded the stationery and crossed over to the dresser.

The rolling and pitching of the ship caused her to wish she had left the chocolate cake on the dessert tray. She became dizzy as her condition worsened, and she barely made it to the toilet as a rush of diarrhea hit her.

I don't believe I'm this sick. I'm used to crewing on a sailboat. Damn it, stop this constant bobbing. Where the hell was Blackwell tonight?

A soft, but steady knocking on her cabin door interrupted Nancy's jumbled thoughts.

Not now.

"Who is it?"

"Miss Bechet, it's the ship's nurse; I was told you are seasick. I brought some medicine to quiet your stomach and help you sleep."

"Thank God." Nancy hesitated and tried to focus on something—anything—that wasn't moving, but it was no use. The cabin was spinning. She took a deep breath and managed to stand long enough to open the door.

"Please be seated on the bed." The nurse rushed past Nancy and into the bathroom. A moment later she emerged with a glass of water and pulled a dark brown bottle from her medical bag. Measuring some powder into the water, she stirred the mixture and handed the glass to Nancy.

"You won't care for the taste, but it will stop you from feeling seasick."

Nancy swallowed as much of the liquid as she could tolerate and slumped back on the bed. The nurse was right, she didn't like it. Almost immediately she had problems swallowing and began to drool. It required a great deal of mental effort for Nancy to concentrate. Her vision became blurred, an unidentifiable jumble of shadows and flashes of light.

"Who are you?" Nancy whispered hoarsely, almost inaudibly with the leathery voice of a three pack-a-day smoker.

She could no longer control her writhing body. It was a struggle to breathe as her throat constricted. Nancy involuntarily doubled up, every muscle fiber pulled piano-string tight. Her mouth opened in a tortured, silent scream. She no longer thought of getting well, she just wanted the pain to end.

Savoring every exquisite minute of the struggle, the nurse sat in a chair next to the dresser and observed Nancy with the concentration of a predator, claws firmly planted, waiting for its victim's life to slip away.

This whole incident is inconvenient, most inconvenient.

Grabbing a magazine from the dresser top, she flipped through the pages, but just as quickly slammed it closed and tossed it across the cabin.

See how powerless you are. What are you experiencing —pain, fear, terror?

The nurse sprang up and hurried over to the bed and checked Nancy's neck for a pulse. Abruptly seizing Nancy's head, she wrenched it to one side so their eyes met.

"No, you can't die yet. Not yet."

The nurse back-handed Nancy across the face. "Look at me when I'm talking. Look at me! Remember my face in your soul. I'm the last living thing you'll ever see."

An expression of disappointment swept over the nurse's face as Nancy's gaze froze, eyes wide open. She stopped thrashing and expelled the remaining air from her lungs in one low raspy gurgle.

The nurse sat back in the chair and lit a cigarette.

They always die too quickly.

Chapter Twenty-one

When Vincent and Marie entered the lounge from the grand foyer they were confronted by an elaborately carved teak bar positioned prominently along the back wall. Two rows of multi-shaped liquor bottles lined glass shelves in front of a huge gold framed mirror mounted behind the bar. Etched glass doors, allowing passage onto the promenade deck, stood on each side of the bar. A small group of passengers sat at a table quietly talking about the day's events.

Marie tightened her grip on Vincent's arm and pulled him closer as she whispered in his ear. "Would you look at the mural above the gaming tables. It's immense."

"Yes, it is large with a similar theme to the murals in the dining salon. I'm becoming used to the artist's style, but still I don't care for his use of unnatural, arbitrary colors." Vincent wound his watch as he looked around the lounge.

"I thought you liked Post-Impressionism?"

"I do, but so far all the murals we have seen are just commercial wall coverings, not art. They only provide color to the room. The artist has not put passion into his work." Vincent turned toward the back of the lounge. "There's Briana and the others over there on the right. Let's not stay too long."

Marie's eyes softened as she glanced up at Vincent and smiled. She pressed his hand to her lips and kissed the finger tips. "We could leave now."

"Briana has seen us. It's too late."

Vincent and Marie continued past a line of booths to a grouping of over-stuffed chairs where Charles and the others were seated.

Briana held a dry martini while Charles and James sipped twenty-year-old brandy from snifters they occasionally swirled as they savored the warm fragrance. Life for these travelers was good.

"Glad you could stop by." Charles stood as he greeted the young couple. "May I offer you a nightcap?"

"Thank you, I'll have what you're drinking; Marie never developed a taste for alcohol, but will have ginger ale with a twist of lemon."

Charles raised his hand and caught the steward's attention while he introduced James to the new arrivals.

"I understand that you have done some climbing in the Alps," James said. "I know I don't look like it now, but in my youth I climbed in the Dolomites; although, today the stairs in my building challenge me more. I would love to swap climbing stories with you."

"I brought a small album of pictures to show friends in California and it would be a pleasure to share them with you tomorrow."

"I look forward to seeing them." James eyes sparkled as a broad smile swept over his face. He reached into his coat pocket and offered Charles and Vincent one of his prized, hand rolled Havana cigars. Soon the robust aroma of cigar smoke filled the air as Charles, James, and Vincent explored the world's current problems while the ladies listened politely.

"How do you feel about the Japanese interference in China?" Charles asked. "What do you suppose they are really up to?"

"It's all about money," James said, exhaling a rolling cloud of cigar smoke. Several interested passengers drew closer when they overheard his comment.

"I couldn't disagree more." Charles shifted in his chair. "The root of the problem goes back to the end of the Great War with the Treaty of Versailles and the founding of the League of Nations."

"What's Versailles have to do with Japan?" James slowly tilted his brandy snifter and held it just below his nose. "The Japanese had a relatively small role in the Great War."

"Western countries rejected their request to have a racial equality clause included in the League of Nations Covenant and the United States passed the Japanese Exclusion Act to stop Japanese immigration into the States. These acts attacked their pride and increased their militaristic sentiments. The United States never has

155

recognized the importance of pride and saving face in the Oriental culture."

Vincent ran his hand through his wavy black hair and took a deep breath. "Being from France, I can tell you we are more concerned about Germany than Japan. We have already dealt with the Germans once this century and are presently fighting a war of espionage and counter-intelligence as German spies cross our border in increasing numbers disguised as refugees from Nazi tyranny."

"Chamberlain has Germany under control; France and the rest of Europe have nothing to worry about." James looked directly at the others and grinned knowingly. "Mark my words. It's the Japanese who will eventually be the problem."

Olivia tiptoed up and silently sat down beside James. She winked and smiled as their eyes met.

Vincent swirled his cognac. "An acquaintance of mine in Paris speaks of boycotting the Japanese as a way to curb their expansion."

"Now you're talking." James leaned forward and rubbed his hands together. "A boycott makes perfect sense. It would be a major contribution to world peace. Japan can't fight for an extended period without foreign trade."

Charles put down his empty snifter and shook his head.

"I don't think a boycott can become effective in time to stop their further expansion. In fact, a boycott might be perceived as yet another affront to pride and face, further increasing resentment and causing war to break out sooner."

"Well in my opinion, a boycott of German and Italian goods certainly has not stopped German rearmament or

German and Italian aggression in Europe and Africa," Vincent said. "War will come. It's inevitable given world events. We will surely be at war within a year."

"That sounds like a self-fulfilling prophecy. I hope you're wrong for all our sakes." James leaned back.

"Have either of you read *The Great Pacific War* by Hector Bywater?" Charles asked.

"No." Vincent and James spoke in unison and then looked at each other in surprise.

"It was a novel published almost fourteen years ago describing an ocean war between Japan and the United States. In it Japan attacks the United States Pacific Fleet near the Philippines. The war starts in 1931 and the Philippines and Guam fall to the Japanese. I won't tell you any more about the book; you will have to read it yourselves."

Briana interrupted, giving Charles her burn a hole in a nickel look again.

"Gentlemen, you've talked long enough about world affairs. We ladies would like to discuss a happy future with our newlyweds. Vincent, how did you two meet?"

With that, the eavesdroppers departed as fast as they had arrived, leaving Briana and the others to continue their conversation without an audience.

"We met in February 1936 while I was attending the Canet-Cluse Police School for inspectors." Vincent took Marie's hand and looked into her eyes. "A mutual friend introduced us on a blind date. We became engaged by the end of the year, but waited three years to marry.

"Where are you assigned?" Charles asked.

"I am currently an inspector in the French National Police working in Paris."

"How do you like police work?" James inhaled from his cigar one last time and extinguished it in the ashtray.

"It has always been interesting to me. I have wanted to be a police inspector ever since I was a little boy. I used to hide in the closet and read mystery stories when it was past my bedtime. Mother knew, but she never told father. I have read each one of Sir Arthur Conan Doyle's Sherlock Holmes stories at least three times."

"I enjoy reading Holmes myself," James said. "What is your favorite?"

"That's easy, *The Valley of Fear.*"

"Why is that?" Olivia asked.

"Doyle wrote *The Adventure of the Final Problem* as the last of the Sherlock Holmes stories. To my horror, Professor Moriarty killed Holmes. My childhood hero was dead. I just knew Holmes couldn't die, and I was devastated, until Doyle wrote *The Valley of Fear.* Holmes wasn't dead after all, and I was elated. It satisfied my need to have good overcome evil. I guess that's why it's my favorite."

"I'm at the other end of the literary scale." Marie's eyes lit up. "I have to admit I like comic books. It must be the little girl in me. I don't suppose anyone else here reads comics?"

Everyone looked around and smiled timidly. It was obvious by their blank stares that considering comic books as a serious literary art form had eluded them.

"Go on, my dear," Briana said.

"I like comics because you always know who the bad guys are, and they receive their due in the end. In real life you may not know who they are until it's too late."

"And they may never be caught," Vincent said as he peeked at his watch.

The snifters and glasses were empty and the glow from the cigars had long been extinguished. James and Olivia were beginning to politely yawn.

"Charles, we should say goodnight." Briana tugged on Charles' hand. "This has been a pleasant evening. We'll join you all in the morning for breakfast."

Charles and Briana stood and left the lounge. It didn't take long for the others to follow their lead and retire as well.

Tanaka Yashiro had been sitting at the bar casually talking with two Japanese businessmen since 10:30 this evening. He was facing the large mirror observing the entire lounge. Yashiro and Schulte were scheduled to meet in the lounge just before midnight, but neither agent knew what the other looked like.

Yashiro pursued a Bachelor of Arts degree in civil engineering at Purdue University for three years starting in 1927. However, the Great Depression changed his family fortunes and required him to drop out of school and return to Japan. Shortly after his return, Yashiro joined the Japanese Black Dragon Society, and in the early thirties worked as an intelligence agent for Colonel Akashi in

China. In 1938 he was selected to attend Nakano, the newly formed Imperial Japanese Army's Intelligence school for espionage training. His selection was due in part to the years Yashiro had spent in the United States.

Just before midnight the two men bid good night to Yashiro and left him sitting alone at the bar. Now only Yashiro and two other passengers remained in the lounge. Yashiro wondered which one was his German contact, both appeared to be European. One passenger was much older, probably in his sixties. He didn't seem to be waiting for anyone, but that might just reflect his many years of experience as an espionage agent. The body language and mannerisms of the younger passenger portrayed someone who was comfortable, but edgy. After considering his options Yashiro spoke to the bartender.

"What is the gentleman over at the far table drinking?"

"Macallan Scotch on the rocks."

"Please take him a fresh drink with my compliments."

After delivering Schulte's drink, the bartender returned to Yashiro and poured him a glass of Takara sake saying, "The gentleman wonders if you might join him."

Yashiro moved to Schulte's table and introduced himself as a textile distributer in Central and South America. He was relieved to have made the correct choice. They remained silent for a moment and sipped their drinks.

The other passenger in the lounge was sitting nearby and leaned in as he overheard the introductions. He turned and looked toward Schulte and Yashiro and finished his drink. He stood and walked over to their table.

"I didn't mean to eavesdrop, but I couldn't help but overhear you. We have something in common; I'm also in the textile market. Might I impose and join you?"

Schulte's menacing stare provided the answer: there was no room at the table.

The old man started to speak, but closed his mouth as his jaw clinched. He glanced toward the foyer and departed without saying another word.

Schulte sat quietly until after the bartender had cleared the old man's table and returned to the bar.

"Why did you sit at the bar for so long? Didn't you notice me over here?"

"I waited until the lounge was almost empty."

Yashiro finished his sake and pulled out a matchbook. Opening the cover, he wrote down his cabin number and handed it to Schulte. Yashiro rose and strolled past the bar to the promenade deck.

The passageway was empty when Schulte approached Yashiro's cabin. After a series of light taps, Yashiro opened the door and motioned for Schulte to enter.

"The loud American had it right, their fleet is the key to victory in the Pacific."

"Do you have a cigarette?"

Yashiro opened the desk drawer and removed a pack of Golden Bat cigarettes and a book of matches.

"Lotus Bar, what's this?" Schulte closed the matchbook cover and lit a cigarette.

"It's a nightclub I operate catering to American sailors in Panama. Keep the matches. I pass them out where ever I go. They are a good advertisement."

"My understanding is that after the mission in Brazil is finished, I travel to Buenos Aires and wait for new orders."

"I have something for you." Yashiro retrieved a sealed manila envelope from behind the dresser mirror.

It was unusual for an agent of the Japanese Black Dragon Society to carry orders for a member of the Abwehr; however, since 1934 the two countries had been working closely together toward a common goal in South America.

The envelope was sealed with red wax and an impression of Admiral Canaris' signet ring. Schulte sat down at the desk and decoded the contents.

"This directs me to coordinate with you in Panama."

"Yes, I asked for Abwehr assistance because we needed someone with your special talent. There are some areas in the Canal Zone my agents are not able to adequately observe. The authorities are watching the movement of Orientals more closely as the situation deteriorates in China. After you conclude negotiations in Brazil, you are to meet me in the port city of Recife. I have something else for you." Yashiro removed a plainly wrapped package from the closet and placed it on the desk.

Schulte took out a Walther PPK pistol and a box of cartridges, but set them both back on the wrapping paper without inspecting them and turned away.

"Not big enough?"

"I would rather carry a knife. A gun attracts too much attention."

"What about using a silencer?"

"Guns with silencers still make noise and aren't as quiet and personal as a knife. Death should never be impersonal, but dispensed intimately and savored like a deep red Burgundy."

"Well, I can keep the pistol, if you don't want it." Yashiro pursed his lips as he stared at the desk.

"I lost my knife in New York and didn't have time to replace it before we sailed. I will find another in Havana, but until then this will do." Schulte took a deep drag and crushed the cigarette butt in the ashtray. "Is there anything else?"

"No." Yashiro turned away as the door opened. "I won't contact you again until Recife."

Chapter Twenty-two

Sunday, August 6, 1939
Atlantic Ocean

By mid-evening Captain Ashcroft had ordered signs posted at all hatches leading to the weather decks warning passengers to stay below deck for their safety. Any crewmen going on deck were required to wear a line securely attached to the ship's structure. Throughout the evening the storm escalated, pounding the open decks with an endless barrage of waves and torrential rain. The sea was relentless as it toyed with the *Southern Cross* The worst weather hit with a vengeance in the early morning hours shortly after one.

But seven hours later, just before sunrise, the storm winds were exhausted and had faded into a mild breeze that no longer tossed the *Southern Cross* about. At times the morning sun glinted from behind a wall of diminishing clouds, heralding the possibility of a quiet day at sea.

Many passengers elected to skip breakfast in hopes of catching up on lost sleep. Those who came returned to their assigned seats and were soon discussing last night's storm.

Most ate a simple fare of hot or cold cereal, toast, and tea or coffee, choosing to stay away from rich foods that might antagonize an already tender stomach.

Briana placed her napkin beside her plate and stirred a lump of sugar into her coffee.

"I'm not surprised Nancy missed breakfast. The color had drained from her face by the end of dinner last night. I am sure she felt far worse than she let on."

"Yes, I noticed her distress also," Olivia said. "She must have had a rough time during the storm and remained in bed to recover."

"We should have helped her to her cabin." Briana touched Charles' hand.

"Yes, dear." Charles glanced around the dining salon.

James unconsciously brushed some crumbs from around his plate and onto the floor. "Well, if we don't run into Nancy by lunch, I'll have someone look in on her."

"Dad, what about Mary?"

"She is probably just exhausted. This trip is Mary's second time on an ocean liner. Last night wasn't the best time to develop sea-legs. Don't worry, I'm sure we will see her on deck this morning."

Vincent and Marie Bedeau, Phillip and Helen Lansing, and Robert Blackwell were seated at a table in the far corner of the dining salon.

Phillip set his tea cup down. "Robert, we missed you at dinner."

"I hope you are feeling better," Marie said. "So far, I haven't become seasick, but judging by the number of passengers missing from breakfast you were not alone."

"Thank you for your concern. You're right. The last twenty-four hours weren't enjoyable, but I am much better now. I shouldn't have celebrated the night before we sailed. I don't know what I could have been thinking."

"What business are you in?" Helen asked as she shifted closer to Robert.

"I'm in the Foreign Service. Next week I start work for the Passport Control Officer at the British Embassy in Havana. It's a new assignment for me, and I am looking forward to seeing Cuba for the first time."

"What does the Passport Control Office do?" Marie asked.

"We issue visas to foreign travelers wishing to visit the UK and help British subjects in matters pertaining to their passports. Have any of you been to Cuba before?"

"Marie and I have never been out of Europe so we're excited about spending the day sightseeing. We hear the Cubans are warm and hospitable. So far this trip has been enjoyable; everyone we have met has bent over backwards to help us."

Phillip had been studying Robert's face as Vincent talked.

"I feel like we have met before, but I am not sure when or where." Phillip poured some cream into his coffee as he watched Robert's eyes.

"It's possible, but I don't remember meeting you. We might have passed on the pier or weather decks when the ship was loading yesterday, although I felt sick and retired o my cabin as soon as I boarded. The only people I remember were the ship's nurse and my cabin steward; beyond that, yesterday was just a blur."

"It does not matter. Most likely I saw you in the crowd on the pier. It is sometimes better to abandon one's self to destiny."

Robert abruptly pushed away from the table and stood.

"Napoleon was wrong; destiny is overrated. I must be going. I have wires to send and some other business to attend to. I didn't contact my family before we sailed from New York. I'm sure they are wondering how my trip is going."

"I trust you will have a pleasant morning and continue to improve," Phillip said. "I am sure we will meet again before dinner."

"Yes, possibly."

After Robert had left the dining salon, Phillip turned to the others and said, "Have you ever come across someone you are positive you have met before but cannot remember where? It bothers me when I cannot place a face. Robert not only knows his Shakespeare, but also knows something of Napoleon. What an intriguing fellow."

"If you don't focus on it, I'm sure the connection will come to you when you least expect it," Helen said.

Marie and Vincent excused themselves from the table. They wanted to go for a swim in the on-deck pool. The idea of swimming in a pool full of fresh water in the middle of an ocean of salt water appealed to Vincent's sense of the surreal, and Marie just wanted to work on her tan.

Helen picked up the copy of Steinbeck's new book she was reading. "Phil, let's go for our morning constitutional while the sun is out. We haven't had a chance to explore the ship yet."

Phillip nodded to James and the others as he and Helen left the dining salon. Now that the storm had passed, the ship didn't roll much as it cut through the water. "We might play some shuffleboard later if the weather holds out."

By mid-morning the sky was blue and the sun warmed the constant parade of deck walkers as they circled the ship. Charles and Briana had settled into a pair of comfortable deck chairs on the glass-enclosed garden deck where Briana was reading an article in the August *Reader's Digest* on why President Roosevelt shouldn't be allowed to run for a third term, and Charles was working on a crossword puzzle.

"This one has me stumped. What's an eleven letter word meaning underhandedly inducing someone to do something unlawful that begins with 's' and ends in 'on'?" Charles asked.

"Subornation," Briana quickly responded with a smile. It was obvious she liked coming up with the words that stumped Charles. He always asked, and she knew he secretly hoped she wouldn't know the answer. It was a game they played.

Charles looked out at the sea. "I'm glad it's cleared up. It would have been a shame to spend our whole trip trapped

)elow deck in the cabin. I trust it will be sunny when we
'each Havana."

"How do you think Mary and Nancy are feeling?"
3riana looked up as she turned to the next page. "I hope
hey're not still seasick. We haven't seen either of them
his morning."

A young steward approached the Jefferys. "Doctor
[effery? Captain Ashcroft would like to speak with you. If
/ou will please follow me."

"I'll catch up to you later," Charles said. "I wonder
vhat the captain wants."

"As long as the sun stays out I'll be right here. Why
lon't you leave your crossword with me. I can finish it now
hat you have all the hard words filled in. I'm almost
hrough with this *Reader's Digest*."

"Funny," Charles grumbled, but he did leave the
)uzzle.

Chapter Twenty-three

"Come," Captain Ashcroft said. "Please close the door and be seated."

The captain's office was richly appointed. Large paintings of sailing ships locked in epic sea battles adorned dark walnut paneled walls. An ornately engraved brass sextant rested at one corner of the captain's teak desk. A barrister book case sat under the porthole behind the captain, and a large teak table surrounded by chairs filled the right side of the office. A tin of Player's Navy Cut cigarettes lay beside an empty coffee cup on the desk.

The captain was clean-shaven with close cropped grayish-brown hair and a square jaw line giving him the appearance of a military officer. He wore tortoise framed reading glasses low on his nose; and whenever he spoke, he would tilt his head slightly down and look over them.

Charles' lips parted when he recognized Vincent Bedeau sitting in a leather chair next to the captain's desk.

Vincent flashed a strained smile and cleared his throat as Charles sat down.

"I believe you and Inspector Bedeau have already met. Would either of you like a cup of coffee before we get started?" the captain asked as he refilled his cup.

Vincent declined, but Charles said, "By the look on your face, I'm going to need a good deal of black coffee before we are through."

A steward filled a cup with fresh coffee and placed a tray with cream, sugar, and a carafe next to Charles.

"That will be all," the captain said.

"Yes sir."

The captain waited until the steward closed the door and then he turned and faced Charles and Vincent.

"Let's cut to the chase. We have a situation. Shortly after the ship sailed from New York, a man and his wife and their one year old daughter became sick. The couple ate breakfast in one of the local waterfront diners before boarding the ship. Doctor Beck, the ship's doctor, diagnosed them as having food poisoning."

"Mild food poisoning should not be a lasting problem for the parents," Charles said. "The effects of food poisoning, in particular dehydration in a one year old, can be life-threatening. Do you know how the child is doing?"

"The little girl is in our sickbay. She was quite ill last night and was admitted to receive additional care. However, her condition has greatly improved this morning. She could be returned to her parents later today, depending on what you determine."

"The timing of the family eating breakfast and becoming sick certainly points to a strong possibility they contracted food poisoning from something they ate, but in my mind it still raises concerns over how their daughter became sick."

"Late this morning the shipboard problem multiplied greatly. Less than an hour ago one of our passengers was found dead in her cabin. Apparently she died last night in her sleep. A bedroom stewardess discovered her body when she went to make up the cabin this morning. Doctor Beck diagnosed the passenger as having died from cholera and has reconsidered his original diagnosis of the family. He now believes we have the beginnings of an epidemic onboard and wants to quarantine the ship. I don't have to tell you how grave the implications are."

"Cholera!" Charles said. "That's quite a leap from food poisoning. Cholera is not generally spread through direct contact between people. It is caused by infection with the bacteria Vibrio Cholerae and can be transmitted via infected fecal matter, food, or water."

"Upon learning about the death of our passenger, I called the purser and determined she had items in the ship's safe. I had hoped the contents of her safe-deposit box would help identify her next-of-kin. The box contained a United States passport and four sealed envelopes. The passport indicates she returned to the United States from England through the Port of Boston on January 18th of this year."

"It sounds like there may be more going on than simple food poisoning," Vincent said.

"What is the dead woman's name?" Charles asked.

"Miss Nancy Bechet." The captain picked up a gold pen from his desk and leaned back.

Charles stared at the captain in disbelief and cleared his throat.

"What can I do to help?"

"I need a second opinion about Miss Bechet's death. My first concern is to protect the passengers, but prematurely declaring we have cholera aboard would be a disaster, if it were not the case. I don't know whether she died of natural causes, sickness, or if foul play was involved. The ship's master-at-arms is not trained to investigate potential crimes, so Inspector Bedeau has agreed to be in charge of the investigation. He recommended I contact you for a medical evaluation."

"I will gladly do anything I can, but I'm not a forensic pathologist. It's not likely we are dealing with cholera since it's more of a concern in third-world countries where sanitation can be a problem. However, cholera could still be a possibility, since some of the ship's passengers may have come from countries other than the industrialized nations, but I am sure you don't have an epidemic."

"Thank God for that." The captain nervously rolled the pen between his fingers then set it on the blotter.

"Where are the recovering parents?" Charles lit his pipe.

"They remain in their cabin, isolated from the other passengers."

"Would you please call Doctor Beck for me," Charles said. "I would like to consult with him about his patients. I have some specific questions concerning the child and where the family was before they joined the cruise."

"Before I call, I should tell you Doctor Beck is not at all happy about my asking for a second opinion. This ship has been his personal domain for the last five years, ever since he retired from his private practice in Shanghai, and joined my crew. He doesn't like being questioned or second-guessed. In fact, he threatened to quit when I told him of your involvement. He was so irritated I felt I needed to order him to cooperate with you whenever you request help but to otherwise stay out of your way. I'm afraid I didn't help the situation."

"I hope this doesn't develop into an adversarial relationship between Doctor Beck and myself. I am often called to mediate opposing opinions between colleagues during research projects. Sometimes it can be quite difficult if the disagreement is fueled by rigid personal opinion instead of facts."

The captain dialed the phone, spoke to Doctor Beck, and then handed the receiver to Charles.

"Hello, Doctor Beck. I'm Doctor Jeffery. Captain Ashcroft asked if I would consult with you concerning your recent food poisoning cases and the death of Miss Bechet."

There was silence on the other end of the phone line.

Charles waited for a response, but when none came he continued, "How is the little girl doing?"

Another long delay and then Doctor Beck said, "Fine."

"Are there any signs of extended gastric distress or pyrexia?"

"No."

"Are all vital signs normal?"

"Yes."

"Did you speak with the parents and determine if they had been out of the United States any time in the last thirty days?"

"Yes."

"Yes, what?" Charles tightened his fist and bit his lip. It was obvious Doctor Beck was not the least bit interested in cooperating.

Doctor Beck exhaled loudly and said, "Yes, I talked with them."

"Were they out of the United States in the last thirty days?"

"No they weren't. Now look Doctor Jiffy, I am busy and don't have time to answer a lot of meaningless questions."

The phone went dead.

"Sounds like you two hit it off rather well," Vincent said.

"Right, at least the child is recovering."

"I'll speak to Doctor Beck about his professionalism," the captain said.

"Don't bother, it will only serve to incite him further. He is curiously defensive, but his attitude doesn't matter to me. Whatever is disturbing him is his problem, not mine."

"Very well." Captain Ashcroft turned to Vincent. "I don't want to alarm the other passengers. Your investigation should be as discreet as possible, but this issue needs to be resolved quickly. The limited resources of the ship are at your disposal."

"Is there a cabin we can use during the investigation?" Vincent asked.

"I had the cabin adjoining Miss Bechet's emptied as a precaution, based on Doctor Beck's concern over cholera. You may use the vacant cabin."

"Has anything been disturbed since Miss Bechet was found?"

"No, her cabin has been locked. Doctor Beck wanted to have her body removed, but since I wasn't sure what we were dealing with, I ordered him to leave everything as he found it. I have directed the master-at-arms, Mister Hopkins, to prevent anyone that I have not personally authorized from entering her cabin."

Vincent peered up from his notes. "Has Mister Hopkins had any formal police training?"

"No, he hasn't. He was a boatswain's mate for six years in the United States Navy before joining my crew four years ago. We don't normally deal with anything other than the occasional passenger who has overly indulged and just needs to be shown to his cabin. We don't have a brig or even a pair of handcuffs for that matter."

Vincent's shoulders slumped with disappointment as he drummed his fingers on the arm of the chair. He glanced at the floor and took a slow, calculated breath.

"I could have used the help of someone with knowledge of police procedures . . . well, we'll work with what we have. Please ask the ship's photographer to meet us in the vacant cabin. We'll need photographs of the scene regardless of the outcome of the investigation."

"We should move quickly. At this temperature and humidity, conditions will deteriorate rapidly," Charles said. "We've already lost valuable time."

"I'll need to interview the bedroom stewardess later today." Vincent turned to the next page in his notebook. "What's her name?"

Captain Ashcroft adjusted his glasses and looked at a card on his desk. "The bedroom stewardess' name is Miss Kate Gatti. This is her first time at sea. She's a new employee and is just eighteen. She was distraught but has been resting quietly in her cabin ever since the ship's nurse gave her a mild sedative."

"For now we can allow Miss Gatti to continue to rest," Vincent said. "When she wakes would you please have her write a statement of the events as she remembers them."

"Would you have a steward contact my wife and tell her not to wait on lunch for me?" Charles asked. "I'll catch up with her this afternoon."

"Inspector Bedeau, would you like to send a message to your wife?"

"No, I had a feeling I might be occupied for awhile after your steward contacted me, so I told Marie not to expect me until later."

There was a lull in the conversation as the captain gazed through the porthole behind his desk. Suddenly he turned to Charles and Vincent and leaned forward. "I can't afford to have this ship quarantined in Havana. It is imperative we resolve this issue before we reach Cuba or we may not be allowed to dock. I hope we aren't dealing with a communicable disease."

"So do I." Charles rubbed the back of his neck and looked up. "So do I."

Vincent wrote a few sentences in his notebook and put his pen away.

The captain returned to staring out the porthole, but not focusing on anything in particular. The silence in the room spoke volumes.

Charles shifted in his chair and glanced at Vincent. "Captain, I couldn't help but notice you wear a class ring from the United States Naval Academy at Annapolis. When did you graduate?"

"Class of 1921." The captain turned away from the porthole and started toward the door.

"I have a nephew who hopes to be appointed next year," Charles said as he stood.

"I wish him luck. If you will follow me I'll escort you to Mister Hopkins. Let us hope we can clear this matter up quickly."

"We should have no problem reaching a conclusion by mid-afternoon," Vincent said as they walked down the passageway.

Chapter Twenty-four

The captain led Charles and Vincent to the cabin adjoining Miss Bechet's. Knocking once, he opened the door. The master-at-arms jumped to his feet and appeared to brace, but just as quickly relax. It was apparent that years in the service had ingrained an automatic response to authority that wasn't easily forgotten. Hopkins had the appearance of an honest, hardworking man who intended to spend his life at sea. His right hand had been severely injured in a line handling accident while he was in the United States Navy, and his master-at-arms job allowed him to be at sea without having to endure the rigors of a job as a boatswain's mate.

"Sir."

"Mister Hopkins, may I introduce Inspector Bedeau and Doctor Jeffery. They're investigating the death of Miss Bechet."

"Yes sir."

"I will leave you gentlemen to your work as I need to complete some ship's business before we reach Cuba."

The captain opened the door and stepped into the passageway, but then turned back. "Mister Hopkins, expect the ship's photographer to arrive soon. In my absence, anyone Inspector Bedeau authorizes may enter the cabin and no one else."

"Yes sir."

The captain addressed Vincent and Charles as he closed the door. "Please contact me in my office when you have made a determination."

Vincent pulled out his notebook and pen.

"Mister Hopkins, has anyone other than the bedroom stewardess and you been in Miss Bechet's cabin since you arrived?"

"Old Doc Beck entered twice. Once right after the body was found and then just a little while ago."

"Twice? Well, I don't want him to enter her cabin again."

"Yes sir," Hopkins said as he locked the door.

"Please describe what occurred starting when you arrived at Miss Bechet's cabin. Include anything you saw or touched."

"There's not much to tell." Mister Hopkins shook his head. "Miss Gatti called me just after eleven hundred hours this morning saying something had happened to one of the passengers. I met her at the cabin and asked her to wait outside while I investigated. I found a woman lying on the bed. She had been sick, too sick to remove her jewelry and undress. I confirmed she didn't have a pulse and her pupils were fixed. I exited the cabin and locked the door. I contacted the captain, and have been on guard ever since."

"Please take time this afternoon to write out a statement covering what you just told me. It can be notarized later."

There was a knock on the door. It was the ship's photographer who looked more like a mad scientist than a member of the ship's crew. He was in his late fifties, average height, thin, with balding white hair. A camera bag was draped over his right shoulder, and a tripod was tucked precariously under his left arm. His shirt was partially untucked and a copy of this month's Racing Form stuck out of his back pocket. It was obvious his life was photography; and he thought only of shadows, lighting, and camera angles, unless he was at a horse race playing the longshots.

"I'm Inspector Bedeau and this is Doctor Jeffery. We need your expertise. I appreciate your coming down on such short notice."

The photographer fumbled with his tripod as he held out his hand. "Rick Waters. Pleased to be of service."

"Well Rick, do you have any qualms about photographing a dead body?"

"No sir. Served as a combat photographer during the Great War with Pershing's First in France and have taken pictures of just about anything you can imagine and some things you wouldn't want to."

"Before we start I will provide you with a map of the room. When we enter the cabin do not touch anything. Take only the photographs I ask for. Please indicate the location and orientation of each photograph on the map. We need to proceed quickly, but deliberately. There won't be a second chance. Do you have any questions?"

"Nope, but no one told me what to expect. Sounds like we'll be taking a lot of pictures. I need to pick up more flash bulbs and a close-up lens from the lab, and I should load all of my extra film holders."

"Go ahead. Doctor Jeffery and I need to enter the cabin first to look things over. We shouldn't be in there for more than a half hour. Don't discuss this case with anyone else. We need to keep things as quiet as possible until we have made a determination."

"I understand. I'll return as quickly as I can."

"The ambient temperature this morning is already well over eighty," Charles said. "and the closed cabin is probably above ninety. Miss Bechet's body has been sealed in there for over twelve hours. There are some items we'll need from the sickbay before we enter the cabin.

"Here, use a page from my notebook."

Charles wrote out a list and handed it to Mister Hopkins. "It's not much—just rubber gloves, masks, sample bottles, and Vicks."

The two adjoining cabins had identical, but mirror-image floor plans. Vincent made a sketch of the cabin layout for himself and one for Rick while he waited for the items from the sickbay. He had just finished the second sketch when a steward knocked on the cabin door.

Charles opened the door, but stopped the steward from entering the cabin. The steward handed Charles a box.

"Queer lot of stuff. What you gonna make?"

Charles paused for a moment. "We have a gentlemen's bet about Vicks floating on water."

"Right, guv'nor," the steward said with a puzzled look as he turned and strolled away shaking his head. "Now I've heard it all."

Shortly after the steward departed, someone rattled the door knob and pounded on the door. Hopkins unlocked the door and found a red-faced Doctor Beck standing in front of him breathing hard and puffed up like a toad.

The doctor was in his sixties with a full head of snow white hair and a ruddy complexion punctuated by a disproportionately large, red nose. He was much shorter than Vincent and greatly overweight for his height, which may have explained why he was sweating like a poker player who should have folded and had just been called.

Doctor Beck tried to push his way into the cabin, but Hopkins stood in the doorway and wouldn't let him pass.

"Doc, you ain't authorized to come in here."

"Who says?"

"Inspector Bedeau gave specific orders."

"Who's this Inspector *Bidet*? That's my patient in there and I have a right to be here. He can't tell me what I can and can't do." Doctor Beck tried once again to force his way past Hopkins by thrusting his black medical bag through the open door.

Vincent rushed to join Hopkins at the door.

"Your patient is dead, and this is a police investigation. You can not enter the cabin."

"We'll see about that." Doctor Beck's face became beet-red as he stormed off in a fit of rage.

Vincent locked the door. "That was some show."

"Yes sir," Hopkins said.

Vincent turned toward Charles and rolled his eyes. "Do you think he's protecting his rice bowl or is something else driving the doctor?"

Vincent and Charles smeared Vicks on their masks and pulled on rubber gloves.

"Doctor Beck's wounded ego is the last thing on my mind."

Chapter Twenty-five

The cabin was dark; the curtains still closed from the night before. When Vincent reached for the light switch he said, "Only Hope was left within her unbreakable house, she remained under the lip of the jar, and did not fly away'."

"What's that you're saying?"

"It's from the *Pandora Myth* by Hesiod."

A cabin full of Vicks could not have prevented the overpowering stench from penetrating their masks. Vincent and Charles involuntarily recoiled against the door as the ghastly scene came into focus.

It was apparent from her condition that Miss Bechet had been suffering from nausea and diarrhea. She lay face up on the bed, her body contorted and frozen in a hideous display of writhing agony. Her auburn hair was no longer styled and beautiful, but matted and caked. Her ashen features recorded her last silent scream. Her delicate fingers had clawed at the bed covers so violently that several of her nails were broken.

Charles' hands trembled as he turned away. He drew the curtains back and swung the porthole open. "She was so young." He stared at a flock of gulls as his eyes began to glisten. "I wasn't prepared for this."

Vincent started to speak, but stopped and focused on the twisted figure laying in front of him. He reached forward, gently pushing her eyelids closed, and crossed himself.

Charles cleared his throat and returned to the foot of the bed. "Let's get to work. I'll examine Miss Bechet while you search the cabin."

Vincent moved away from the bed and began to look around. "This must have been more than seasickness," he said as he approached the dresser and started going through the drawers. "This place is a mess." He paused and glanced at Miss Bechet. "It's curious that she's still fully dressed, but I haven't seen any of her jewelry. Mister Hopkins mentioned jewelry. Every woman has a jewelry case."

"The first thing my wife does when we turn in for the night is remove her makeup and jewelry. You didn't find a pearl necklace or earrings on the dresser? She wore them last night at dinner."

"No, they are not here." Vincent closed the drawers and moved to the writing desk. "Did she smoke?"

"Not that I know of. Why?"

"There are several cigarette butts in this ashtray." Vincent carefully picked them out and placed them in an envelope.

Charles rolled Miss Bechet onto her side. "She has expelled a great deal of yellowish diarrhea, indicating the digestive system was not processing food normally. There was something in her system her body wanted desperately to purge."

"When do you believe she died?"

"The lividity and the state of rigor mortis indicate she has been dead for at least twelve hours, but it's hard to be specific without an autopsy, and in this heat I would just be guessing. As I mentioned before, I'm not a forensic pathologist, I'm a research scientist with a medical degree. Miss Bechet sat with us at dinner last evening until about nine, when she left the table to go to her cabin. I'd say she died before midnight last night." Charles retrieved a blanket from the closet and covered Miss Bechet's body.

"She looks like the cholera victims I saw in pictures from the late 1800's," Vincent said. "Maybe Doctor Beck is correct and she died from cholera."

"Poppycock. It is not likely that she died from cholera. Based on the passport information the captain gave us, Miss Bechet came directly from England and was in the United States for over six weeks before boarding the *Southern Cross*. The last cholera outbreak in the States was an epidemic in the early 1900's."

"Isn't cholera spread by mosquitos?"

"You're thinking of malaria. Cholera is transmitted through ingestion of food washed in water contaminated with cholera bacteria or drinking the contaminated water directly. The ship operates under the strictest sanitary controls for food preparation and manufactures its own fresh water supply by distilling sea water. Bacteria would not survive the distillation process."

"If not cholera, what then?"

"Even though Miss Bechet suffered from watery diarrhea and vomiting, her state of dehydration is not so great as would be seen with cholera. Extreme dehydration didn't cause her death. Instead, I believe she most likely died from ingesting a poison—probably arsenic. The symptoms for cholera and arsenic poisoning are similar. However, she suffered hematemesis."

"Hema-what?"

"Sorry, she vomited blood. I'm surprised Doctor Beck didn't make the connection since he practiced in Shanghai in the twenties when cholera was a constant concern and must have seen a number of cholera cases. Hematemesis is a clear sign we are not dealing with cholera but might be dealing with an extremely toxic poison. For example, less than a teaspoon of arsenic could result in coma and death within hours."

Charles wrote out a note and handed it past the door to Hopkins. "Please send this to Captain Ashcroft. I need these supplies as soon as possible. I believe the zinc anode and battery electrolyte can be obtained from the ship's engineering officer."

"What are you sending for?" Vincent asked.

"We need to know if Miss Bechet was given arsenic," Charles said. "We'll conduct a Marsh Test."

"So you think she was murdered?"

"Yes, without a doubt. There can be no other explanation."

"Murdered . . . for what reason?"

Charles paced back and forth with his hands clasped behind his back. Suddenly, he spun on his heals as if he had been struck by a bolt of lightning.

"I'm sure we can make it work. We'll test for the presence of arsenic. In my laboratory in San Francisco it would be a simple and accurate test, but on this ship . . ."

"Great, at least something about this investigation will be simple."

"Well, not exactly. We are on a passenger liner with no laboratory equipment. We'll have to improvise and modify the test to accommodate our circumstances, but I think we can pull it off." Charles clapped his hands together.

"Let's move out of here for now," Vincent said. "We could use some fresh air while we work things out." He glanced at Miss Bechet's covered body. "I didn't expect we would be dealing with a murder."

Neither the blanket nor the closed door stopped the haunting image of Miss Bechet from following them into the other cabin.

Charles sat motionless at the writing desk for a moment with his head in his hands. Vincent stood and silently stared around the room without making eye contact with Mister Hopkins.

The silence was broken when Rick entered carrying an armload of photographic equipment.

Taking a deep breath Charles said, "Well I guess we better get on with it, hadn't we?" He picked up a pen and filled out the labels on four small glass bottles and slid them toward Vincent.

"What are these for?"

"I can't go in there right now." Charles' lips compressed into a thin line as he looked away. "If you don't mind, would you please obtain two samples of vomit and one of diarrhea. Fill the fourth jar with the residual liquid from the glass beside her bed."

"Does it matter how the samples are taken?"

"No, just don't contaminate them."

Vincent tucked the bottles in his pocket and turned to Rick. "Can you use your cameras while wearing a surgical mask and rubber gloves?"

"Never done it, but I don't see why not. I had to work in a gas mask during the Great War."

"I wish we didn't have to do this," Vincent said. "It's not pretty in there." He paused and pulled his mask up. "Are you ready to take some photographs?"

"Set as I'll ever be."

As Rick and Vincent moved into the adjoining cabin, Rick tried to show the face of a war-hardened veteran; however, it was clear from his reaction when Vincent removed the blanket covering Miss Bechet that he was deeply affected.

"Are you all right?"

"Yep, ready. Just needed to catch my breath and refocus my thoughts. I'll be fine."

"Let's start by taking a series of photographs in the bathroom." Vincent felt once Rick began working he would become professionally detached as he concentrated on the mechanics of using his equipment.

"Take a general area series from the doorway, clockwise, ending at the commode on the right with close-ups of the sink and the trash can."

As he snapped the last photograph Rick asked, 'Anything else in here?"

"Make sure you have a close-up of the small brown bottle in the trash can."

"Got it."

"Great," Vincent said. "Step out here while I recover the bottle as evidence. We'll deal with the main cabin next. How do you feel?"

"Better, I didn't expect—"

"I know, neither did I. Do you want to take a break?"

"No, let's keep going. As long as we are working, I'll be fine."

The heat and humidity were causing the cabin to ferment with the smell of decaying flesh, vomit, and diarrhea. Vincent read the labels on the sample bottles.

"I wish Charles would have collected his own damned samples," Vincent mumbled under his breath as he turned toward the toilet.

"Rick, please take sequential, general area photographs of the main cabin and then we'll concentrate on the bed and Miss Bechet." Vincent knew that by now Rick was emotionally detached from the scene and would be able to photograph Miss Bechet.

Vincent had deliberately avoided looking at Miss Bechet while Rick had been working in the bathroom, but now he was forced to confront her contorted body as they prepared to take the final series of photographs. He paused and whispered, "*La danse macabre*, the dancing skeleton of death takes us all, sinners and saints alike."

It took ten minutes to finish photographing the scene, and by then they were both emotionally exhausted. Vincent pulled the blanket over Miss Bechet and turned to the door.

While Vincent and Rick were in Miss Bechet's cabin, Charles had sent for more supplies and set up a curious configuration of jars, stoppers, and hoses on the writing desk which he and Mister Hopkins had moved into the center of the cabin. The assembly looked more like it belonged in the Tennessee backwoods making moonshine than in a shipboard cabin determining the cause of someone's death.

Vincent placed the sample bottles on the desk and turned to Rick. "Thanks for your help. How long before I can review the proofs?"

"I'll have them back to you in a little over an hour. It doesn't take long to process black and white film; but after that, the film has to dry before we can print the proof sheets."

"We'll still be here," Vincent said as Rick closed the door.

Charles picked up the samples, one at a time, and held them up to the light. "The sample from the drinking glass is contaminated."

"I'll go back and see if there is anything left in her glass."

"No." Charles took a deep breath. "I'll go. It's not your fault. I shouldn't have asked you to do my job."

Charles prepared another bottle. He hesitated at the door and took a deep breath before entering Miss Bechet's cabin.

A moment later Charles returned carrying an empty bottle. "There was no more liquid in the drinking glass."

"I'm sorry."

"Don't be. We'll use the sample you obtained and hope for the best. I'll filter it through a clean mask. The test will require only a small amount; and if it gives us the answer we're looking for, we won't need to test the other samples."

"What will we observe during this test? I'm sure you know what you're doing, but I've never seen a lab setup like this before."

"You're not likely to ever see another one, either." Charles talked as he worked. "In this jar we'll mix some battery electrolyte, containing about fifty percent sulfuric acid, with half of the liquid from Miss Bechet's drinking glass. We'll heat the mixture with the candle flame and collect vapor in the second jar."

"What are these gray particles?" Vincent pointed to the second jar.

"They're thin metal shavings I scraped from the zinc anode. The vapor from the first jar will react with the zinc, and, if I'm correct about the arsenic, produce arsine gas that will flow into the third jar and be collected. When we have enough gas, we'll release the clamp in the third jar's vent line and ignite the escaping gas while holding this small china bowl upside down over the flame."

"Why is the bowl sitting in a tub of ice?"

"We need to have a cold surface to quickly condense the product from the final step. If there is arsenic in the liquid sample, there will be arsine gas in the third jar, and when it's burned, a black mirror-like deposit will form on the cool surface of the bowl. Any more questions?"

"You lost me with the anode. What is a zinc anode?"

"Anodes are used to prevent corrosion of metal that is in contact with saltwater. The zinc corrodes instead of the ship's hull or equipment. By the way, would you mind opening the porthole behind you? Arsine gas is poisonous, and we wouldn't want to become sick."

Charles pulled a wooden match out of the box and struck it on the bottom of the table.

"Please hand me the bowl."

He released the clamp on the vent hose and held the match near the open end of the hose. Nothing happened. There was no flame at the vent of the third bottle.

"I was positive it was arsenic." Charles looked at the surface of the clean white bowl and shook his head.

"Now what?"

"We'll have to disassemble the apparatus, clean everything, and start over using one of the other samples. It could take hours."

Charles' head dipped as he shuffled over to the porthole to collect his thoughts.

Vincent examined the test assembly. He rubbed his forehead and turned toward Charles.

"Aren't all the hoses supposed to be connected?"

"What? Charles hurried to join Vincent at the desk. "What did you say?"

"This hose isn't connected."

"Sometimes I'm so careless." Charles stared at the hose. "How could I have missed something so simple?"

Charles attached the hose and checked the rest of the connections. "That's why you should always have someone review your work. It's the little things that trip you up. I forgot the first rule of experimental work: The devil's in the details."

Charles repeated the test sequence using the remaining liquid from Miss Bechet's drinking glass.

Vincent watched intently as Charles held a match to the released gas from the last jar. A low, sooty flame flickered under the bowl and went out.

"There! Just as I suspected, arsenic poisoning. Here, take a look." Charles handed the bowl to Vincent. "We now know how, but we still don't know who or why."

There was a knock on the cabin door. When Hopkins answered, Rick entered carrying the proof sheets.

"Yes, these are all good. Thanks for being so quick."

Vincent used a pen to mark the proofs.

"Please make prints of the selected negatives; but before you leave, take photographs of this test apparatus and the deposits on the china bowl."

"Mister Hopkins, have Miss Bechet's body bagged and placed in one of the ship's cold storage lockers where it won't be disturbed," Vincent said. "It won't be a pleasant task, but it's all right to have someone clean Miss Bechet's cabin now. We have collected all of the evidence we are going to find. Continue to maintain guard on the cabin, and let no one enter without my permission."

"Yes sir. Do you want to be notified when it's clean?"

"Please, I may need to look at it again."

"Mister Hopkins, I have a question concerning Doctor Beck," Charles said.

"Shoot."

"Well, I'm curious, do you know anything about the doctor's background? I mean before he became the ship's doctor?"

"No sir, just that he's a loner, and he and Miss Pennell are close friends."

"Miss Pennell?" Vincent asked.

"She's one of the ship's nurses. Miss Pennell and Doc Beck spend a lot of time together in the evenings, but I don't think they got anything going. Mostly they just talk and drink. I think they console each other about their past mistakes; everyone has regrets."

"We will be with Captain Ashcroft if you have any questions," Vincent said. "Rick, please make three copies of the photographs and send them to Captain Ashcroft. Do not show them to anyone. Place the negatives in a sealed envelope and have the purser lock them in the ship's safe."

Vincent and Charles exited the cabin carrying the sample bottles and bags of evidence and headed toward the captain's office. The passages were almost empty. Most passengers were either in their cabins dressing for dinner or still on deck enjoying the cool evening breezes.

Charles glanced at his watch. "No wonder I'm hungry. We missed lunch. What do you make of this case?"

"I suspect there's more to good Doctor Beck than meets the eye."

Chapter Twenty-six

Vincent and Charles remained silent as they threaded their way through the passageways. When they reached the captain's office, Charles turned toward Vincent.

"I am sure this hasn't been the honeymoon cruise you and Marie had planned on."

"Well, not exactly." Vincent's eyes narrowed as he glanced at Charles and lowered his voice to a whisper. "It sure hasn't."

Charles knocked on the captain's door.

"Come. Please be seated."

Captain Ashcroft crushed out his cigarette on the rim of a polished brass ashtray and glanced over the top of his glasses at Charles and Vincent.

"Gentlemen, what have you determined?" The captain leaned forward.

"Miss Bechet was murdered by arsenic poisoning," Charles said. "She did not die from cholera as Doctor Beck believes. The family with food poisoning and this case are not related. Presently we have no leads to a killer, nor do we have a motive."

"A murder on my ship. No one has ever died, let alone been murdered, on the *Southern Cross*. Never. This is terrible. You said *killer*. Meaning we will be looking for a single individual?" The captain took a sip of coffee and lit a cigarette.

"Yes sir, that's our belief," Vincent said. "Miss Bechet was comfortable unlocking her cabin door late at night. If there had been more than one person when she looked through the peep-hole in the door, I'm sure she wouldn't have willingly opened the door. There would have been signs of a struggle. No, the murderer had her confidence and was let in freely. She either knew the murderer or they presented themselves in a position of authority, possibly as a member of the ship's crew."

"The murderer may be a member of my crew?"

"Not necessarily, the murderer may have worn a disguise; like a stewardess. Someone so common to ship's routine as to not be questioned. We found several cigarette butts in an ashtray near Miss Bechet. The intruder must have spent at least twenty minutes in the cabin."

Vincent moved over to a large map of the world mounted on the wall to the right of the desk as the captain finished his coffee.

"When did the ship leave the territorial waters of the United States?"

"Around four hundred hours this morning."

"What's the country of registry for the *Southern Cross*?"

"The United States, and her home port is New York. The company transferred her registration last year as conditions in Europe became more unstable. Is that important?"

"Miss Bechet's murder occurred last evening while we were in United States territorial waters, so the FBI has jurisdiction over this case. Frankly, we are lucky to have them involved instead of dealing with some island-nation with questionable resources."

"I'll send a radiogram to Miami as soon as we are finished," the captain said.

"I asked Mister Hopkins to move Miss Bechet's body to one of the ship's cold storage lockers." Vincent returned to the seat next to Charles and stretched back to relieve the tension in his shoulders. "The locker needs to remain secured until the FBI takes custody of the body."

The captain handed Vincent a typewritten page. "The purser prepared this list of the passengers who have cabins near Miss Bechet's. I also had him assign a safe-deposit box for your use. When you are ready, it will be secured in the ship's safe."

"Is that it?" Vincent pointed to a gray metal box sitting on top of the barrister bookcase.

"No, this one contains Miss Bechet's valuables. After you called, I had it returned to my office. I thought you might need access to her passport."

"Splendid."

The captain transferred the box to his desk and removed Miss Bechet's British passport and the sealed envelopes. Each envelope was addressed and stamped to a post office box in a different country: Cuba, France, Germany, and Spain.

"I wish I could open these envelopes," the captain said, "but I have no authority to interfere with the mail."

"This is a murder investigation and, until the FBI arrives, I am the investigating officer." Vincent leaned back in his chair and folded his arms. "The contents of the envelopes may provide some insight into Miss Bechet's murderer. I'll open them and sort out the legalities later. When a bureaucracy is involved, it's easier to receive forgiveness than to ask for permission."

Three of the envelopes held sizable sums of currency and additional passports, each from the country written on the envelope. The passports all had Miss Bechet's picture, but were issued under different names. The fourth envelope held a list of names and addresses in Cuba, but it wasn't clear what the people on the list had in common. Some names were obviously Spanish, but others appeared to be Japanese and German.

The captain stared at the pile of money and fake passports covering his desk.

"Why all of this subterfuge?"

"It's apparent to me that Miss Bechet was a foreign agent. We may never learn where her loyalties were." Vincent placed a French passport in the pile.

"Ship's records show she was traveling alone to Havana," Captain Ashcroft said.

"Not alone," Vincent said. "When you have a dead spy it means there's a live spy hiding somewhere. He or she is our killer."

Charles rubbed the back of his neck. "Spies, agents, and espionage. What have we uncovered?"

"We should approach this with caution." Vincent put his pen down. "We don't want to reveal we know Miss Bechet was a spy or that she was murdered. The murderer obviously is not concerned about leaving a dead body to be found, for he or she made no effort to conceal the murder."

"I sense we have uncovered a nest of hornets and are about to poke at it with a short stick." The captain peered out at the sea and drummed his fingers on his desk.

Charles thought for a moment and said, "We should allow people to think Miss Bechet died from pulmonary aspiration resulting from extreme seasickness. The passengers won't know about her diarrhea and vomiting of blood, so the story is plausible and will allow us time to investigate without raising suspicion."

"Pulmonary aspiration, you mean she choked to death?"

"Sorry, I got technical again. Yes, she choked to death."

"What about the safety of my passengers?"

"Unless they're spies, they shouldn't be in any danger," Vincent said. "This was an attack directed at a specific person. The issue was between two spies either covering up some espionage activity or revenging a previous transgression."

"So for now we let the killer think they got away with murder?" The captain leaned back in his chair and pulled on his right earlobe.

"Yes, Charles and I believe that's the best plan of attack."

Captain Ashcroft surveyed the contents of Miss Bechet's safe-deposit box again and shook his head.

"I almost wish we were dealing with something as straight forward as cholera." He paused and lit a cigarette. "I'll start the rumor with the housekeeping staff about Miss Bechet's death by choking. It will spread soon enough throughout the ship."

"Is there an empty cabin on a different level of the ship we can use to continue the investigation?" Vincent asked. "It will be more convincing if we no longer show an interest in Miss Bechet's cabin. I would like to speak with the bedroom stewardess tonight after dinner. Let's say, around nine."

"I should have a cabin for you within the hour. I believe one of our deluxe suites is empty. The suite will provide more space than one of our normal cabins. I'll let you know the cabin number before dinner. The bedroom stewardess will be there at twenty-one hundred hours tonight."

Vincent leaned toward Charles and slid forward in his seat.

"I'd appreciate it if you would keep working with me on this case."

"If you think I could quit now, you're wrong. Miss Bechet's murder has become personal for me."

"I think we should follow the ship's normal schedule as much as possible to add to the deception."

"This is Saturday and the ship arrives in Havana on Monday," Charles said. "We don't have much time to uncover the killer. I am not sure how we can follow the ship's schedule and work on this case at the same time."

Chapter Twenty-seven

Charles met Briana as he rushed down the passageway toward their cabin. She had just left, but turned and walked back to the cabin with him.

"I was ready to send out a search party. What were you doing for so long?"

"Remember that Miss Bechet didn't feel well after dinner last night? Unfortunately, she died sometime during the night from pulmonary aspiration. The bedroom stewardess found her this morning."

Charles' ears blushed as he avoided direct eye contact with Briana. He looked down and started to unbutton his shirt.

"I'm sorry to hear that," Briana said as she rubbed Charles' back. "Miss Bechet was such a vibrant young lady with her whole life in front of her. What a horrible way to die. Has her family been notified?"

"The captain sent a radiogram early this afternoon."

"Why did he involve you in her death?"

"He asked me to provide a second opinion."

"Why would he need a second opinion? Was her death questionable? Doesn't he trust the ship's doctor?"

"The ship's doctor made some assumptions the captain wanted reviewed before he notified his home office. Briana, you ask too many questions."

"Do you mean her death was misdiagnosed?"

"The doctor has been on the ship's crew for over five years and has not kept up with the changes and advancements in the medical field since he retired from private practice. The captain just wanted a second opinion. Can we not talk about it for now?"

"Certainly, dear." Briana redoubled her massage effort on Charles' shoulders as she pressed her thumbs into his trapezius muscles as if she was drilling for oil.

"Ouch!" Charles jerked away.

"Sorry, was that too hard?"

"I hope no one else becomes sick. The ship is not prepared to handle much more than sunburns and scraped knees." Charles shook his head as he leaned over to untie his shoes.

"I finished your crossword puzzle and started reading a new book," Briana said as she stroked Charles' temples. "Early in the afternoon I saw Marie Bedeau sitting by herself on the promenade deck; so I joined her. We chatted for hours."

"That's nice, what did you two talk about?" Charles opened the closet and tossed his shirt in a laundry bag and folded his pants on a hanger. "I spilled some chemicals on these. I flushed the area with water, but they need dry cleaning."

"We talked about things, you know, that girls talk about—romance and dreams for the future. Marie mentioned the captain sent for Vincent. I wonder what that could have been about?"

"I don't know," Charles said. "It's late and we should dress for dinner. I'm starved. I missed lunch." A blush returned to Charles' ears as he stepped into the bathroom and turned on the shower.

Briana set out Charles' tuxedo while steam and the sound of cascading water filled the bathroom.

The warm water felt good, but it couldn't wash away the haunting images of Miss Bechet filling Charles' mind. He stood in the shower with the spray pounding at the back of his neck and tried to clear his thoughts.

"Are you feeling sick? You're usually not this quiet."

"Sick? No," Charles replied as he wiped the mirror and began to shave. "I was daydreaming about our trip through the Canal."

There are so many loose ends. The more we find out, the less we know. The death of Miss Bechet was so senseless. Her last minutes must have been filled with sheer terror and a complete sense of helplessness. How can someone consider life so meaningless and cheap they would callously throw another human being away like a piece of spoiled meat?

Briana stretched out on the bed reading an article in *Reader's Digest*, as Charles shaved and dressed for dinner. She smiled when she noticed the mess he had made out of his tie. She had tried, but couldn't persuade him to wear a clip-on.

Charles believed in the tradition of a hand tied bow tie, just like his father wore, but he never could tie one of those damned things correctly. His efforts always ended up looking like Buster Brown's lop-eared dog—all scrunched and twisted to one side.

"Have you ever wondered what we'll be doing this time next year?" Charles asked while Briana repaired his tie.

"What made you think about next year? Are you sure you feel all right?" Briana touched Charles' forehead. "We could have the steward bring dinner to the cabin."

"I feel fine, really. We'd better hurry or we'll miss the first course."

B riana and Charles strolled arm in arm to the dining salon. Their mood was not so festive as the night before. The steward seated them at their assigned table with Olivia and James. The table was set for five, Miss Bechet's place setting was conspicuously missing, but there was another empty place at the table. Mary Channing was not at dinner.

"Olivia and I were shocked to hear Miss Bechet died last night under such disturbing circumstances," James said. "I hope she didn't suffer."

"One never knows what tomorrow will bring," Briana said. "We can only live each day to its fullest and take tomorrow as it comes."

"Did anyone talk with Miss Channing today?" Charles asked.

"I forgot all about her." James jumped up and summoned the maitre d'.

"Would you please have someone look in on Miss Channing to make sure she is not ill."

The maitre d' sent a steward to Miss Channing's cabin as the others continued with dinner. When the plates were cleared, almost everyone left a portion of the meal untouched. Conversation at the table was slow and subdued.

"I hope Miss Channing is resting and isn't sick." Charles was well aware of Doctor Beck's incompetence and hoped Miss Channing wasn't having to count on the good doctor for anything but an aspirin.

The steward brought the dessert menu and refilled the water glasses.

"I think I'll have the cherries jubilee and some dark coffee, please," Olivia said. "Do you want anything, Father?"

"I'll have just coffee, thank you."

The steward left and the table fell silent until Charles spoke up.

"James, where are you and Olivia traveling to?"

"We're going to Berkeley to visit my sister. She's a law professor at the University of California School of Law at Berkeley. I haven't seen her since I retired last year."

"I'll bet you're looking forward to catching up on family news," Charles said. "Bree and I have friends at the university, and we often spend weekends camping in the hills east of Berkeley."

"We plan to spend some time this September hiking in Yosemite National Park," James said. "My sister and her husband are avid naturalists."

"Did you have time to meet with Vincent Bedeau and look at his climbing pictures?"

"Yes, we met this morning at the pool," James answered. As he talked, a smile returned to his face and his eyes lit up. "After Vincent and his wife had finished swimming, he joined me in the library with his photograph album. He has some fantastic pictures and many astounding stories. I always enjoy talking about past adventures with a fellow mountaineer."

"What do you think about the recent German climbing expeditions?" Charles asked. He didn't know much about mountain climbing, but he had read the newspapers and seen the newsreels in the theater. It seemed German climbing expeditions were trying to climb every peak in the Himalayas.

"Well to be frank, I'm a little tired of all the Nazi propaganda, trying to prove the Aryan race is superior to everyone else. I don't mean to belittle the physical accomplishments of climbers like Anderl Heckmair on the North Face of the Eigar last year. The climbers deserve all of the recognition they receive."

"Would anyone care to adjourn to the lounge for a game of Mahjong?" Olivia asked.

"I'm sorry, but I have some matters to attend to before morning," Charles said. "Most of my day was taken up with Miss Bechet's death, but Bree might join you."

"I think I'll call it a night and crawl into bed with my new book," Briana said. "Charles and I will see you in the morning."

"Olivia, I'll meet you in the lounge," James said. "I want to check with the maitre d' to find out if there is any word on Miss Channing."

The Lansings, the Bedeaus, and Robert Blackwell were finishing dinner at their table in the far corner of the dining salon.

Phillip wiped his mouth and placed his napkin beside his plate.

"Last night's storm was frightening. I have never felt so insecure. When the sea is calm, one feels in control; but when the sea demonstrates her power, one is reminded just how precarious life is."

"I vividly remember visiting friends on Long Island Sound a year ago when the Long Island Express hit," Helen said. "The storm last night frightened me more because we were not on land."

"I'm sorry you two had such a rough night of it. Vincent and I slept through the night. I guess the excitement of sailing from New York tired us out more than we thought."

"Did you hear one of the passengers died last night due to complications from seasickness?" Helen said.

"Oh my god, who?" Marie asked.

"I think her name was Nancy Bechet," Helen said. "We never met. I heard she was traveling to Havana. It's tragic. You're not supposed to die when you are young."

There was silence at the table as everyone weighed their own mortality. After a moment Robert spoke. "'When I consider every thing that grows, holds in perfection but a little moment.'"

"Was that from Shakespeare?" Phillip asked. "Possibly from Sonnet 29?"

"It was Shakespeare, but it's the first line of Sonnet 15," Robert said.

"You are right . . . my mistake." Phillip folded his napkin beside his plate. "I have not read Shakespeare since high school."

Helen and Phillip's eyes briefly met.

"Robert, after your initial encounter with seasickness, how did you manage last night?" Helen asked.

"The ship's nurse gave me something to help me sleep. I slept soundly all night and missed most of the storm. Today I've enjoyed the sun and the fresh sea air. I feel like a new man. Most of this morning I relaxed on deck and read."

"I saw you this morning as Briana Jeffery and I passed through the sun deck," Marie said. "You were halfway through *Peer Gynt*. I admire you for being able to read Ibsen and drink vodka on the rocks in the morning after being seasick last night."

"Well, a little hair of the dog," Robert said. "However, I think the dog is about to catch me, and I should turn in before he bites again. It has been a long day, and tomorrow afternoon we dock in Havana. I'll see you in the morning."

After Robert had departed, Vincent said he had a natter to clear up. Marie, Phillip, and Helen adjourned to he lounge for an after dinner drink.

"Robert is certainly an fascinating fellow," Helen said is she, Phillip and Marie approached a grouping of over-stuffed chairs in a far corner of the lounge. "He knows Shakespeare and reads Ibsen. Not many people his age spend time reading classical literature. I wonder what other nterests he has."

"Yes dear, I look forward to discussing Shakespeare vith him again."

Chapter Twenty-eight

Miss Gatti was waiting in the living room of Cabin 25 when Charles and Vincent arrived. She was surprisingly tall and wore a simple white uniform accentuating her long slender limbs. She wore no makeup. Her brown hair was pulled back tightly and tied in a bun. For a young woman of eighteen she already looked rather matronly. From the redness and puffiness of her eyes, it was obvious she still felt the effects of finding Miss Bechet's body.

Vincent studied Miss Gatti's written statement and asked her a few more questions attempting to put her at ease. She confirmed Mister Hopkins' version of events but added nothing new. He had one more question to ask. He hesitated and then looked her squarely in the eyes.

"Did you notice if Miss Bechet was wearing jewelry or see any jewelry in the cabin when you looked around?"

"No!" Miss Gatti twisted her handkerchief into a tight roll as her voice trembled. "I didn't look around. As soon as I saw the lady, I ran out of her cabin and called Mr.

Hopkins." Her hands began to shake and her eyes filled with tears. "Are you accusing me of taking something?"

"No, by no means." Vincent's shoulders rounded as he folded his hands in his lap. "It just puzzles me that we didn't find any of her jewelry in the cabin when we searched it. No, I am not accusing you of taking anything."

Miss Gatti turned away and covered her face as she began to weep.

"Please accept our sincerest apology for having to put you through this interview," Charles said. "You have been very helpful. If we have more questions, we will contact you. I hope you feel better in the morning.

Charles had observed Miss Gatti during the interview. After she stepped from the cabin, he lit his pipe and glanced at Vincent. "She strikes me as an honest girl. I don't think she had anything to do with the disappearance of the jewelry. Frankly, I'm surprised she was able to talk at all, considering her age and what she has been through."

"I didn't expect she would provide us with any new information," Vincent said. "Although, I'm disappointed she didn't notice Miss Bechet's jewelry."

"Well, I'm sure jewelry was the last thing on her mind this morning."

Vincent opened the list of passengers with cabins near Miss Bechet's. "We need to determine if any of these people saw or heard anything last night. Let's start with Bill and Margaret Cates. They're in the cabin directly across the passageway from Miss Bechet."

It was a little past ten when Vincent knocked on the Cates' door. Bill answered and invited Charles and Vincent in. The Cates owned a horse ranch north of Billings, Montana. Bill had sunbaked, leathery skin and furrowed features earned through almost seventy-one years of working the range. His jet-black hair and lean six-foot frame contradicted his age. Margaret had been equally honed by a life as a Montana rancher's wife and could obviously work stride for stride beside Bill.

They had heard about Miss Bechet's tragic death and were eager to help.

"We were returning from dinner last night," Margaret said, "and as we turned the corner toward our cabin, we saw that poor girl trying to unlock her cabin door. She had trouble putting the key in the lock, so Bill opened the door for her. We offered to send for help, but she refused, saying she was just a little under the weather and would be better in the morning."

"I wish we had known how sick she was, we would have done more," Bill said. "She closed the door, and we retired to our cabin and got ready for bed."

"Did you observe anything else during the night?" Vincent asked.

"Margaret and I read for an hour or so before we went to sleep. About twenty minutes after we had climbed into bed, we heard persistent knocking on her door. It took a while for her to answer. When I looked through the peephole in our door, I saw a nurse entering her cabin."

"Can you describe her?"

"She had black hair tied in a bun and was about five and a half feet tall, slender, and in her mid-thirties."

"How do you know she was a nurse?" Vincent asked.

"I overheard her say she was the ship's nurse and she was wearing a white dress, white shoes, white stockings, and a nurse's cap. You know, one of those funny looking caps they all wear. She carried a small black bag like a doctor's bag."

"How long did she remain?"

"She left about twenty-five minutes later, at eleven o'clock. I remember the time because I had just finished the last chapter in my book, and I noticed the clock on the nightstand as I turned out the light."

"Did either of you hear anything else during the night?"

"No, Margaret and I slept through the night. The storm didn't bother us. In fact, we kind of enjoyed it."

"If you think of anything, please contact Captain Ashcroft. It's important that you do not discuss this interview with anyone else. Thank you for your help."

Vincent and Charles proceeded from cabin to cabin talking to the occupants. It was almost eleven before they finished interviewing the occupants of the last cabin on the passageway. Everything came up blank; no one had seen or heard anything. The passengers were eager to help; however, they had all been asleep by ten o'clock last night.

"We need to talk to the ship's nurse. She may be the last person to have seen Miss Bechet alive."

It was late, so Vincent called Miss Dixie Pennell to ask if they could interview her tonight. She was in her cabin reading and said she was willing to talk with them.

215

It didn't take long for Vincent and Charles to make their way to Miss Pennell's cabin. As soon as she opened her cabin door, it was obvious she was not the person the Cates had seen enter Miss Bechet's cabin last night. She was a little over five feet tall with short red hair and in her early fifties. Her large horn-rimmed glasses magnified her eyes to Peter Lorre proportions.

"Miss Pennell, I am Doctor Jeffery and this is Inspector Bedeau. We are investigating the death of Miss Bechet. We would like to ask you some questions if it isn't too late in the evening."

"Sure, come on in. Can I fix you gents a drink?" She said with a heavy Texas accent.

"Not for me, thanks," Charles said.

"Me neither." Vincent stepped in and stood beside Charles.

"Well, if you don't mind I'll just work on my Scotch while we talk. That girl's death is a real tragedy. If there's something I can do, just ask. I'm a night-owl and I read until one or two in the morning."

"Did you go to Miss Bechet's cabin last night around ten-thirty?"

"No, I met Doctor Beck in the lounge for a nightcap a little before eleven."

"Are you the only nurse on the ship?"

"No, Miss Clara Bauchman is the night nurse. Clara, Doctor Beck, and I are the entire medical department. I've

)een a ship's nurse for almost eight years, and, to my knowledge, this is the first time anyone has died on this ship. I wish someone would have called when that poor girl first became sick. I might have been able to do something. Dying from pulmonary aspiration is not a pleasant way to go. I wouldn't wish that on my ex-husband, the bastard."

"Would you please describe Miss Bauchman," Vincent asked.

"Sure, she is about five and a half feet tall with black hair, in her mid-thirties. She speaks with a slight German accent."

"How long has she been a member of the medical department?"

"Only a short time. Less than two years ago she moved from the Hamburg Amerika Line where she had worked as a ship's nurse for five years."

"Do you know where she was last night?"

"She was in the ship's sickbay caring for a little girl. Clara cared for the little girl at night, and I watched her during the day. We had hoped to discharge the little girl to her parents on Saturday, but her condition worsened."

"Could Nurse Bauchman have left sickbay during the evening?"

"I suppose, momentarily; however, the little girl required close monitoring. We were able to step out for brief periods, but I know Clara was in sickbay last night from at least eight until shortly before eleven. She called me when the little girl spiked a temperature around seven-thirty, and I joined her in sickbay until just before eleven when I went to meet Doctor Beck in the lounge."

"Was Doctor Beck in the lounge when you arrived?"

"No, he showed up at about quarter after eleven. He said he got tied up somewhere and forgot the time."

"Are there any nurses' aides?"

"No."

"Do you mind if I ask you about Doctor Beck," Charles asked.

"Ask away."

"Are you close friends?"

"We're just drinkin' buddies. That's all. He likes to drink and I like to drink; so we drink together. I keep my social distance from men since my divorce."

"I understand Doctor Beck joined the ship's crew five years ago after he retired from his practice in Shanghai," Vincent said. "Do you know anything about the time he spent in China?"

"Well, a little. He's told me things from time to time. You know, when you're sitting around, late at night, reminiscing about old times and telling tall stories."

"He's overly distraught and uncooperative about our involvement in Miss Bechet's death," Vincent said.

"I can tell you he doesn't like anyone prying into his business. He used to become testy when I would question him, so I learned to keep my mouth shut."

"What about his time in China?" Vincent asked again.

"I shouldn't be telling you this and you didn't hear it from me, but he has some demons that haunt him. He went to Shanghai with the high aspirations of a new doctor fresh from his internship and ready to make a difference. The years and life in Shanghai were hard on him, and he became depressed and slowly turned to self-medication. In 1929, there was an epidemic; cholera I believe. He misdiagnosed a number of patients and wasn't available when their relatives tried to reach him. Two of the patients died before anyone else could intervene. Their ghosts still chase him. No one else on this ship knows about this and I already wish I hadn't said anything."

"What you've told us will go no further," Vincent said.

"The life of a ship's doctor is fairly quiet, with few challenges beyond an occasional scrape or upset stomach. I know advances in today's medical field have passed him by, but he's fine here as the ship's doctor. When he makes a mistake, I just correct it without bothering him. That way he still has his pride, if he has nothing else. Do you understand?"

"Yes I do," Charles said as he gently touched her left forearm and smiled.

"I have one last question, if I may," Vincent said. "We find it curious that a set of pearl earrings and a pearl necklace belonging to Miss Bechet are missing. There was no jewelry case anywhere in her cabin. I am puzzled why Doctor Beck would need to enter Miss Bechet's cabin multiple times long after he had determined the cause of her death."

"I don't know. You'll have to ask him. I am sure he would not take anything from a passenger's cabin. He's as honest as a Texas church deacon at a Sunday afternoon barbecue. Whenever he has borrowed money from me, he has always paid me right back. I think he likes to play poker with some of the deck hands but loses more than he can afford from time to time. I don't mind loaning him money."

"Thank you for your time," Vincent said. "If anything else comes to mind Doctor Jeffery and I are using Cabin 25, or you can contact us through Captain Ashcroft."

"I want to reassure you there is nothing you could have done to save Miss Bechet," Charles said as he and Vincent stepped into the passageway.

Vincent and Charles retreated to Cabin 25. Charles opened the porthole and gazed out into the darkness. The fresh salt air and the sounds of the *Southern Cross* moving through the water drifted into the cabin. After a long silence he turned toward Vincent.

"We seem to have reached an impasse," Charles said as he lit his pipe.

"The killer is obviously someone with professional skill at hiding his or her true identity," Vincent said. "I am not sure what we should do next."

"Perhaps, we could compare a passenger list with the list of names from Miss Bechet's safe-deposit box."

"I'll ask Captain Ashcroft if he will send us a list of passengers and indicate those with safe-deposit boxes."

"The copy of the names from Miss Bechet's box is in the top drawer of the desk. Someone on her list might be a passenger on the *Southern Cross*, although I don't think it will be that easy."

Chapter Twenty-nine

'Who is it?" Vincent opened the cabin door to find Miss Pennell glaring in the passageway. Her nostrils flared as her face flushed scarlet-red.

"You won't believe what just happened. That son of a bitch had the gall to involve me in his stupid mess. If I'd had a gun, I would have shot him on the spot." She pushed past Vincent and paced defiantly in the middle of the cabin. Her fists were clinched so tightly the knuckles bulged out bone-white.

"What happened?"

Miss Pennell took a deep breath and spun around to face Vincent. "Shortly after you and Doctor Jeffery departed, Doctor Beck showed up. He brought me a damn pair of pearl earrings. After what you said about Miss Bechet's jewelry, I accepted them, but told him I was not feeling well and needed to turn in. I waited until he left and came right up here. I can't believe he would steal earrings, let alone from a *corpse*, and then give them to me. What gall."

Miss Pennell thrust an envelope containing two white pearl earrings at Vincent. He looked at them and handed the envelope to Charles.

"Is this the pair of earrings Miss Bechet wore Saturday night?"

"Sure looks like them."

"I would like to retain these as evidence," Vincent said.

"I don't give a tinker's damn what you do with 'em. They ain't mine. That stupid old fool." She stamped her feet and stood scowling in the middle of the cabin as her temples throbbed and her fists snapped open and closed. "This takes the cake."

"Thank you for bringing them up here tonight. I'll contact you tomorrow for a written statement," Vincent said as he opened the door.

After Miss Pennell stomped out, all Vincent and Charles could do was look at each other in disbelief.

"What could Doctor Beck have been thinking?" Charles asked. "He removed this jewelry from a dead body like a grave robber. I'm stunned."

Even though it was almost midnight, Vincent called Captain Ashcroft to provide him with an update and request a complete list of passengers and safe-deposit box holders.

"Captain, we believe Miss Bechet's killer entered her cabin around ten-thirty last night disguised as a nurse. Earlier tonight we questioned your day nurse, Miss Pennell. After talking to her, we don't believe either she or the night nurse, Miss Bauchman, had anything to do with Miss Bechet's death."

"So that clears my medical staff of any involvement?"

"Well, not exactly. As far as we can tell they had no involvement with the murder, but there was an incident where Doctor Beck took some jewelry from Miss Bechet's cabin."

"What? Did I hear you correctly? Doctor Beck stole from Miss Bechet?"

"That's the way it appears. We have a pair of pearl earrings Doctor Beck gave Miss Pennell tonight. Charles believes Miss Bechet wore the same earrings last night at dinner."

"I always thought of Doctor Beck as being a bit odd, but he never struck me as a thief."

"I am sorry sir, but I want to question Doctor Beck tonight. He obviously knows more than he has revealed."

"I'll call him as soon as we are through and have him meet us in my office."

"I would rather surprise him in his cabin, if you don't mind."

"I will meet you at the doctor's cabin in five minutes."

Vincent received directions to the cabin and turned to Charles. "I need to speak with Doctor Beck, and I think it would be best if you weren't around. I will meet you back here as soon as we have finished. Why don't you try to rest."

"I'll compare Miss Bechet's list with the passenger list as soon as it arrives. I couldn't relax anyway. We have to be looking at the answer; we just haven't recognized it."

Chapter Thirty

Vincent and the captain met in the passageway leading to Doctor Beck's cabin. The captain loudly rapped on the door several times before there was a response.

"Who is it?"

"Captain Ashcroft and Inspector Bedeau. We need to speak with you."

"Come back tomorrow. I'm in bed."

"No, we need to see you immediately," the captain said.

The sound of breaking glass and muffled swearing could be heard through the door.

The captain knocked again, only more emphatically this time. "Doctor Beck."

The doctor finally opened the door. He reeked of gin and was fully dressed—including his shoes. He clearly had not been in bed. The cabin was a mess. An almost empty bottle of gin and a glass sat on the nightstand beside the ed. An empty bottle and a broken glass lay on the floor next to a pile of dirty clothes.

"Well, get in here and close the damned door. What he hell do you want at this hour?"

"Doctor Beck, Inspector Bedeau has some important questions to ask you concerning Miss Bechet." The captain's eyes widened and his lips remained parted as he ooked around at the squalor the doctor lived in.

"Earlier this evening you gave Miss Pennell some ewelry you took from Miss Bechet's cabin," Vincent said.

"I don't know what you're talking about." Doctor Beck poured the last of his gin into a glass and drank it without pausing.

"Miss Pennell brought us this pair of pearl earrings and said you gave them to her." Vincent held the earrings out for the doctor to see.

The doctor stared at the earrings, and leaned forward without saying a word.

"Where is the necklace?" Vincent asked.

Doctor Beck didn't respond. He rolled the empty glass n his hand and stared at the floor.

"Doctor Beck, where is the necklace?"

The silence in the room was heavy as the doctor's right hand began to shake and the empty glass slipped to the floor. Finally he spoke in low, hushed, almost inaudible tones.

"I don't know what you're talking about."

"Doctor, we know you are lying." The captain moved toward the doctor. "Do we have to search your cabin?"

The doctor's lungs slowly expanded and his lower lip began to quiver.

"It . . . It's over there in the top drawer of my dresser in her jewelry case." He continued to look at the floor.

"Why did you take it?" Vincent asked.

The doctor slumped farther forward on the bed as he buried his face in his hands.

"I noticed her jewelry when I was leaving her cabin. I thought about it as I filled out her death certificate. At first I didn't plan on returning to her cabin, but since Miss Bechet was dead I thought no one would ever find out— and she didn't need the stuff anyway. It was like a dream. I found myself standing in her cabin with the jewelry case in my bag. It was just an impulse; something a ten year old would do in a dime store for a candy bar."

"You're not telling the whole truth," Vincent said. "You took the jewelry case from her dresser, but you also removed the pearl earrings and necklace from her *dead* body."

Vincent and the captain stood staring at the doctor. The captain's jaw muscles tightened and his face reddened as the doctor began to speak.

"Last night while you were investigating Miss Bechet's death, I came to my senses and tried to return the jewelry case. I hoped her cabin would be empty, and I could return the case before anyone noticed it was missing; however, you wouldn't let me in. I should have just thrown the damn stuff overboard, but I couldn't. Tonight I gave Dixie the pearl earrings and was going to give her the necklace for her birthday next month. Don't ask me why. I guess I didn't think anyone would recognize the pearls. I'm not sure what I was going to do with the case and the rest of the jewelry."

Vincent retrieved the jewelry case and placed the earrings inside. There wasn't much else in the case except two plain silver rings and a pendant.

"Is this all that was in the case?" Vincent asked.

"Yes."

"Did you remove anything else from Miss Bechet's cabin?"

The doctor sat straight up and faced Vincent.

"No, do you think I'm a common thief?"

Vincent didn't respond. However, the captain had something to say.

"Doctor Beck, You are relieved of all duties as this ship's doctor, and you are restricted to your cabin. Breakfast will be brought to you. I want you cleaned up and in my office at zero seven hundred tomorrow morning. This whole incident is unbelievable. Frankly, I'm extremely disappointed. I trust I will not have to lock you in your cabin."

The doctor just rocked back and forth on the bed and stared at himself in the dresser mirror.

Vincent picked up the jewelry case as he and the captain turned to leave. "I have one more question. Do you smoke?"

"Yes."

"What brand?"

"Lucky Strike."

The captain and Vincent exited Doctor Beck's cabin and rejoined Charles in Cabin 25.

"What did Doctor Beck have to say for himself?" Charles asked.

"He eventually broke down," Vincent said, "but tried to rationalize his actions. We recovered the rest of her jewelry and this case. Anything stand out in the lists?" Vincent set the jewelry case on the desk.

"No, the lists were a dead end. I find it hard to believe Doctor Beck would stoop to stealing, especially something as trivial as a box of inexpensive jewelry. He certainly has the resources and opportunities to purchase much finer jewelry at any of the ports-of-call this ship visits."

"Now that we have Miss Bechet's jewelry, Doctor Beck is the least of my worries," the captain said. "There's another more serious problem. I didn't want to bring it up until we talked with the doctor, but just before I joined you my crew completed an exhaustive search of the ship for a missing passenger who may have fallen overboard some time last night. She is nowhere to be found."

"She?" Charles asked.

"A middle-aged woman from Geneva was traveling alone to San Francisco."

"Mary Channing?"

"Yes, but how did you know?"

"She sat at our table last night at dinner," Charles said. "What an unfortunate tragedy."

"Her bed wasn't used," the captain said.

"Perhaps she visited one of the exposed decks after dinner and fell or was swept overboard during the storm," Vincent said.

"If she did, she must have ignored posted signs prohibiting use of the weather decks," the captain said. "Last night's storm was intense, with thirty to forty foot waves most of the night. Early yesterday morning we responded to a distress call from a yacht floundering between Miami and Nassau. Fortunately we rescued the last crew member just before the yacht was swamped and sank." The captain tilted his head and looked over his glasses at Charles and Vincent. "I'm afraid that if Miss Channing was on deck last night, we'll never find her."

"She was talkative at dinner," Charles said. "A few of us met in the first class lounge for a night-cap after dinner, but she excused herself, saying she was tired and wanted to retire."

Vincent fell silent as he interlaced his fingers behind his head and leaned back in his chair. He tilted his head upward and closed his eyes. After a few moments he jumped to his feet.

"Captain, even though it's past midnight, Charles and I had better look at Miss Channing's cabin tonight."

"Very well. I will be in my office, if you need anything."

"There may be a connection between Miss Bechet's death and Miss Channing's disappearance," Vincent said as he opened the door. "The two events are too unusual to be a coincidence."

Chapter Thirty-one

"Will you require anything else?" the steward said as he opened the door to Miss Channing's cabin.

"No, not at this time, thank you." Charles shifted his attention from the steward to the interior of the cabin.

The cramped space did not have an ocean view like the more expensive outside cabins. Instead a picture of palm trees lining a beach was displayed in place of a porthole. The space was filled by two single beds and a night stand stuffed against the back wall. The dresser was crowded next to the closet. A plain metal reading lamp was centered above each headboard. No space remained for a writing desk; there was barely enough room to walk between the beds, yet the cabin felt strangely empty.

Miss Channing's bed was just as the steward had left it the evening before. The spread was turned down with a single gold-foil wrapped chocolate candy on the pillow. The steward had folded one of the bath towels into the hape of a cute little bunny and set it on the pillow beside he candy. The other bed was untouched.

"It appears she didn't return after dinner last night," Charles said as he turned away from the closet. "I don't see he dark green velvet evening dress she wore last night."

Vincent stepped aside to allow Charles to pass.

"I hesitate to say this, but old people sometimes have nood swings and become despondent." Vincent bit his lip. 'Is it possible she jumped overboard?

Opening the top drawer of the dresser, Charles pulled ut a few items and inspected them.

"I don't believe she would have deliberately jumped. Miss Channing was traveling to visit her sister's family in Monterey and seemed in high spirits. During the onversation at dinner she mentioned a young nephew and low much she was looking forward to seeing him for the irst time. She was fatigued by the long trip, but by no neans despondent."

"Can you imagine someone wanting to kill a middle-ged housekeeper from Geneva?"

"No, the only plausible explanation is that she wanted ome fresh air before going to bed and somehow missed the osted warning signs and ended up on one of the weather lecks where she was swept overboard."

Vincent leaned against the door and slowly considered he cabin as a whole. Rubbing his forehead, he glanced at Charles.

"We haven't found the make up or toiletries one would xpect a woman to travel with." Vincent paused and pursed us lips. "I can't put my finger on why, but this cabin loesn't feel right."

Charles turned from the dresser and sat on the edge of the bed. He tapped his fingers slowly on his knees.

"Curious, there was no luggage in the closet and nothing of a personal nature in the dresser. The cameo pendant she wore the other night is missing. It's as if we were in a display window at Goldberg's on Market Street. We're only missing the mannequins. Except for the clothes hanging in the closet or in the dresser, you wouldn't know anyone was assigned to this cabin."

Vincent stepped into the bathroom, used the toilet, and then returned.

"Everything has been staged. For whatever reason, we're surrounded by an elaborate hoax. We will not find anything that leads to Miss Channing here."

"I agree." Charles looked at his watch and moved toward the door. "It's almost one. I'm sure Bree and Marie turned in long ago; we should do the same. Sunrise will come all to quickly."

As Vincent approached the door a glint of light between the nightstand and bed drew his attention to the floor. He bent down and lifted a corner of the bedspread.

"This must have slipped off the back of the nightstand and not been missed." Vincent handed Charles a small, clear bottle with a black metal lid.

"The label has been stripped off." Charles studied the bottle for a moment. "But it's obviously a saccharin bottle," he said, removing the lid and inspecting the contents. "These tablets aren't the same color as saccharin. They have a brownish tinge and saccharin is pure white."

"Why would someone remove the label from such an ordinary product?"

"Probably to prevent anyone from tracing the bottle."

Charles thoughts returned to the end of dinner Saturday night when Miss Channing gave Miss Bechet some saccharin—most likely from the bottle he was holding. Miss Bechet was in a happy and talkative mood until finishing her coffee. After that she became ill and excused herself from the table. Everyone assumed she was seasick, but now Charles was beginning to have his doubts. He touched one of the tablets to his tongue and quickly rinsed his mouth with fresh water in the bathroom.

"Initially there was a slight bitter taste to the tablet before the sweetness of saccharin came through. I believe these tablets have been treated with an emetic."

"What's an emetic?"

"It's a drug that can cause a person to rapidly expel the contents of their digestive tract through vomiting and diarrhea. You may not be familiar with Ipecac, but it's sometimes administered in hospital emergency rooms in cases such as a potential suicide, where a patient has ingested a poisonous substance. The active ingredient in Ipecac is emetine and the reaction depends on the dose."

"Why would Miss Channing give Miss Bechet something like that?" Vincent asked.

"My guess is she wanted to make Miss Bechet feel sick so she would go directly to her cabin after dinner. Based on the description the Cates provided, I think Miss Channing impersonated a nurse in order to gain Miss Bechet's confidence and trick her into opening her door."

Vincent's eyes narrowed and he pulled out his notebook and pen. "If that's the case then Miss Channing is the mystery spy we have been looking for, and with her disappearance overboard our problem is solved."

"Don't be so sure. We have another possibility concerning her disappearance: she didn't fall overboard during the storm, but is still alive and hiding on the ship."

"Well, at least we know what she looks like."

"No," Charles said. "We know what she *looked* like Saturday night, but not what she *looks* like now."

"So we're searching for someone who is lurking in the shadows and doesn't want to be found?"

"That pretty well sums it up."

"What about the saccharin bottle?"

"The first thing we should do is attempt to verify the use of an emetic. I remember a simple test for emetine. If I can obtain the chemicals I need on the ship, I think we can conduct a basic test in short order; or you could just take a couple of these tablets, and we can observe what happens."

"Not on your life."

"Just kidding, it's a late-night, laboratory joke, besides we don't have enough time to wait for you to become sick. The ship's galley uses chlorinated lime to make a weak chlorine solution for disinfecting fresh fruits and vegetables."

Charles picked up the phone and dialed Captain Ashcroft's office.

"Sir, would you have a steward deliver two medium sized glass bowls and some chlorinated lime from the ship's main galley to Cabin 25? Vincent and I are leaving Miss Channing's cabin and will be there shortly."

"What have you found out about Miss Channing's disappearance?" the captain asked.

"We should know more in half an hour."

The ship's passageways were nearly empty as Charles and Vincent made their way back to Cabin 25. Most of the passengers were fast asleep, and the night crew was busy cleaning the ship.

"In my college freshman chemistry class we conducted a test for emetine in ipecac root," Charles said. "We crushed the root to expose the inner pulp. Then we combined the pulp with acid and allowed the mixture to soak liberating the emetine. We filtered the mixture to remove the pulp and then sprinkled chlorinated lime over the remaining liquid. A bright reddish orange color indicated emetine was present. We'll attempt to produce the same reaction using some of these tablets."

In less than ten minutes a steward knocked on the door to Cabin 25 with a box containing the glass bowls and chlorinated lime.

"You gentlemen sure move around." The steward looked at Charles. "Anthony, a steward on day shift, told me about your bet. How did your experiment with Vicks work out?"

Charles stared blankly at the steward until he remembered his previous conversation.

"Oh yes, I won the bet and proved to my friend that Vicks floats on water."

"I could have saved you the trouble," the steward said as he turned and walked away. "Vicks is petroleum based and oil floats on water. Everybody knows that."

Charles closed the door and set the supplies on the desk. "I wish everything in this case was that obvious."

"I'm amazed at your resourcefulness," Vincent said as he watched Charles prepare for the test. "Can you turn lead into gold?"

Charles smiled as he crushed three of the saccharin tablets in a glass bowl and mixed the powder with some battery electrolyte remaining from the modified Marsh Test.

"How long do we have to wait for results?"

"If this works, we'll observe a color change as soon as we sprinkle the chlorinated lime over the mixture. Here, I'll let you do the honors." Charles handed Vincent the lime.

"I remember when I was a young boy playing with my Gilbert chemistry set . . .well, that was cookbook chemistry, not seat-of-the-pants chemistry like we're doing now." Vincent's eyes lit up as he sprinkled the white powder on the liquid. "I'll be. The mixture in the bowl turned bright red and proves your theory about an emetic."

"Not exactly, we're not using a laboratory with pure chemicals and exact measurements. Although saccharin tablets contain mostly benzoic sulfinide and a salt, other chemicals could affect the reaction. I just guessed at the amounts of reactants needed. Chemical analysis is an exact science, and right now we are not all that exact. The FBI lab will perform a complete analysis of the tablets, but for now the reaction we observed tells me we have something more than saccharin."

"We can go no further tonight. It's nearly two o'clock
n the morning and we should get some sleep."

Vincent called Captain Ashcroft. After a short
:onversation the captain requested to see them in his office
)efore they retired for the night.

The captain was sitting behind his desk drinking a cup of
)lack coffee. He didn't look like he had been awake since
'our yesterday morning. Not only had he been dealing with
Miss Bechet's murder and Miss Channing's disappearance,
)ut he also had a ship to operate.

"Would either of you care for coffee?"

"None for me, sir," Vincent replied.

"I'll pass too. How can you drink coffee at two in the
norning?"

"It's an acquired habit from standing years of mid-
vatches on the bridge. I can drink a cup of coffee just
)efore going off watch and fall asleep as soon as my head
lits the pillow. What have you found?"

"We have developed a theory concerning Miss
3echet's murder and Miss Channing's disappearance,"
Vincent said as he turned to Charles.

"Yes, as we searched Miss Channing's cabin, we
·eached the conclusion it was staged, no one actually
)ccupied the cabin. As we were about to leave, Vincent
'ound a bottle containing what appeared to be adulterated
;accharin tablets. It is our belief the spy we are looking for

in conjunction with the murder of Miss Bechet was masquerading as Miss Channing."

Vincent handed the bottle to the captain. "I don't believe she planned on leaving this behind."

"I thought saccharin was white," the captain said.

"Normally it is," Charles said. "However, the brownish tinge to the tablets indicates to me they have been treated with a substance that caused Miss Bechet to become sick and go directly to her cabin. Sometime between ten and eleven Miss Channing came to Miss Bechet's cabin disguised as the ship's nurse and gained entry. She administered arsenic and killed Miss Bechet. Miss Channing did not fall overboard last night. She is hiding somewhere on the ship."

"Gentlemen, we have been wasting our time searching the ship for someone who doesn't want to be found. No wonder we couldn't find her." The captain suddenly stood and turned away. "How can we apprehend this person— this Miss Channing?"

"She could be impersonating a stewardess, someone working in the ship's laundry, or another passenger," Vincent said. "She is obviously an expert in the art of disguise. Charles, you sat across the table from her during dinner the other night. You didn't notice anything strange or out of the ordinary did you?"

"No, she appeared to be a woman in her mid-fifties on her way to visit her sister in Monterey. Her conversation flowed without hesitation. There was nothing to cause me to doubt her."

"My point exactly," Vincent said. "You sat no more han five feet away from her and didn't notice anything abnormal."

Charles stretched back in his chair and thought for a moment. "Wait, I remember one peculiarity from our dinner conversation. When I talked about my field of research, I was surprised she knew the term Orthopoxvirus, much less that she knew smallpox was a virus in that family. She commented how effective smallpox was as a weapon of war. Her comment struck me as unusual then, but now as I look back, it was telling. She obviously knows more about pathology than you would expect from a mid-fifties housekeeper."

"Gentlemen, back to my original question. How do we apprehend this person?"

"I think the disappearance of Miss Channing was part of the killer's plan all along," Vincent said. "Nothing has happened so far that would cause the killer to suspect we know Miss Bechet was killed or Miss Channing's disappearance was anything other than an accidental fall overboard during the storm. Let's keep it that way."

"Makes sense," Charles said.

"We have a dead spy and a live spy. Your passengers aren't in danger as long as the spy believes no one has uncovered the real story. Captain, I recommend we circulate a story that Miss Channing suffered an unfortunate accident during the storm and is presumed to have fallen overboard."

"I don't believe we have a choice in this matter. I hope everything doesn't unravel before we can gain control of the situation. FBI agents are flying down from Miami this morning and will board the ship prior to our docking in Havana. I'll inform their office in Miami of the developments concerning Miss Channing." The captain paused and clinched his fists. "I should have listened to my wife; I'm really too old for this crap."

Chapter Thirty-two

Steel had called the FBI field office in Miami the morning he *Southern Cross* sailed from Manhattan to talk with gent Jack Masters. They had worked together on an organized crime investigation two years before in Florida and, despite Masters' impulsive nature, they both received commendations for their work. Masters occasionally jumped in before he understood how deep the water was or where the rocks were, and that is probably why Masters worked in Florida, not New York City or Los Angeles.

Some people in the agency referred to Masters as a "cowboy," a label that fit him, because his family owned a two thousand acre cattle ranch near Fort Davis in West Texas. As a boy growing up on the ranch, he had always wanted to be a Texas Ranger, but his career led him to the FBI instead. He spoke with a slow Texas drawl. Folks in Fort Davis said given half a chance, he could "talk the tail off a lizard." Masters carried himself like a professional wrestler or football player, standing six-foot-four in his alligator hide cowboy boots. He often wore a white Stetson which made him appear even taller. It was a good thing he worked in Miami and not Washington; J. Edgar would not have approved of the boots and hat.

Steel briefed Masters concerning the circumstances surrounding Otto Vogt's murder at Penn Station and informed him about Clive Smith's two MI6 agents onboard the *Southern Cross*. Everything was under control. After all, the German was isolated on a ship headed to Havana with two of Smith's top agents. It was only a matter of time before they developed leads to the German. What could go wrong?

In a word, everything, and in short order. Masters called Steel when he received Captain Ashcroft's wire disclosing Miss Bechet's murder. Apparently the German had discovered the identity of one of the MI6 agents and the agent had paid the price. Smith had no way of contacting his second agent until he boarded the *Southern Cross* in Havana. Smith and Steel were no closer to identifying the German than they were when they emerged from the Bellevue Morgue early Saturday morning.

Steel booked seats for Smith and himself on the red-eye to Miami. It was imperative they reach Havana before the *Southern Cross* docked and the passengers disembarked. This was not an ordinary murder case where the usual suspects could be rounded up and questioned until the murderer broke down in a sweat and confessed. They certainly couldn't overrun the ship with agents like a band of Caribbean pirates plundering for gold. The investigation had to be handled more subtly.

Smith and Steel needed to neutralize a situation that had gotten out of hand and had the real potential to become a major career-changing event.

Masters met Steel and Smith as they exited the Miami airport. At eight in the morning the sun burned hot in the cloudless blue sky. Steel mopped his brow and removed his jacket.

"Howdy. You boys sure got down here faster than a scorpion on a hot rock. I didn't expect you for another twenty minutes. How was the flight?" Masters captured Smith's right hand with a crushing grip as they shook hands.

"As good as can be expected, for a red-eye," Steel said. "I hate last minute bookings. I usually end up sitting next to some fat guy who takes up half my seat, talks the whole flight, spills coffee on me, and always needs to go to the can at least five times in a three hour flight."

"Hey, I know that guy," Masters said with a broad smile. "He's my brother-in-law, Cooter."

"During this flight I enjoyed the company of a woman with a little boy who was practicing to be the fat guy on my next flight. Little Billy ricocheted up and down the aisle banging on the seats screaming he wanted to go home. The woman became upset with me when she asked if little Billy was bothering me and I said yes."

"I don't care for flying at all." The color still hadn't returned to Smith's face as he rubbed his right hand. "It took all the courage I could muster to climb on the plane in New York. I prefer to travel by boat or car."

Steel looked at Masters as he lit a cigarette. "Yep, between chain smoking and talking non-stop all the way from New York, Smith nearly drove me crazy. He must have asked the flight attendant where the emergency exits were located fifteen times, if he asked once."

"I'm with Smith. I prefer to drive or take a train when I can," Masters said. "I hate to fly. There's not enough leg or head room in those sardine cans and as soon as anyone sneezes everyone else gets sick."

"Speaking of travel, how do we reach Havana?" Smith asked.

"A Catalina will pick us up at Opa-Locka and drop us in Havana."

"What kind of boat is that?"

"It's not a boat," Masters said as he winked. "It's a plane, a Navy PBY—kind of a flying boat. They almost never sink."

"Oh . . ." Smith clinched his fists as he fell silent.

"The plane and its crew are on hot standby. The flight to Havana shouldn't take more than an hour. It won't be as nice as the flight you two just finished, 'cause a PBY isn't nearly as cushy as a DC3, and the Navy doesn't have a cute little stewardess to bring you mixed drinks and peanuts on a silver tray. In fact you won't find anything *cute* about the flight."

"As long as little Billy isn't on the plane," Steel said. "I'll be all right."

"I'm afraid there's more bad news," Masters said. "I received a radiogram from Captain Ashcroft while you boys were in the air. There is another problem. They discovered the identity of a woman who they think killed Smith's MI6 agent, but now she's missing. They haven't been able to find her onboard. Other than that, everything's under control."

"Did you say woman?" Steel asked.

"Yep, that was the message from the ship."

"Now we're dealing with two spies, a man and a woman," Steel said. "Great, just great."

"Look at it this way. The odds just doubled on finding at least one of them."

"Is that a bit of your West Texas logic?" Steel's posture stiffened. It was obvious he wasn't happy about the possibility of having to deal with co-conspirators.

On the way to Opa-Locka, Masters stopped at the office to check for any last minute information. The drive to the Navy base was uneventful and the time mostly filled with Masters' folksy tales of armadillos, snakes, and of growing up on a West Texas ranch. Smith was introduced to the concept that everything living under rocks in Texas pretty much tasted like chicken when cooked over a mesquite fire. Masters' command of frontier cowboy knowledge kept Smith transfixed as Masters gave new definition to the term "tall tale."

Steel sat quietly and smiled as he watched the expression of amazement grow on Smith's face. He had experienced Masters' "wild west" show before. The depth of Masters' yarns was dependent on the gullibility of his audience and Smith's expression made him look like he was fresh off the bus.

By the end of the ride to Opa-Locka it became clear Masters had an innate ability to come out on top, that like a cat dropped upside down from a tree, he would always wind up landing on his feet; no matter how the events of the next few days unfolded, he would find a way to deflect any failures. Gum never stuck to Masters' boots.

The navy-gray PBY embodied Smith's greatest fears. It was huge and noisy with its two powerful Pratt & Whitney radial engines already thundering. Imposing three bladed props churned the air. The smell of burned high octane gas surrounded the plane and spilled into the spartan cabin. Most of the interior was packed to the top with cargo. The only space remaining contained four seats facing each other located at the rear of the plane. Masters' long legs meant no one would be able to sit in the seat facing him, so that left two seats available for Steel and Smith. One of the seats faced forward and the other faced backward. By their reaction, neither Smith nor Steel appeared keen on the seating arrangement.

"I'll flip a coin to decide which one of you lucky boys gets to face the back of the plane during the flight," Masters said. "Smith, you're the guest, you call it." Masters pulled a silver dollar from his pocket and sent it rocketing skyward. He caught it as it fell and loudly slapped it on the back of his hand.

"Call it."

"Heads," Smith mumbled. "Is this some kind of western vigilante justice?"

Masters grinned and moved his left hand, uncovering the coin for all to see.

"Sorry, it's tails." Masters glanced at Smith and winked. "Looks like you'll be flying backwards all the way to Cuba, but it's better to be sitting backward when the plane crashes."

Smith cinched the seat belt tightly around his waist and sat as rigid and unmoving as a death row inmate about to meet Old Sparky.

The rumbling of the engines reverberated through the drafty cabin as the PBY lumbered into the air. Smith soon lost sight of Opa-Locka and all hope of a safe landing. The plane wasn't designed for passenger comfort, but they did have a large thermos of hot navy-black coffee.

Smith and Steel had to shout above the engine noise to talk, but that didn't stop them from debating where the German was headed. Masters listened to them for awhile, but then tuned their conversation out as he looked at the whitecaps on the water far below.

"My gut tells me the Panama Canal is the target," Steel said above the roar in the cabin. "The German will remain on the *Southern Cross* until it reaches Colón, on the East Coast of Panama. Recent FBI intelligence reports indicate there are a number of Nazi and Japanese operatives working in the Canal region. We know they're gathering information on Canal operations and looking for weak points to disrupt and sabotage the Canal."

"What about the notation in Vogt's wallet about Panama Shipping and Export Limited in Rio de Janeiro?"

Smith said. "The German is leaving dead bodies like a trail of bread crumbs in the Black Forest. Vogt's reference to the *Southern Cross* was right on the money. I believe the German and his female collaborator are headed to Rio de Janeiro."

"You're wrong. What possible interest could the Germans have in Brazil? It's mostly jungle, and a hell of a long ways from the States."

"MI6 believes the Germans want an airfield in Brazil. The shortest flying distance across the Atlantic is between Dakar on the bulge of French West Africa, and Natal on the eastern bulge of Brazil. It's well within the range of the German Heinkel He 111. A few years ago a French airplane took less than fifteen hours to fly from Dakar to Natal."

"Straight across the South Atlantic?" Steel shifted in his seat.

"That's right. The Germans don't have long range bombers that can fly across the North Atlantic and reach the United States directly."

"Dakar and the rest of French West Africa are firmly under French control," Steel said. "They won't just hand Dakar over to the Germans."

"That may not always be the case. The Germans have expressed more than a passing interest in North Africa. France and England have signed a mutual protection pact with Poland. Hitler is about to attack Poland, and may turn his attention to France and England after that. We know another world war is on the horizon and this time it won't be confined to Europe."

"French West Africa and Brazil are still a long way from the States."

"Not so far a German bomber flying overland from Brazil couldn't refuel on the way and drop bombs in the heartland of the United States."

"I still think it would be easier and quicker to sabotage the Panama Canal with a bomb," Steel said. "The Canal could be out of commission for a long time with just one well placed, hand-carried bomb."

Smith didn't like the possibility of being wrong so he changed the subject.

"What's our next step when we reach Havana?"

"We meet with Captain Gomez of the Cuban National Police as soon as we land," Masters said. "I briefed him by phone before we left Miami, and he is more than happy to have the FBI proceed with the case."

"Have you worked with him before?" Smith said.

"No, his name came up once in Miami during a smuggling investigation, but beyond that I know nothing about him. Probably just another low-level government entrepreneur."

The Catalina landed in Havana Harbor and taxied to a pier. The agents hurried to a gleaming black Packard limousine. As soon as Smith closed the door, the limousine sped away heading toward central Havana. It shot down narrow cobble-stone streets past women rolling cigars on card tables and old men playing dominoes as they sat under convenient mango trees. Feathery topped palms rustled in the breeze and stretched for the sun. The scent of ripe mangoes, guavas, and bananas flooded into the Packard as Smith rolled his window down.

It was ten o'clock when they squealed to a stop in a cobble-stone plaza in front of a plain, tan colored building, with coral-limestone block walls and tall windows overlooking the plaza. Each window above street level opened onto a separate balcony protected by black wrought-iron railing.

As the agents stepped from the Packard, Steel was submerged in the rich aroma of freshly roasted coffee and Cuban bread coming from a street vendor's cart at the other end of the plaza. Smith and Steel hadn't eaten since they boarded the red-eye in New York.

Masters glanced at Steel as the Packard drove away.

"You don't have time. We have to get inside. Gomez is waiting."

Steel mumbled something inaudible under his breath as they moved up wide tile steps lined with potted palms. A green patina covered plaque mounted to the right of the entrance announced "*Policia Nacional.*" Masters pushed open a pair of weathered mahogany doors and entered the lobby.

"That's my last flight on a PBY," Smith said. "I'll take a boat back to Florida, even if I have to row, or I'll live in Cuba the rest of my life. My ears are still ringing."

"Clive, I think you'll become accustomed to living here." Steel winked at Smith. "The Cubans have a wonderfully rich culture that embraces foreigners, but you vill have to switch from warm Barclay's beer to cold Bacardi rum if you want to fit in."

"There will be plenty of time for beer and rum after the German is caught," Masters said.

The Spanish red tile from the steps flowed into the lobby and covered the floor contrasting with freshly white-washed walls. A large electric fan slowly wobbled in the middle of the high ceiling chasing flies as they aimlessly darted back and forth in the currents.

As Spanish was a second language to Masters, he became the spokesman for the group. He approached a Cuban National Police officer sitting at a desk near the back of the lobby and cleared his throat.

"*Tenemos una cita con el Capitán Gómez.*"

"I speak English. Captain Gomez is on the next level, third office on the right."

They hurried up the stairs to the second floor. Captain Gomez's aide met them at the top of the stairs and escorted them to a waiting area.

"Please acquire a seat. Captain Gomez will be accepting you shortly," the aide said.

As the agents sat on lumpy chairs waiting for an audience with the captain, a number of distinguished-looking people paraded through the captain's office. It wasn't often Captain Gomez received foreign visitors so he was obviously making sure Steel, Smith, and Masters understood how important he was. The agents sat in the waiting area facing a large colorful map of Cuba and a larger-than-life painting of someone in a dark pinstriped suit on the far wall. After several minutes of silence

Masters started to nervously drum his fingers on the chair arm and Steel shifted his gaze from the pinstriped suit guy.

"Who the hell's that?" Steel whispered.

"Laredo Brú the president of Cuba," Smith said. "He's the current puppet for Batista. Shh, it's best to not talk about it in public."

Twenty minutes crept by and Masters began to frown and tap his foot.

"This delay is getting under my skin," Masters whispered. "I'm going to find that aide."

Just as Masters stood, Captain Gomez swooped into the room like a long lost friend. The smell of his cheap dime-store cologne filled the air, crowding all of the more pleasurable aromas from the room. The captain was portly with pomade-slick black hair, thick bushy eyebrows, and a scrubby excuse for a mustache.

"Señores, welcome to Cuba. I trust your flight was not too long," Gomez said with a lisp. "I know most military shuttle flights are exercises in diminishing endurance."

"We arrived in one piece," Masters said as he and the others shook the captain's hand. Then, ever the diplomat, he said, "Thank you for seeing us on such short notice. You are very gracious."

"If you will join me in my office I have information for you."

Captain Gomez dispensed Cuban cigars from an ornate silver humidor as the agents seated themselves around a heavy Spanish cedar table in the center of the office. The room was light and airy with a pleasant breeze from an open window behind the captain's desk. A Cuban flag stood prominently on a stanchion to the right of the captain.

Smith wondered how anyone could keep such an organized desk and get any work done. The pencils were lined up side by side according to length, with their precisely sharpened points all facing in the same direction. The captain obviously had too much time on his hands.

"Señores, may I offer you a drink or some coffee?"

"We had better stick to coffee, the darker the better, since we haven't eaten anything solid today," Masters said.

Steel smiled when the captain sent down to the plaza for some food. Maybe he wasn't such a bad guy after all. In no time at all his aide entered the room with a tray holding steaming bowls filled with fried plantains, black beans and rice, and an ample supply of broiled pork.

"The SS *Southern Cross* is on time and will arrive outside Havana Harbor at noon today. Our customs officials and the harbormaster will board the ship approximately one hour before she docks."

"That doesn't give us much time," Masters said. "We would like to board with your people. Do you have any suggestions on how we can do it without raising suspicion?"

"My aide will measure Señores Steel and Smith for customs officer uniforms. I am sure we have some that will fit. However, as far as you are concerned, I think it will be easier to smuggle you aboard in a coffin, that is if we can find enough people to carry it."

Everyone in the room except Masters laughed, but Gomez was right. Masters' legs were too long for him to wear any of the "official" pants Captain Gomez provided. Masters was able to find a harbor pilot's coat and cap.

Luckily he was already wearing neutral colored pants and black shoes and from a distance didn't look too bad.

It took less than twenty minutes to answer all of Captain Gomez's questions. It became obvious he was not the least bit interested in personally dealing with a bunch of entangled German and British spies, considering the volatile state of world affairs.

Steel and Smith emerged onto the plaza wearing Cuban customs officer uniforms and looked sharp as hell, but Masters still stuck out as a cowboy from West Texas. His coat appeared as if it had been in the dryer too long. The sleeves were a little short and it was tight across the chest making it hard to conceal his shoulder holster and 38 Colt Special.

"I will contact my agent while you two meet with Captain Ashcroft," Smith said.

They would have a limited amount of time to debrief the involved parties once they boarded the ship. They could slow the docking of the *Southern Cross* a little to give them more time to comb the ship for the German and his associate; however, they didn't know what either one of them looked like, or what roles they were currently playing. The hope was that Smith's agent had uncovered information about the identity of the German.

"Even though it appears the spy has an accomplice, we need to remain focused on the German we have tracked from New York," Smith said. "This situation may quickly deteriorate with over five-hundred passengers in the mix. The ship's docking has to appear to be going according to schedule, with no delays. Otherwise the German will become suspicious. Once the *Southern Cross* moors at the ier and the gangway is in place, passengers will expect to go ashore."

"It is imperative we capture the German before any passengers leave the ship or we may never see him again," Masters said.

Steel thought for a moment as a puzzled look swept across his face.

"But with only the vague description from the witnesses at Penn Station, where do we start?"

"We start by talking to Blackwell," Smith said as he shaded his eyes and stared toward Havana Bay.

Chapter Thirty-three

Monday, August 7, 1939
Ten Miles From The Cuban Coast

A fresh, warm sea breeze blew across the deck and swirled into every corner of the ship. Anticipation of a new adventure filled the air as the faint blue-green outline of Cuba beckoned on the horizon. Passengers excitedly strolled around the weather decks hoping to find a good view of Cuba as the *Southern Cross* pulled into port. Since the *Southern Cross* would be in port for over thirty-six hours, many were looking forward to spending time on solid ground after the fierce weather they had endured.

A few passengers were planning to spend the afternoon enjoying the horse races at Oriental Park. Post time for the first race was two-thirty this afternoon, so they would have to hurry once the ship docked if they didn't want to miss the start of the race. Rick, the ship's photographer, already had all of the winners circled on his racing form. Clearly he expected to make a bundle, maybe never have to work again. At least that was his plan, but mostly he would end up throwing his money away on the ponies.

Briana sat near the pool and half-heartedly tried to read. Her chin dipped to her chest as she avoided the gaze of the other passengers. Charles had told her at breakfast he was sorry he couldn't go ashore until late in the day. She had been aimlessly turning the pages in her book for a few minutes when Olivia strolled up.

"Good morning, is this seat taken?"

"No, I was hoping someone would come by." Briana looked up and flashed a weak smile. "My mind isn't on reading anyway. How is your father this morning?"

"Oh, he is enjoying the trip; he does so like to travel. By the by, I haven't seen Charles this morning. Is he working with Vincent Bedeau on something?"

"I don't think so. Charles has some minor business to attend to and won't be joining me until later."

"I'm sorry to hear that. I don't suppose he would be working on the disappearance of Miss Channing?"

"Not that I know of."

"It is a shame we have had two tragedies since leaving New York. Well, I have to meet Dad in the lounge, I must be going. I hope Charles won't be delayed long."

Shortly after Olivia left, Marie approached and plopped down in the deckchair next to Briana.

"How's the morning been for you?"

"It has been pleasant except Charles is still busy. So I guess I'll be on my own for most of the day. What about you?"

"Vincent is working on something, but he won't talk about it."

Briana sat up in her chair and touched Marie on the arm.

"I have an idea. Why don't we tour Havana on our own? Charles and I still have the car reserved for the day. It would be a shame not to use it."

"I would love to visit Havana with you, but you must let me pay for lunch."

"Then it's all set." Briana closed her book. "I'll check with Charles before we leave and agree on a time to meet later in the day. He can bring Vincent with him, since they appear to be working together, and we can have dinner at the Hotel Sevilla."

Marie's smile faded as she sat silently watching a pack of seagulls glide back and forth beside the ship. Finally she looked at Briana.

"Vincent won't tell me anything."

"You'll become used to not knowing what your husband is thinking. It comes with the territory. Would you like something to drink?"

"Iced tea with lemon, please."

"You just missed Olivia Howell."

Briana stopped a passing steward and ordered two iced teas with lemon. Then she and Marie returned to planning their day.

Charles and Vincent met in Cabin 25 right after breakfast to review the information they had gathered before the FBI joined the *Southern Cross*. They felt pressured to identify anything they might have missed.

Vincent stood, looking out the porthole, while Charles made notes at the writing desk. They had finished studying the crime scene photographs and their case notes for the third time. They had a lot information about what had happened, but not much about why or who. There was a sense of desperation in the room; time was running out.

"Let's see if we can apply some logic to what little evidence we have." Charles eyes widened as he slid his chair closer to the desk.

"We believe Miss Bechet was a spy and Miss Channing is most likely also a spy," Vincent said. "With all of those passports we can't say who Miss Bechet—"

"I mean let's start before that."

"When?"

"Before the *Southern Cross* sailed from New York."

"New York?"

"Yes, while I stood on deck watching the dock workers and line-handlers on the pier ready the ship for departure, I noticed a lone woman in her sixties standing in the shadows some distance from the gangway."

"There were a lot of people on the pier in New York. Why does a sixty-year-old woman stand out in your mind after all that has happened?"

"I remember her *because* of all that has happened. The scene was peculiar as she didn't appear to be waiting for anyone yet didn't attempt to board. With her travel bags sitting beside her, she was obviously a passenger on the *Southern Cross* and could have boarded anytime."

"Maybe she just didn't want to deal with the crowd of people going up the gangway? You know how some people are about crowds and noise."

"There was more to it. She was intently watching each passenger as they checked in and ascended the gangway. She attracted my attention because she was so obviously concentrating on the face of each passenger, as if looking for someone."

"Possibly she intended to join someone onboard. You know, a traveling companion."

"It was more as if she wanted to avoid someone. She was almost the last passenger to board and didn't appear to meet anyone before she disappeared below deck. As I think back on her, she resembled our Miss Channing, although a bit older."

"So why make the connection now?"

"I don't know. It's just one of those loose ends that rattle around in your brain and pop to the surface when least expected. I was lying in bed this morning thinking over the events of the last few days when a picture of Miss Channing jumped into my head. I'm always studying people in a crowd. It's one of my pastimes. It drives Bree up the wall. She says it's not polite, and one day someone's going to punch me in the nose."

"Do you think the old lady on the pier was Miss Channing?"

"I don't know, possibly. No, I'm not sure." Charles' brow furrowed as he shook his head. "She could have been someone who was taking her first cruise and apprehensive, or it could have been something else. However, I think there was more to her than met the eye."

Charles paused and turned toward the porthole as he ran his hand through his hair.

"I never used to think about spies; now everyone looks like one."

"These days spies are so adept at disguises," Vincent said. "One could sit right next to you on the bus and you would never know it."

"Or at dinner?" Charles said. "Miss Channing is our prime suspect considering her cabin and what we found or didn't find. All we know about Miss Channing is what she told us at dinner Saturday night. We naturally want to believe what people say about themselves. Our relationships are developed within an expectation of truth."

"The passenger list has a Miss Mary Channing traveling alone to Los Angeles," Vincent said. "Her nationality is listed as Dutch. She had to show a Dutch passport when boarding in New York."

"Miss Channing's uncommon knowledge about smallpox and the doctored saccharin tablets we found in her cabin lead me to believe she was schooled in the dark art of using chemical weapons. There is no other plausible explanation for the abrupt change in Miss Bechet's health at the end of dinner on Saturday. Miss Channing wouldn't give James Amherst any saccharin, even though we now know from what we found, she had almost a full bottle. The tablets had already reached their intended mark, so there was no need to make James sick or attract attention."

"How would Miss Channing know Miss Bechet would drink coffee and take saccharin tablets from her instead of using sugar from the table?"

"I believe the tainted saccharin was just one of many weapons available to her, and the opportunity to utilize the tablets presented itself at the end of dinner. Given other

261

circumstances the weapon used may have been entirely different. The only constant was that Miss Bechet was the target."

"This person, Miss Channing, is so practiced at putting on makeup and wearing a disguise that she may have been a professional actress before becoming a spy."

"That may be true, but our unanswered question is, what role is she playing now?"

There was a knock on the door. When Vincent answered, Captain Ashcroft was standing in the passageway with a pot of coffee and three cups.

"Please come in. We didn't expect to see you this morning, sir."

"I received a wire from the FBI. The two FBI agents and a British agent are waiting in Havana. When they board, I'll have them escorted to this cabin. The ship will dock on time, so you'll have about an hour after they board before we tie up at the pier. The passengers will be free to go ashore as soon as the gangway is in place."

"I will be glad to turn over this case to the FBI, but an hour won't give them much time."

"Thank you for bringing the coffee," Charles said. "I need the caffeine."

"I figured as much."

"We'll need access to the safe-deposit boxes and to Miss Bechet's body and cabin after the FBI has joined us," Vincent said.

"I will station two stewards outside this cabin who will be at your disposal and the purser will stand by in his office. Is there anything else I can do for you before I go to the bridge?"

"No, sir. I think we have all we need," Vincent answered. "I only wish we had the killer in custody."

"Doctor Jeffery, do you require anything else before I leave?"

"No, sir. There isn't much we can do, except continue to go over our information in hope of discovering something we missed."

"Then I'll see you gentlemen after we dock." With that, the captain exited their cabin and proceeded to the bridge.

Vincent looked at his watch and suggested they take a break for about an hour to relax and catch up with their wives before they fell any deeper into the doghouse.

As they walked down the passageway leading to the weather deck, Charles slowed. His expression was stark as he looked down. Vincent walked on a little further and then turned back.

"What's wrong?"

"Shortly, the case will be in the hands of the FBI, but you will never be able to tell Marie what we have been doing for the last three days."

"I know."

Briana and Marie were still sitting in deck chairs on the sun deck by the pool when Charles and Vincent located them.

"Well look who's here," Marie said. "We wondered if you two had fallen overboard. Did you meet with the captain again this morning?"

Vincent's and Charles' eyes met in silence.

Some passengers sat nearby, but no one appeared to have heard Marie's question except Robert Blackwell, who was sitting under the cabana by the edge of the pool, still reading Ibsen's *Peer Gynt* and drinking vodka on the rocks. Robert paused and looked up.

"Steward, would you bring me another vodka on the rocks?"

Blackwell lit a cigarette and returned to reading.

Phillip Lansing strolled past, hesitated, and returned to where Blackwell was sitting.

"Excuse me, but may I borrow a cigarette from you? I seem to have forgotten mine in the cabin."

"Help yourself."

"Thank you, I was about to have a nicotine fit. You saved my life. Well, I must be on my way. Helen is up here somewhere." With that Phillip strolled off to the other side of the ship where he found Helen near the bow, leaning against the handrail and watching the porpoises swim in the wake of the ship.

"They always do that," Phillip said as he approached.

"Always do what?"

"The porpoises always swim with ships whenever the ships enter or leave port. It is a good omen. You know, like seeing a rainbow or a red sky at night. It is a sailor thing."

"You're in good spirits this morning, Phil. Since when did you take up smoking?"

"The water is blue, the weather is fair, and we are about to pull into Havana, Matey. Who knows what precious treasures we may find?"

"Matey? Phillip what's in that cigarette?"

"Nothing, dear." Phillip took the last drag on his cigarette and tossed it into the water. "Now I understand why American cigarettes are in such demand overseas."

They stood at the handrail a little longer and then moved to a pair of empty deck chairs to watch the parade of passengers as they circled the sun deck. Phillip made the comment that the passengers looked as nervous as a group of virgin sailors about to hit their first foreign liberty port. Helen couldn't help herself as she burst out laughing. Phillip wasn't normally a morning person.

"Something has you going. You sure you haven't been at the bar already this morning?"

"No, it is just a good day to be a poet and be alive. I finally solved a problem I have been working on for days."

"What was that?"

"I will tell you later, but I need to discuss it with somebody else first."

Chapter Thirty-four

Schulte watched from the promenade deck as the *Southern Cross* slowed long enough for the motor-launch to come alongside and discharge its passengers. The Cuban customs agents, the harbormaster, and his "staff" came aboard and were greeted by the ship's first officer, who escorted them from the main deck.

"Smith . . . damn it. How did he get here? I should have slit the old man's throat at Penn Station Friday night."

Schulte plunged down the stairs and dashed through the passageways toward a cabin several decks below. Adrenaline surged through Schulte's veins as the ship closed in.

"Martha, are you sure we haven't left anything behind?" an elderly gentleman said as he set two bags outside their cabin door. He looked up just as Schulte careened past and knocked him back into his cabin.

"Get out of my way, decrepit old fool!"

The man's wife hurried to the door to help her husband up and confront his assailant, but the passageway was empty.

Two bells sounded over the ship's intercom as Schulte shoved past a steward pushing a cartload of luggage, knocking the top bags to the floor.

"Hey, watch where you're going," the steward said as he bent over to pick up the bags.

Schulte turned the corner and jumped down the narrow stairs, guided only by the handrails. Cabin 228 lay just ahead.

"Where's the key? Shit, where's that damned key?" Schulte's hands frantically fumbled through empty pockets.

"At last."

The door flew open and slammed shut with a crash. A "Do Not Disturb" sign swayed violently on the doorknob and almost fell to the floor.

"No time to waste." Schulte's breath came in anxious bursts like a trapped fox about to chew its leg off. "Less than an hour to change."

There was a knock at the door.

"Sir, it's the steward. Will you be placing bags in the passageway?"

"No. Don't bother me. I can take care of myself. Leave me alone." Schulte flew into the bathroom and dumped the makeup kit on the counter.

"Damn it. I don't have time for this."

Chapter Thirty-five

Captain Ashcroft and a steward met the boarding party on the main deck.

"I'm sorry there isn't time for pleasantries, but we will dock in under an hour." The captain turned to the steward. "Please escort these gentlemen to Doctor Jeffery and Inspector Bedeau in Cabin 25."

Inspector Bedeau closed the door and everyone crowded around a small oaken table located at the center of the cabin.

"What have you found out?" Masters said.

"Doctor Jeffery performed some rudimentary chemical analyses. From the results we concluded one of the other passengers, Miss Mary Channing, poisoned Miss Bechet, but we still haven't determined her motive." The inspector landed Smith a likeness of Miss Channing. "It's possible that Miss Channing may be a foreign agent."

"Not one of mine," Smith said as he passed the likeness to Masters.

"The ship's crew has searched the ship from top to bottom, but Miss Channing has disappeared without a trace. An examination of her cabin yielded nothing other than a bottle of tablets we believe were used to incapacitate Miss Bechet. The file folder on the table includes a complete report of our findings, affidavits from the witnesses we interviewed, and photographs of the crime scene."

Masters leafed through the file folder and returned it to the table. "Do you have anything else?"

"We did have an unrelated event where a jewelry case was taken from Miss Bechet's cabin after she died," the inspector said. "However, we were able to recover the case and its contents."

It took a few more minutes to answer all of the questions. When the briefing was completed, Smith opened the file folder and turned to the pictures of Miss Bechet.

"This was one of my agents." Smith's voice cracked as he placed the pictures face down on the desk and turned away. "It's Nancy Bechet. I'll need to see her body to make an official identification, but from the pictures I'm sure it's she."

The room fell silent. Doctor Jeffery glanced at Inspector Bedeau and shifted uncomfortably on his feet.

"Although we only briefly met, my wife and I quickly developed a bond with Miss Bechet."

"She had that effect on people," Smith said as he regained his composure. "May I see the jewelry case."

"It's in the ship's safe." The inspector picked up the phone and called the purser's office. "Please deliver the safe deposit box containing Miss Bechet's jewelry case to Cabin 25."

"It will be here momentarily," Inspector Bedeau said turning toward the others.

Smith took a deep breath and let it out slowly. "I need to locate my other agent. Blackwell should have seen me board the ship and already contacted me. I'm concerned he's in trouble."

The inspector looked surprised. "Robert Blackwell?"

"Yes, do you know him?"

"I have met Blackwell. He takes his meals at the same table as my wife and I. He was seasick the first day after leaving New York and didn't join us for meals until Sunday morning."

"That's just like Blacky. He wasn't seasick, just hung over from a night on the town. Serves him right, the bounder. He never learned the meaning of moderation. Do you have any idea where I might find him?" A smile returned to Smith's face with the prospect of learning what Blackwell had discovered about the German.

Inspector Bedeau glanced at his watch. "At this time of day my wife has seen him sitting on the sun deck reading Ibsen and drinking vodka on the rocks."

"Ibsen?" Smith's expression turned to one of concern. "Ibsen doesn't sound like the Blacky I know. He wouldn't read anything deeper than the comic section of the daily paper, and he certainly wouldn't be caught dead with vodka in his glass. He's a dyed-in-the-wool gin and tonic man. Never could stand that Russian crap; believed vodka should be used to remove paint."

"Blackwell seems quite well-read," Inspector Bedeau said. "He always interjected poetry during our conversations and even quoted a line from one of Shakespeare's sonnets at dinner the night after Miss Bechet was killed."

"Blacky couldn't tell a joke, let alone repeat a line from Shakespeare. He wouldn't know a poet even if the bugger bit him on the ass. Describe this mysterious Mister Blackwell to me."

"He's Caucasian with a slight build, weighs about 140 to 150 pounds, has dark brown hair, is clean-shaven, and stands about five and a half feet tall. I would guess he was in his early thirties. He's kind of a pretty-boy."

"That's not Blacky. By any stretch of the imagination Blacky couldn't be called *pretty*. He's almost six feet tall and weighs near 180 pounds with gray-black hair. I won't say he's fat, but he shows his mileage. In his late forties with a lightly pock-marked complexion, he always has a five o'clock shadow."

Smith's fists clinched and his nails dug into his palms.

"That Nazi bastard has killed another of my agents."

"We can't be sure Blackwell is dead," Masters said. "He could just be tied up and locked in a closet."

"Spies don't leave loose ends . . ." Steel's voice trailed off as he realized what he had just said.

While the others talked, Inspector Bedeau picked up a pencil and note pad from the desk and started to sketch a likeness of Blackwell from memory.

"My agents were assigned to this case at the last possible moment." Smith shook his head and looked at Masters. "They had no idea what was coming and didn't know whom to look for. They were supposed to observe the ship for anything unusual or anyone who appeared out of place. *That's all*."

Smith exhaled loudly through tight lips as his body tensed. A look of resolution swept over his face.

"The German could have assumed the role of a tourist and gotten away scot-free. He must have recognized Bechet and Blackwell and thought they were on to him."

Except for the ticking of the alarm clock on the desk, the cabin became graveside-quiet. No one spoke or even dared breathe. It was clear from the charged expression on Smith's beet-red face and the veins pumping in his neck that he was ready to dismember the first Nazi he found.

After what seemed an eternity, Doctor Jeffery cleared his throat.

"Just before you arrived, one of the passengers told me that he felt Robert Blackwell was not who he claimed to be. Professor Lansing believed they had met sometime in the past and finally recognized Blackwell as an actor he had seen in a number of plays in Germany."

"Why didn't you bring the professor up sooner?" Smith's eyes flared as he spun to face the doctor.

"Until a minute ago I didn't know Blackwell had anything to do with this case."

"What makes Lansing such an expert on German actors?"

"He's a professor in the drama department at the University of California in Los Angeles specializing in Shakespearean and contemporary German drama. He wrote a book about German theater and has conducted research in Germany for a number of years."

"So what about this actor?"

"He had made an impression on the professor because of the wide variety of roles, male and female, that he played with ease. However, he dropped out of sight in the early thirties. The professor said the actor's stage name was Hans Zimmerman and he is positive the man pretending to be Blackwell is Zimmerman."

"We need to talk to Professor Lansing without delay."

There was a knock at the door. Inspector Bedeau took the safe deposit box from the steward. "Thank you. Please quickly locate and escort Professor Lansing to this cabin."

The inspector unlocked the safe deposit box and handed the jewelry case to Smith. It was a small rosewood box, not ornate. A simple brass hasp secured the lid, and a strip of half-round decorative molding accented its base.

Smith studied the case and, removing its contents, thoughtfully arranged them on the table.

"Not much to show for a life's work." He began to replace the jewelry in the case, but stopped when he recognized a silver Celtic spiral ring he had given Miss Bechet a number years ago as a token of a growing friendship. A relationship he had always hoped would go further, but it was not to be. They had just remained friends.

I don't believe she still has this ring—ten years and a lifetime later.

Smith's eyes began to glisten as he remembered Nancy. He wiped his eyes and started to place her jewelry in the case, but held back the ring and slipped it into his pants pocket. As he closed the lid he noticed an almost imperceptible misalignment where the molding joined in one corner.

"Cor, wait a minute. What have we got here?"

Smith examined the case for a minute and then slid the bottom to one side. A piece of paper fell onto the floor. He picked it up and saw "Channing" and "Chris Schulte, Paris 1936" scrawled on a piece of the ship's stationery. The writing was not typical of Nancy's beautiful penmanship. It was sloppy and appeared hastily written, almost drunken.

"In 1936 Miss Bechet was working undercover in Paris." Smith handed the note to Masters. "She was tracked by a German agent named Chris Schulte, but was able to elude him."

Inspector Bedeau reviewed the passenger list. "There's no passenger by that name."

"Miss Bechet must have recognized the German agent as one of the passengers," Doctor Jeffery said. "Possibly disguised as Miss Channing."

"We're already hunting for Channing and this Zimmerman character," Masters said. "Does this mean we should be searching for a third German? It's going to be hard enough finding one Nazi spy on a ship crawling with

German tourists, let alone finding a pack of 'em. This case is turning into a scorpion race to hell and we're losing."

Inspector Bedeau set the sketch of Blackwell on the desk and reviewed the passenger list again.

"Blackwell was assigned to Cabin 228."

Doctor Jeffery rotated the sketch to get a better look. 'Say that's a good likeness. It looks just like Blackwell, I mean the impostor."

"If we're going to hog-tie these agents, we need to move quickly," Masters said as he looked at his watch. 'The ship docks in less than forty minutes. We should concentrate on locating the agent impersonating Blackwell since he is our most credible lead. Any description of Channing, including Inspector Bedeau's likeness, is useless. By now the agent has changed into another character."

"I concur," Smith said. "We'll split the inspector and doctor up since they have both seen Blackwell's imposter. Inspector Bedeau has spent the most time with the impostor so he and Steel should observe the main deck while Masters, Doctor Jeffery, and I search Blackwell's cabin."

Doctor Jeffery picked up the phone and requested a steward with a master key meet him in the main starboard stairway leading to the 200 level.

Masters handed Steel the drawings of Channing and Blackwell. "If you spot someone who resembles either of these sketches, place him under surveillance. He may not know we are on to him, so go easy. We don't want to spook him or he'll burrow in deeper than a black-legged Louisiana tick on a dog's butt."

Chapter Thirty-six

A steward met Doctor Jeffery and the others at the top of the starboard stairway and followed them down to the head of the passageway leading to Cabin 228. In the distance they could see a "Do Not Disturb" sign hanging from the door knob.

"How long has that sign been there?" Masters asked.

"Ever since we left New York on Saturday," the steward said. "I've not entered that cabin for the last three days and, frankly, I didn't want to after encountering Mister Blackwell the first day out. I thought he was on deck, but to my surprise he was in the cabin lying on the bed. He jumped up and slammed the door shut, nearly cutting my fingers off, and yelled that if he needed anything he would ask for it. Quite rude."

Masters glanced at Smith and slipped his Colt from its shoulder holster. He flipped the cylinder out, verified all six chambers were loaded, and slapped it back in place. He moved onto the balls of his feet and focused on the door to Cabin 228.

"I hope we surprise the German in the cabin. He won't go down without a fight. A shoot out in the cabin will be messy, but not nearly as bad as one surrounded by innocent passengers."

Smith looked at the other cabin doors lining the passageway. Someone needed to clear the occupants.

"Steward, please give me your coat and master key; then go to the far end of the passageway and block the stairwell to prevent anyone from entering from that end."

Smith put on the steward's coat and hurried to the first cabin. He quietly tapped on the door.

"It's the steward ... I came to verify your dinner reservations for tonight." When no one answered, he used the master key to ensure the cabin was empty and quickly moved to the next. When he reached the end of the passageway, he knocked on the last door.

"Who is it?" A voice came from the other side of the door.

Crap, someone's inside.

"Ship's steward."

An elderly gentleman opened the door.

"We're not ready to have our bags picked up."

Smith could see a woman packing a suitcase at the far end of the cabin.

"You and your wife need to leave immediately," Smith whispered.

"What? You'll have to speak up," the man said loudly as he cupped his hand to his ear. "What did you say?"

"You have to excuse my husband," the woman said as she joined them at the door. "He's hard of hearing. Can I help you."

"There is an emergency, and I have to ask you to leave your cabin immediately. You will be able to return for your bags later."

She looked at Smith without responding. He was sure by now they had lost the element of surprise and said the only thing he could think of.

"Ma'am, we don't have time. Please, you need to leave now. Several poisonous, Brazilian jumping sea snakes have been seen on this level. We can't let you stay here until they are trapped. You need to be very quiet; they are attracted by noise and attack without warning."

"What's he saying?"

"Shush." She grabbed her husband's arm and pulled him into the passageway. He started to say something, but she quickly covered his mouth. "Shush, Fred. Be quiet."

Smith ushered the couple to the steward and returned to Masters and Doctor Jeffery.

"All clear."

"What was all that about?"

"Jumping sea snakes. I'll tell you later."

"Doctor Jeffery," Masters said, "please stay at this end of the passageway until we call for you. We don't want you hurt. Smith, you ready?"

"Right." Smith became aware of a steadily escalating sense of foreboding as he drew his Webley forty-four and checked the clip. "Maybe we'll get lucky and surprise the German sitting on the commode—taking a crap. That would suit me just fine."

Masters moved to one side of the door and Smith the other. Using the master key, Smith quietly unlocked the door. Masters pushed the door open and jumped through the doorway, ending up behind the bed, as Smith switched on the overhead light.

"Clear," Masters said.

Smith rushed to the closed bathroom door and, standing to one side, threw it open as Masters covered him. When the door slammed against the wall, Smith looked in the mirror and saw the bathroom was empty. Clothes were strewn everywhere.

"Clear."

Smith motioned his gun toward the closet door. Masters nodded.

The unmistakable stench of decay filled the air. It reeked like the back alley of an Oklahoma slaughterhouse on a hot summer night. Smith knew what it meant but hoped he was wrong. No one wanted to take the next step, but someone had to. Masters edged up to the closet and cracked the door open. It was empty except for a large black steamer trunk.

"Cabin's clear. Come on in, Doc, and close the door," Masters said, throwing open the only porthole for some air. "Damn, this place stinks. Smith, give me a hand. Let's pull his trunk out."

Smith and Masters grabbed the nearest leather handle and began to pull.

"Easy, it's heavy," Masters said as they moved the trunk into the center of the cabin. "What a smell."

"Damn trunk's locked."

"Not for long." Masters whipped out the largest folding knife Smith had ever seen and popped the brass hasp open with a snap.

"I know I'm not ready, but . . ." Smith drew a deep breath and opened the trunk lid just far enough to glance inside. His worst fears were soon confirmed. A man's bloated, decaying body was stuffed inside. He recognized a signet ring belonging to Blackwell on the swollen little finger of the man's right hand. Smith slammed the lid shut as his hands began to shake and perspiration covered his brow.

"It's Blacky, I told him not to wear that damn ring when he was on assignment."

Smith rushed toward the open porthole reaching it just as nausea overwhelmed him. He was in the unfamiliar position of not being in control. Instead of anticipating and planning the next move, he was only able to react as the case continued to rapidly spin out of control.

"Damned German." Smith used his handkerchief to wipe the vomit from his face as he crossed to the bathroom to rinse the bile from his mouth. When he returned, he glared at Masters.

"Blacky shouldn't have ended up like that. This Nazi has my undivided attention. I'll find him, even if it takes the rest of my life."

"Let's see what we can uncover in this cesspool," Masters said. "Maybe the Nazi forgot something that may help us figure out what part he's playing now. We need to hurry. The ship docks soon."

Masters and Smith searched the main cabin while Doctor Jeffery examined the bathroom. They didn't know what they were looking for—just any scrap of information that might lead them to the Nazi before he got away or killed again.

Smith jerked the drawers out of the dresser one by one. He dumped their contents onto the bed and tossed each drawer on the floor. The drawers held a mixture of men's and women's clothes, but he saw nothing of help to the investigators.

Masters edged up to the bed and looked through the items strewn on the bed hoping to find anything Smith might have overlooked in his haste to seek revenge.

"Look at all these women's clothes. Cripes, this guy's a cross-dresser. What the hell is this?" Masters pointed to a white dress, white shoes, cap, and black wig sitting near the edge of the bed.

"That's the disguise he used to fool Miss Bechet," Doctor Jeffery said from the bathroom, "There's a complete stage makeup kit in here—wigs, eyebrows, glasses, beards, and more. This Nazi could be disguised as anyone by now. A Nazi hiding on a ship of five-hundred passengers and who knows how many crew members."

Masters spotted several poetry books, including a copy of Ibsen's *Peer Gynt,* lying on the nightstand next to the bed. He opened the *Peer Gynt* to the title page.

"There's an inscription in here: 'To Chris with all my love, Elsa.' I wonder who Elsa is? I'll bet this 'Chris' is the same 'Chris Schulte' mentioned in Miss Bechet's note and might even be Professor Lansing's 'Hans Zimmerman' since this book is in Blackwell's room."

Smith slammed his fist on the dresser. "That ties it! The nurse's uniform, the book inscription, and your UCLA professor identifying the person pretending to be Blacky as Zimmerman all point to Channing, Schulte, and Zimmerman being only one person. We are looking for one agent who assumed the role of the ship's nurse, Miss Channing, and then Robert Blackwell. This Zimmerman or Schulte is a one man acting troupe."

Masters glanced around the cabin trying to put everything they had found in perspective.

"This cabin gives me the creeps. Can you imagine sleeping and casually reading poetry next to a dead body in the closet? This guy's sick."

"He's more than that," Smith said. "He's a time-bomb, not exhibiting the subtlety or self control of an under-cover agent, but only the callousness of a serial killer. There is another agenda in his actions; he's gone rogue. I doubt even the Abwehr could control him now. His rampage started last year when his girlfriend was killed by a subway train in Brooklyn."

Masters picked up an open pack of Haus Bergmann Privat German cigarettes laying next to an ashtray jammed with cigarette butts.

"When does this guy *not* smoke?"

"That's the same brand of cigarettes Vincent and I found in Miss Bechet's ashtray," Doctor Jeffery said from the bathroom.

Masters looked in the trash can sitting beside the bed. It contained a number of empty cigarette packs along with several empty vodka bottles and a lot of cotton balls.

"I understand the cigarettes. This guy's from Germany, but what the hell are the cotton balls for? Some of these butts have lipstick on 'em. Are you sure it's one person?

Maybe we should be looking for Channing *and* Schulte or Zimmerman?"

Smith stopped what he was doing and glared at Masters.

"We just have one Nazi who is a chain smoker and sometimes wears lipstick. I don't give a damn. This spy will be a dead Nazi if I have anything to say about it."

Masters looked down as the public address system announced the *Southern Cross* would be docking in thirty minutes.

Doctor Jeffery stepped out of the bathroom holding a dark green velvet evening dress. "The makeup kit and the other items confirm this guy was the actor Professor Lansing spoke to me about. This was the dress Channing wore at dinner our first night at sea. I remember it because I thought it was strange to be wearing a high neck, heavy velvet evening dress on such a humid night. Later, I asked Bree and she said Miss Channing was just old fashioned."

"The dress confirms Miss Channing and the German spy are one and the same," Smith said. "The high neck was probably used to hide his Adam's apple. In London, the female impersonators sometimes wear chokers. You know a band of velvet or a wide necklace around the middle of the neck."

"After going through all this crap, have we found anything that will help us catch this psychopath before he leaves the ship?" Masters asked as he picked up a drawer and slid it into the dresser.

Smith stooped to pick up the next drawer and hand it to Masters.

"Hold on, what's that?" Masters asked.

Smith turned the drawer over and removed the torn remnants of a brown envelope taped to the bottom. He looked on the floor and found the rest of the envelope under the bed.

"The contents of this envelope were removed in a damn hurry," Smith said.

Masters crawled on his hands and knees and looked under the bed.

"What are you searching for?" Smith asked.

"I don't know, just looking. Maybe something fell out of the envelope. Anyone got some matches?"

Smith handed Masters a matchbook from the nightstand.

Masters finished searching under the bed and crawled over to the dresser. He struck a match. In the initial flare Masters noticed the glint of something metallic.

"Well, just look what the cat drug home." Masters removed a half-hidden key from the seam between the rug and the floor molding behind the dresser.

"Looks like a safe-deposit box key," Smith said.

"The Nazi knows we are looking for him. He wouldn't have abandoned his books, cigarettes, and makeup kit if he didn't believe we were close. We have upset his rhythm and now he's starting to make mistakes."

Masters read the matchbook cover as he handed it to Smith. "This guy really gets around. These are from some dive in Panama called the Lotus Bar."

"The matches could be from anyone," Smith said as he tucked them into his pocket. "Matches have a way of getting around. Doctor Jeffery, was there anything in the bathroom to indicate what disguise we should look for?"

"No. All of the makeup was tossed into the kit with nothing left on the counter. There was a pile of men's clothes on the floor and several pair of men's and women's shoes in one corner by the shower. No way of knowing from the shoes or makeup kit if the German is disguised as a man or a woman."

"I'm sure he intended to leave the ship disguised as Blacky, until he recognized me as an MI6 agent," Smith said. "He panicked knowing Blacky was the first person I would look for. Cor, for all we know the German could look like Pope Pius by now."

"Blackwell has been dead for some time," Masters said. "He probably was killed as soon as the *Southern Cross* sailed from New York, even before Miss Bechet. Blackwell was the first victim."

"No, not the first," Smith said, "and probably not the last. This guy enjoys killing. I'm positive this is the same bastard who killed a Nazi spy at Penn Station last Friday night and three of my agents in Baltimore before that."

"We have the stage name of Hans Zimmerman and have been referring to the German as 'he,' but based on an obvious skill at wearing disguises, could we be dealing with a woman instead of a man?" Doctor Jeffery asked. "This person portrayed a convincing Miss Channing and ship's nurse. Until now I believed we were dealing with a man, but I'm not sure what to think now."

"The person we're looking for is a man," Masters said. "It would be easier for a man to play the part of a woman than the other way around."

"Look, I've really had it up to here with this man, woman crap," Smith said. "My instinct tells me we're dealing with a man, but it doesn't matter. It took someone with a good deal of strength to place Blacky in the trunk and move it into the closet. There are plenty of strong women in the world who are capable of moving a lot more than this trunk. The ease with which this spy assumes the role of a woman tells me he must be effeminate with fine facial features and probably long, narrow fingers. We know the Nazi was a professional actor before becoming a spy. He's accomplished at putting on disguises and assuming identities, and while we stand here and talk, the spy is escaping."

Smith looked at his watch. Five hundred passengers would be leaving the ship in less than twenty minutes. He thought of the crowd standing on deck and shook his head.

"Damn Nazi has beaten us."

Chapter Thirty-seven

Phillip and Helen Lansing rested in lounge chairs on the sun deck and watched the bustling waterfront as the *Southern Cross* eased into the mouth of Havana harbor. Motion was everywhere as Cubans moved through their daily routine, almost oblivious to the majestic ship's arrival. The shoreline of the harbor was filled with warehouses, buildings, and ships of all sizes. Several small peninsulas jutted into the waterway on the port side, and freighters transferred cargo to piers on the starboard side. The passenger terminal was straight ahead near the central area of town. Two small fishing boats were tethered across the pier from where the *Southern Cross* would eventually dock; the fishermen were busily stowing supplies and completing last minute preparations to depart. They had no time to watch the great passenger liner as it glided past them, for the tide was turning and they would leave soon.

"I did not expect the harbor would be so large and busy," Phillip exclaimed. "One can understand why

Spanish treasure galleons felt secure here. This is an amazing, natural harbor."

"Did you bring extra film?" Helen asked.

"We have four rolls of 120, counting the one in the camera. I do not think we will use it all, but I am sure we can always purchase more film in town if we do."

"Do you have enough flash bulbs?"

"Yes, dear. Everything is in the camera case: film, flash bulbs, lens paper, extra batteries, and light meter. We are all set to visit Havana as soon as they open the gangway. Oh, that reminds me, did you bring the traveler's checks? I do not have—"

"Excuse me, are you Professor Lansing?" a steward asked as he approached.

"Yes, what can I do for you?"

"Doctor Jeffery would like to speak with you immediately. He said it's imperative."

"Dear, please wait here for me; otherwise, I will never find you again. I think I know what this is about, and it should not take long. Can I leave the camera with you? Be careful; my passport is in the case. I will be back shortly."

"I'll be right here until you return," Helen said as she pulled a book out of her bag. "The Joads have just reached California. Steinbeck has me riveted."

"Professor Lansing, please quickly follow me, I'll escort you to Doctor Jeffery." The steward turned toward the stairs leading to the upper deck and Cabin 25.

'**P**hillip, I'm glad they were able to locate you in the crowd," Doctor Jeffery said as he closed the door. "This is Clive Smith and FBI Agent Masters. They are investigating an incident that happened on our way from New York. Mister Smith would like to talk with you about Hans Zimmerman."

"Professor Lansing, I understand you have information about someone who has been passing himself off as Robert Blackwell. I have a few questions, if you don't mind. Would you please describe this person to me? Be as concise as you can, we need to hurry."

"He is about five feet six inches tall with a thin build, possibly around 140 pounds. He is clean-shaven with well-trimmed, brown hair."

"Tell me what made you believe he was an impostor."

"Helen and I did not meet Mister Blackwell until he came to breakfast on Sunday morning. About halfway through breakfast I began to feel he looked familiar, but I could not place him. It bothered me all day. Later at dinner, when we learned Miss Bechet had died Saturday night, we all were shocked."

"Could you please be more succinct?"

"I am getting there. All of us were shocked except Mister Blackwell. He was strikingly cold, not showing any emotion. Eventually he quoted a line from one of Shakespeare's sonnets. It was a curious quote from Sonnet 15 and raised my interest. 'When I consider every thing that grows, holds in perfection but a little moment.'"

The ship's bell sounded. *Ding-ding, ding-ding.*

"Please professor, cut to the chase. We don't have much time."

"His delivery reflected someone who was a trained actor; so I intentionally misstated the origin of the quote to test his knowledge. However, he knew exactly where it came from and corrected me."

"An actor, you say? It's quite a leap from hearing one line of Shakespeare to concluding the person was a trained actor."

"As a professor in the Drama Department at UCLA, I have spent my whole life listening to people deliver lines from Shakespeare, on and off stage, and I know when someone has been trained."

"Anything else?"

"Yes, as I said, I could not connect his face with a name or place; however, I was fairly sure his name was not Robert Blackwell, and he was not from England. Earlier today, I was able to observe him for about an hour from the far side of the sun deck as he read. He was drinking vodka on the rocks, not the typical gin and tonic or Pimm's I expected from a Brit. He appeared to be smoking a foreign brand of cigarettes; so I approached him and asked if I might have one. My suspicions were confirmed, they were German Bergmann Privat cigarettes. The pieces finally came together. He was not from England, as he claimed, but was from Germany."

"Professor, I smoke Camels, but that doesn't make me an American," Smith said. "There must have been something else."

"Everything just fell into place. Everyone is an actor of sorts—even you, Mister Smith. Throughout our lives we

earn to play one character, ourselves. However, the true
ictor can portray many roles with believability and ease. I
ibserved these traits in the person pretending to be
Blackwell. I had studied him as an actor on our summer
rips in a number of contemporary German plays during the
early thirties. His name was Hans Zimmerman; at the time,
ie might have been the best actor in Germany."

"I am curious. You never met Zimmerman personally
lid you?"

"No, I only saw him on stage in plays."

"How could you identify him after nearly eight years if
ie was always in character, wearing makeup?"

"The costumes and makeup could not hide his innate
mannerisms. Each actor has his own style they employ
from role to role. That is why most actors tend to portray
similar characters throughout their career."

"Professor Lansing, Zimmerman is a killer and a
German spy—not just an impostor or a con-man. We need
o intercept him before he leaves this ship. Do you think
you could recognize him among the other passengers?"

"Possibly. There is a chance if I can observe him long
enough."

Smith needed to roll the dice and hoped they wouldn't
come up snake-eyes. He disliked using civilians in a
potentially dangerous situation, but in this instance there
vere no other options. Professor Lansing was their only
iope.

"We need to place the professor somewhere close to
he gangway where he can watch the passengers as they
issemble to disembark from the ship," Smith said. "I think
iis best position would be to stand at the railing on the

promenade deck just above the gangway. He will be able to look at the passengers as they approach the gangway from both directions. Masters, please find Steel and Inspector Bedeau and ask them to join us right away. We have to move fast."

Masters exited the cabin and located Steel and Inspector Bedeau on the main deck. They returned to Cabin 25 and were briefed. The plan was set; Smith hoped it would work, but they only had one more chance to catch the Nazi before he escaped.

"Restraint is in order, for the decks will be crowded with passengers leaving the ship," Steel warned as he looked directly at Masters. "The last thing we need is a wild-west shootout on a ship full of people."

"This ain't my first rodeo," Masters said, meeting Steel's gaze.

Chapter Thirty-eight

'Looks like it's about to rain toads and we don't have an umbrella," Masters said.

Smith scowled and pounded the railing in disbelief as a Cuban military truck sped onto the pier. Twenty well-armed soldiers joined Captain Gomez next to the *Southern Cross* and waited for the gangway to be tied off.

"What the hell is Gomez doing? I thought he was supposed to stay out of this case."

"We've just been bushwhacked," Masters said. 'Everybody has a rice bowl, and we appear to be in his. My guess is Gomez sees this as a golden opportunity to be the hero and maybe even secure a promotion. It looks like he reconsidered his options after we left his office this morning. There's nothing we can do; it's his country. If we're not careful, we could end up as inmates at *Presidio Modelo* learning how to speak Spanish and eating beans and rice twice a day. This just turned into a real Tijuana donkey show."

"Where's the line?"

"If we apprehend the Nazi while he is still onboard then he'll be in the custody of the FBI."

"What if he reaches the pier?"

"Assuming Gomez and his men aren't incompetent and they catch him, we'll attempt to extradite the Nazi from Cuba."

"I'm going to help Steel and Inspector Bedeau on the main deck," Smith said. "We'll need to overpower the Nazi as soon as we spot him before he can pull a weapon and the situation escalates. Doctor Jeffery, for your safety, remain here with Masters until I call you down."

Smith hurried aft and descended a ladder to the main deck. He joined Inspector Bedeau as he leaned on a fire hose rack several frames aft of the gangway. Steel observed the crowd from a location forward of the gangway hidden by stairs that led to the promenade deck.

A familiar face caught Steel's attention. He moved closer and glanced at the sketches Masters had given him.

The eyes, the ears . . . crap, it's the German!

Without hesitating, he charged directly toward the line where Schulte was standing.

Inspector Bedeau and Smith were monitoring the passengers when Smith heard a commotion erupt in the crowd on the main deck forward of the gangway. They raced to find Steel on the deck wrestling with a slightly built man dressed as a priest. Steel had jumped the passenger before he could pull a gun.

"Hold him while I put the cuffs on," Smith said. He couldn't believe their good fortune, they had caught the Nazi. The operation went down smoother than he had imagined.

Steel and Smith hustled the spy from the main deck into a near-by lounge. Maybe now they could get some answers. Smith was practiced in the fine art of persuasion and would soon have this priest singing soprano in the choir.

"Outstanding work!" Masters exclaimed as he rushed into the lounge.

"*Father*, I have to confess I'm a sadist," Smith whispered in German to the priest as he forced the priest's thumb hard against his wrist. "I plan to take you to a dark place only a man like you can appreciate, but where even the devil won't go. You're mine."

There was a loud commotion at the door as two nuns excitedly ran into the lounge screaming in French. Inspector Bedeau intercepted them and herded them to the other side of the lounge while Masters and Steel went through the priest's passport and papers.

"These sure are good forgeries," Steel said.

Inspector Bedeau returned after calming the nuns.

"Stop, he's not the Nazi. There's a slight resemblance, but this man *is* a priest."

"A *what*?" Smith said.

"He's a priest not a German spy. He's traveling with the nuns to work in an orphanage in Panama City. They don't speak English and don't understand what he has done wrong. We've got the wrong man."

"Crap, release him and tell him we are sorry," Smith said, as he and Masters flew out of the lounge and back toward the main deck. The Nazi was still out there. They had just made a costly mistake by exposing their hand and Smith wasn't sure how to recover.

"What a bunch of clowns. The agent ran right past me. Soon I'll be on my way to Brazil. All I have to do is cross the pier and board—"

"*Wieviel Uhr ist es?*" Professor Lansing asked a familiar figure wearing a blue dress what time it was.

"*Es ist zwei*—" Schulte quickly responded without thinking and then glared up at Professor Lansing as he stood, smiling, next to the railing on the promenade deck. The professor tipped his hat and infuriated Schulte even more. The Nazi raced toward the gangway; sending several people tumbling to the deck while others scrambled for cover.

"The old woman wearing the blue dress is your spy," Professor Lansing yelled to Masters and Smith as they appeared on the main deck.

Masters instinctively reached out as Schulte flashed by, but only captured a gray wig and hat. Tossing the items to the deck, Masters turned in pursuit.

Schulte ripped a pistol from the purse and fired several shots, missing Masters by inches. Paint chips flew into the ıir as the bullets ricocheted off the ship's steel structure ınd tumbled into the crowd.

"I've been hurt," a woman screamed as she collapsed n agony.

"Someone help my wife."

"Police! Everyone get down!" Smith thundered as he ıulled out his Webley and took aim. One of Gomez's men vho was already halfway up the gangway swung his semi-ıutomatic rifle toward the charging agent.

Schulte pointed the pistol at the soldier and smiled.

"Elsa, I have missed you."

"Don't shoot!" Smith yelled, but it did no good. The ;oldier didn't speak English. The rapid crack of gunfire lrowned out everything as smoke and the smell of burned ;unpowder filled the air.

Smith heard bullets strike the bulkhead behind Schulte ınd saw the Nazi spin to the right and tumble backwards 'rom the gangway into the water between the pier and the ;hip.

Smith and Masters rushed to the railing and looked ıver the side. They expected to find the Nazi floating next o the pier.

"Where the hell is he?" Smith screamed at Masters. The blood pounded in his ears as he tried to catch his ıreath. He couldn't believe that less than an hour ago he vanted to personally kill the Nazi with his bare hands, and ıow he was trying to save the bastard's life.

Smith and Masters scoured the water below. There vere no signs of the spy, no air bubbles, nothing but a ıandbag floating next to one of the pier pylons.

"He must have been hit," Masters said. "The Cuban should have cut him in half at that range. There's a blood trail on the deck and some more in the water below the gangway. No one could lose that much blood and live for long."

Smith and Masters shoved past the soldier on the gangway and dashed onto the pier. They needed the spy alive, not dead. Masters raced down a wooden ladder extending from the edge of the pier to just above the water. His foot slipped on the second rung from the bottom, and he almost fell head-first into the water. He managed to hold on and land with a thud on a wooden float between the ship and the pier.

Smith strained to see what was going on.

"Get the handbag before it sinks."

Masters fished out the handbag and listened for any sign of the spy. His eyes slowly adjusted to the low light under the pier, but there was no trace of the spy. Eventually accepting defeat, he returned to Smith.

"You're limping."

"I'll be all right, just twisted my ankle. There are too many shadows down there. I couldn't see or hear anything. If the Nazi didn't die when he was shot, he probably was weighed down by his disguise and drowned. The tide is going out and we may never find him, especially when the crabs finish."

Yashiro stood in the background on the promenade deck observing the tumult below when Schulte charged the gangway. As Yashiro quietly slipped below deck to avoid being noticed, he whispered the Japanese samurai principal

)f *Gyokusai*, the shattered jewel. "A great man should die
ıs a shattered jewel rather than live as an unbroken tile."

As quickly as it erupted the scene on the pier subsided.
ʒomez dispersed his men to search the pier and deployed
wo power boats to patrol both sides of the pier. He talked
o one of the soldiers, and then climbed into his jeep and
lrove away.

"That son of a bitch," Smith said. "He showed up to
nake a grandstand play and now that he screwed it up, he's
:vaporated like a ghost. My guess is he was *never* here."

"Bureaucrats are the same whatever language they
peak." Masters limped toward the gangway. "Gomez will
ʃrobably receive a promotion. The next time we meet him
'm sure he won't remember who we are. Let's return to
he ship and clean this mess up before the diplomats arrive.
Ne're going to be busier than a tomcat trying to cover crap
ɔn a marble floor."

*Cor, how hard can it be to find a wounded Nazi in
lrag, wearing a wet blue dress?*

Chapter Thirty-nine

The *Southern Cross* remained unsettled as Smith and Masters ascended the gangway to the main deck. The crew had already escorted the passengers from the weather decks into one of the lounges, the dining salon, or the library and were trying their best to calm and assure them the worst was over. Passengers who had not witnessed the incident were asked to return to their cabins and remain there until notified it was safe to leave.

One passenger had a superficial bullet wound in the arm. Beyond that no one else had been hurt except for a few minor scrapes received when diving for cover. A woman, who was standing in line next to the gangway when Schulte was shot, became hysterical and was taken to the sickbay by the ship's nurse.

The Cubans had secured the gangway and no one was allowed to leave the ship.

Smith and Masters were joined at the main deck railing by Inspector Bedeau, Steel, Doctor Jeffery, and Professor _ansing. Steel carried a list of passengers who were near he gangway when the shooting started. They needed to be nterviewed before they could leave the ship.

Smith continued to stare into the water where Schulte 1ad fallen. "Where could the body have gone? I should 1ave shot first and maybe the Nazi would have fallen on he deck instead of into the water. Damn this business. We 1ave lost an opportunity to uncover his espionage ring. This is just a temporary setback for the Nazis."

While Smith was lamenting what had transpired, a 1teward approached the group.

"Captain Ashcroft would like to speak with all of you. ?lease follow me."

"**B**e seated," the captain said as he poured a cup of coffee. "Would anyone else like coffee before we start?"

"I could use a cup of tea if you have it," Smith said.

The captain asked the steward to bring a pot of hot vater, a selection of tea, and an infuser to Smith. He stood 1t the head of the teak table in his office while the others 1eated themselves along the sides. Pacing back and forth vith a cigarette in one hand and a cup of black coffee in the 1ther, it appeared he didn't know whether to drink coffee 1r smoke his cigarette.

"When can I allow the passengers to leave the ship?"

"As soon as we interview the passengers who were 1ear the gangway, I won't need to hold them anymore,"

Masters replied. "But as far as leaving the ship, that's up to the Cubans and we have no control over them."

"Whom do we talk to on the pier?" the captain asked.

"Steel, please go and try to find someone in authority and press the issue," Masters said. "I am sure they won't make a commitment, but Gomez might make a decision faster if we apply some pressure. When we are finished here, I'll send a wire to Washington to make something happen at the diplomatic level."

"Very well," the captain said. "But please keep in mind a number of my passengers have connections today with other ships to continue their journeys. Those ships won't wait."

Steel excused himself from the others and stepped out of the office.

"Where do we stand with this investigation?" the captain asked.

"Events took on a life of their own when the Cubans showed up," Masters said. "One of the soldiers shot the Nazi as he tried to escape. We believe the Nazi either died directly from gunshot wounds or drowned; however, the body has not been recovered yet, so we can't confirm our suspicions."

"I had a clean shot to the shoulder, but the Cuban fired his weapon first and all hell broke loose," Smith said. "Gomez screwed everything up and then left us hung out to dry." Smith was clearly agitated over the unplanned appearance of the Cubans and Gomez's abrupt departure from the scene.

"I found a key in Blackwell's room. It may be for a safe-deposit box," Masters said. "In his haste to escape, the py ripped open an envelope that was taped to the back of ne of the dresser drawers removing something but losing his key behind the dresser."

Inspector Bedeau looked at the list of safe-deposit box olders.

"There's a box under the name of Blackwell. It's box umber 427."

The captain called the purser and requested the safe-leposit box be delivered to his office.

There was a knock at the door and Steel stepped in.

"I found a lieutenant on the pier who understood Inglish. He contacted Gomez and said the passengers ould leave the ship, but would need to present their papers o the customs agents in the terminal before they will be llowed to leave the pier."

"Good, at least we can start these people on their way," he captain said.

"Steel, where are the witnesses we need to interview?" Masters asked.

"They're in the ship's library."

"Captain, as far as the FBI is concerned everyone xcept the passengers in the library may leave the ship," Masters said.

"Very well." The captain picked up the phone and alled the first officer.

"Let's see if there is anything of interest in the andbag," Smith said as he dumped its contents onto the able. Some of the items were wet, but most were urprisingly dry.

"There isn't much here," Masters said as he started hrough the purse's contents. He opened a passport and a

303

ticket fell to the table. "We have yet another name to add to the long list of aliases this spy used. It's a Spanish passport this time in the name of Mister Chris Remirez, age sixty-three, from Barcelona."

"Obviously, there's no one with that name on the passenger list," Inspector Bedeau said as he looked at the ticket and checked the list. "This ticket, for passage today on the SS *Orion* from Havana to Rio de Janeiro, is made out to Remirez."

"So, the Nazi's destination was Brazil, just as I thought all along," Smith said as he looked at Steel.

In addition to the passport and the ticket there was an unopened pack of Bergmann Privat cigarettes and a wallet containing some Brazilian currency and an identification card in the name of Chris Remirez.

"It looks like we have reached the end of our rope. I agree this spy is the same bastard we have been chasing since New York. And now that the Nazi is dead there's nothing remaining, except to file reports and clean up this mess." Smith was disappointed. The contents of the purse hadn't provided any significant information.

Doctor Jeffery began returning the items to the purse, but stopped and looked up.

"This doesn't feel right," he said as he manipulated the purse. "I think there's something hidden in the lining."

"Let me see." Masters felt the purse. "You're right."

With that, he ripped the lining from the purse causing an envelope to drop onto the table. The envelope contained a key with a tag inscribed "Panama Shipping and Export Limited" and two typewritten pages folded within a one-

)age map. The pages and map were wet from being in the vater but were still legible.

"This is clearly a map of Brazil, but there's something vritten on it in oriental print," Masters said. "I can't make 1eads or tails of the two typed pages. What do you think?" 1e handed the pages and the map to the others.

Professor Lansing picked up the pages and silently ead them.

"These pages are written in German. They do not liscuss anything special. They are just a travel log of a veek long summer boat trip down the Rhine River in 3ermany."

"Then they have nothing to do with the map?" Smith sked.

"There does not appear to be a connection," Professor ansing replied.

"Why would a German spy have a map of Brazil with 1riental writing on it and a travel log of a boat trip on the 1hine hidden in the lining of a purse?"

"Your guess is as good as mine," Steel said.

"One thing for sure, we need to send an agent to 1anama Shipping and Export Limited in Rio de Janeiro to ind out what this key fits," Masters said.

Doctor Jeffery looked at the map while Masters was alking, but then he interrupted.

"The oriental writing is Japanese."

"Couldn't it be Chinese?" Inspector Bedeau asked.

"My wife and I collect Japanese calligraphy as a 1obby," Doctor Jeffery said. "The writing is Japanese, but I an't read it. Hold everything. Look at this."

He picked up the two typed pages and placed them in order, one directly on top of the other. The transparency of the wet paper allowed text on the bottom page to show through the spaces between words on the top page. Professor Lansing stood up and walked over to Doctor Jeffery. When the first page was placed over the second, the letters showing through the spaces seemed random; but when the order of the pages was switched, the letters appeared to have order and possible meaning.

Professor Lansing handed Inspector Bedeau a pencil and note pad as he started to translate from German.

"Please write this down as I read it to you. The first line reads: 3, d, 5, 1, m, s, 3, 2, d, 5, m, w."

"Got it."

Professor Lansing continued, "The second line reads: i, n, a, z, u, m, a, and the third line reads: t, a, g, 2, 0, 1, 2, 3, 9, and the fourth line reads: r, e, c, i, f, e. There is more to this document, but for now let us see if this first part makes any sense."

"So what do you make of it?" Masters asked.

"The first line sounds like latitude and longitude measurements," the captain answered. "Three degrees fifty-one minutes south and thirty-two degrees five minutes west." He went to a map case and brought back a chart showing Central and South America. "That's interesting, the coordinates are not in Brazil, but are located on Fernando de Noronha, an island about two hundred and thirty miles east of Brazil in the Atlantic, nowhere near São Paulo or Rio de Janeiro."

"There's an airfield on Fernando de Noronha," Smith said.

"I think the second line is the Japanese word for lightning," Doctor Jeffery said. "And the third line may refer to claim tag number 201239 for something in storage, maybe the item the key fits at Panama Shipping and Export Limited."

"No. It is a reference to a specific date," Professor Lansing said. The German word for 'day' is 'tag'. I believe the date in question is December 20, 1939, little more than four months from now."

"How did you come up with that date out of those numbers?" Steel asked.

"Europeans write the day, month, and then the year," Professor Lansing said."

"If you follow the shortest line from Fernando de Noronha west to mainland Brazil you end up at Natal," Captain Ashcroft said. "And south about a hundred sixty miles of Natal is the town Recife."

"Most likely *inazuma* is code for someone or an operation. Possibly the Nazi was going to meet someone in Recife on December 20th," Smith said.

The purser arrived with safe-deposit box 427 and placed it on the table in front of the captain.

"This box is heavy." The captain slid it to the edge of the table.

Masters inserted the key he found in Blackwell's cabin and opened the lid. Inside were a list of contacts in Brazil, a set of engineering plans for an airfield runway, and a large sum of Brazilian money. But most amazing of all, it contained eight Deutche Reichsbank one kilogram gold bars. Their embossed Nazi eagle and swastika insignias did not leave their origin in doubt. Everyone in the room stared, speechless, at the unbelievable sight as Masters stacked the bars on the table. They had all seen gold jewelry and coins, but no one had ever seen gold bars, let alone touched them.

"Holy crap." Steel whispered as he exhaled loudly. "What do you think those are worth?"

"Your guess is as good as mine," Masters answered.

"They *were* going to build an airfield in Brazil," Smith said.

"Yeah, looks like it," Masters said. "This is big. I'm classifying the contents of this box and everything to do with this case as *Top Secret.* No one is to discuss any aspect of this case or what we have found with anyone that does not have a need to know. This case is a matter of utmost national security."

Smith's worst fears were just realized. He knew all along if the FBI took control, he would be lucky to find out what day of the week it was let alone what was happening with the case. Masters had just buried everything under a mountain of red tape, and Smith knew he was now on the outside looking in.

"Steel, Smith, and I will be flying back to Miami tonight," Masters said. "I'll turn the material we have over to Washington for analysis. They can piece this together, but in my opinion, we have not seen the last of this issue. We have not recovered the body of the Nazi; so however improbable it might seem, he still could be alive. I agree with Smith, the spy was going to Brazil and the Natal region, maybe Recife. There's a new wrinkle in that the Germans and Japanese appear to be talking to each other.

We have stopped the plot for now, but we are still one step behind."

"And the pale horse approaches quickly on the horizon," Smith said under his breath as he contemplated the endless possibilities.

Why would the Japanese want anything to do with the Germans in the Americas? Is the common denominator the United States and the Panama Canal? The Atlantic is already at risk as Germany builds her U-boat fleet. Is the Pacific next?

Chapter Forty

A steward entered the cabin and approached Captain Ashcroft. He whispered something into his ear. The captain turned to face the others at the table.

"The Cubans have the spy on the pier."

"Great. Now, maybe we can find out some answers," Smith said as he headed for the door.

Everyone raced out of the cabin and ran to the pier. The Nazi lay between two soldiers in the back of a Cuban military truck.

Doctor Jeffery felt for a pulse.

"Well?" Masters asked, "How bad is he hurt? How soon will he be able to talk?"

"The Nazi is dead," Doctor Jeffery answered. He wanted to observe the bullet wounds on the Nazi's right side. He started to open the blue dress and then stopped and stepped back with a look of amazement on his face.

"What's the matter, Doc?" Masters asked.

Doctor Jeffery didn't say a word; he moved to one side so the others could view the body.

They all stood speechless for a moment as they couldn't believe what they were looking at.

"I'll be damned." Masters' eyes widened. "I didn't see that coming. He's a she."

Smith bent down and removed a cameo pendant from the dead spy's neck. "There's an inscription on the back: 'To Chris, love Elsa'. My guess is we are looking at Chris Schulte, who has just played her last role and won't be making an encore."

"Well, the most important thing is the spy and the mission have been stopped," Masters said. "The boys in Washington can sort this mess out. As far as I'm concerned, the case is closed."

Smith detested and admired the German. He detested the spy for the unnecessary killing of his agents, but couldn't help but admire the spy for her ability to convincingly play so many roles. Even Professor Lansing, who had followed the actor for many years, believed Chris Schulte under the stage name of Hans Zimmerman was a man. Smith knew it was only by the thinnest thread of luck that they were able to stop her. From now on Smith would be on his own.

As he contemplated what had recently happened, Smith concluded that Masters was dead wrong. The case was not closed. Masters and Steel would fly home to their comfortable offices and file their reports, and the FBI would lock the case up tighter than a whorehouse on Sunday, to steal one of Masters' West Texas sayings.

Smith shook his head. He had two more agents to bury and his own report to file, but the hunt was far from over.

Epilogue

December 20, 1939
Recife, Brazil

The Hotel Pousada Atlântico was empty except for the lodger in a room on the first floor next to the alley. The room didn't offer amenities and that fit the lodger's mood precisely. The sounds from the freight yard across the street pierced the late night as a lone switch engine transferred boxcars from one spur to another. Each time the switch engine changed direction the engineer would blow the air horn and the rail cars would clank together as the air brakes squealed.

It was a sweltering 87 degrees with 82 percent humidity at almost ten o'clock at night. Yashiro had remained motionless, sweating in bed for over an hour, watching a squadron of flies as they marked time by making aimless rounds over the bed. Neither the ceiling fan nor the open window helped. The fan blade refused to turn when Yashiro flipped the wall switch. All that had happened was that the aroma of hot electrical insulation mingled with the pungent smell from the stockyard down the block. The open window only let in more flies and more noise. Yashiro had discovered the room quickly became unbearable when the window was closed. At least the flies weren't mosquitoes, and maybe the breeze would change direction soon and start flowing from the ocean instead of the jungle.

I hate this place.

Yashiro reached for his cigarettes, but the pack was empty and a quick check of the whiskey bottle on the nightstand showed it had only a few drops at the bottom. He tilted the bottle over his mouth and drained it. Now the bottle was empty.

Damn it, the German should have been here by now. Where in hell is he? The meeting was supposed to be at nine-thirty. Nothing has gone right since I came to this humid hell-hole. I could use a cigarette.

The sound of footsteps in the hall became louder and then stopped as someone knocked on the door. Yashiro turned out the light and cracked the door open.

"It's about time you arrived. Werner, you're late."

"You're lucky I'm here at all. Two thugs jumped me as I came out of the bar down the street. Do you need a watch or a wallet? They won't be needing them."

"They didn't follow you, did they?" Yashiro asked as he turned on the light.

"They won't be following *anyone*." Werner coldly answered.

The unblinking stare of Werner's eyes told Yashiro he didn't need to pursue the matter any further.

"Do you have a cigarette?"

Werner pulled out a pack of Bergmann Privat cigarettes and removed the last two. He lit them and gave one to Yashiro.

"Are these things standard issue for you guys?" Yashiro asked as he exhaled.

"Beggars can't be choosers."

"I would offer you a drink, but I'm out of whiskey."

The sound of a siren grew louder and then faded as an ambulance passed by on the street outside the hotel. Yashiro instinctively looked at the door.

"Don't worry, it's just the meat wagon picking up two new passengers." Werner crumpled up the empty cigarette pack and threw it on the floor. "What about the delivery?"

Yashiro pulled out a brown leather briefcase. Werner opened it and inspected its contents.

"This replaces the funds lost in the Havana incident," Werner said as he removed eight Deutche Reichsbank one kilogram gold bars.

"Too bad about your agent being killed," Yashiro said.

"She was an arrogant bitch and deserved to die. Her actions unnecessarily attracted the attention of enemy agents and almost ended this mission. Besides the loss of the project funds, it is hard to know if the enemy obtained any critical information."

"I was there when she was killed. They probably believe the mission died with her."

"Can't be too sure. I moved the location of airfield construction to deeper in the jungle, making it harder to reach. All because of that damn prima donna. To her, life was just a series of roles. She never considered the consequences of her actions."

"I return to Panama tomorrow."

"I envy you and your involvement with Icarus. I'm only building an airfield, but you, my friend, will be destroying America's greatest engineering achievement."

Werner picked up the briefcase and exited the room. Yashiro sat on the edge of the bed and finished his cigarette.

It will be a relief to return to Panama. I haven't had a decent meal since I came to this miserable place.

Icarus Plot

The following pages contain an excerpt from *Icarus Plot*, a sequel to *Southern Cross*.

Icarus Plot takes place in the Panama Canal Zone in 1940. Tanaka Yashiro has returned to Panama and is ready to implement his plan to turn the Panama Canal into nothing more than a muddy ditch before 1941. Clive Smith and his agents must overcome bureaucratic apathy, a general American belief that the Canal is impregnable, and intentional subversion in Washington DC while they scramble to expose Yashiro's plan.

Icarus Plot will be released in 2012. Updates about my progress on *Icarus Plot* can be found on my website, MysteryAlley.com. I hope you find this excerpt entertaining enough to join Clive Smith and his band of MI6 agents in Panama.

Prologue (Icarus Plot)

March 21, 1940
Colón, Republic of Panama

Perspiration dripped from Tanaka Yashiro's forehead as he slammed his fist against the table in frustration. The other members of the Japanese Black Dragon Society sat, rigidly looking straight ahead, hoping to avoid Yashiro's wrath. The only sounds in the cramped room came from the traffic on Balboa Avenue and the boisterous crowd in the Lotus Bar, one floor below.

Yashiro's face reddened and his speech became deliberate as he leaned to within inches of Toshi Soto. "Stop this petty complaining and focus."

Yashiro pulled back and took a deep breath. Regaining his composure, he forced his extended finger tips against the tabletop and shifted forward as he glowered at the agents.

"Am I making myself clear?"

After a long silence, Toshi cleared his throat and began to speak, slowly at first.

CARUS PLOT (EXCERPT)

"But how long must we take these insults? Army guards detained me this morning at the main gate of Fort Davis. I have visited the administration building many times to repair typewriters, but this time a soldier I have known for years called me 'Jap' and made me wait for over an hour before allowing me to enter the base."

Yashiro's gaze snapped back to Toshi. *Kono yarou!*

"Toshi-san, you will smile and endure these insignificant insults. We are all suffering. Our mission is too critical for personal feelings. Keep in mind why we are here."

Their eyes remained locked in silent combat as a cloud of charged emotion filled the room. No one dared speak, or even breathe. Neither Toshi nor Yashiro looked away until the shrill siren from a passing police car blasted across the balcony and through the second storey window.

Toshi drew a hesitant breath and lowered his head.

"Yes . . . I understand, Yashiro-sama."

Yashiro turned to Makoto Nakamura. "Did the shipment arrive last night?"

"In all, six cases of dynamite are in my storeroom, but we should move them to a safer location."

Yashiro placed his gold rimmed glasses on top of a map showing Panama Canal's defenses and swept his hand across his close cut, salt-and-pepper hair.

"Gentlemen, yesterday was a day of great importance. I secured the allegiance of someone with access to all of the American facilities. The last step needed for Icarus is now in place."

The agents glanced at each other and silently nodded their heads in approval.

Yashiro turned to the dark elm liquor cabinet behind him and removed six small, white Kutani porcelain cups and a narrow necked flask containing Takara sake. He arranged them symmetrically on an antique black and gold lacquer tray and filled five of the cups.

Toshi stood, filled the sixth, and bowed as he handed it to Yashiro.

When everyone held sake, Yashiro offered a traditional toast.

"May the Emperor live for ten thousand years."

"And may our enemies soon feel the sharpness of our swords," Toshi added.

The agents stood and, facing a picture of Emperor Hirohito, raised their cups three times in unison.

"Banzai, Banzai, Banzai!"

Yashiro looked at the others and smiled while the dryness and burn of the rice wine flashed down his throat. Pride and a sense of victory filled his mind.

Now we wait for the rains to come.

Chapter One (Icarus Plot)

April 6, 1940

Colón lay outside United States jurisdiction. It was Mick Jenkins' type of town, wide open with gambling, bars that never closed, and women . . . lots of exotic women. Mick and the Bonner brothers, Alec and Jacob, were British MI6 agents who arrived from Morocco by freighter yesterday and were exploring the local culture.

"God, I love this place," Mick said as he lit a cigarette and exhaled a billowing cloud of smoke. "Can't you feel the energy?"

"You'd like anywhere with this many bars," Jacob said as they exited the Atlantic Nite Club. Jacob and his half brother, Alec, grew up near Whitecastle in the east end of London and spoke with Cockney accents.

Mick's eyes lit up when he noticed a captivating figure wearing a bright red dress with a sparkling floral pattern heading toward them.

"We've gotta learn the lay of the land and here comes one now."

He removed his white Panama hat, revealing slicked-back, jet black hair, and broadcast his best Cheshire Cat smile at the sultry brunette as she approached the Atlantic. The alluring scent of her gardenia perfume filled Mick's thoughts with anticipation when she swayed up to the entrance and reached for the door.

Mick jumped back and pushed the door open.

"Allow me. I'm Mick, and you're . . . ?"

The brunette brushed past him and entered the Atlantic without saying a word. She obviously wasn't the least bit impressed by Mick's grade-B mobster appearance, his gold tooth, or his irritatingly smug chivalry.

Alec adjusted his horn-rimmed glasses as he walked away. "You don't have time. His train arrives in five minutes."

"I know, but . . ."

"But nothing. Remember where he sent us after we lost that German in Manhattan?"

"Yeah, we were lucky to get out of that equatorial pest hole without head lice. I wouldn't give you a bob for the whole poxy place. I still have nightmares of iridescent, green snakes with ruby-red eyes."

"Equatorial?"

"Hey, I'm trying to improve my vocabulary. Someday, I just might write a book and become famous like that fellow, Hemingway."

The shrill whistle from an approaching train sounded repeatedly over the din on the street. They quickened their pace and rounded the corner onto Front Street, moving as if they were Saturday-night cowboys late for a public ianging. Dodging around the shoppers on the sidewalk, hey rushed past the open door of a cafe where the cook vas preparing chicken and plantains. The rich aroma of Caribbean spices and thick clouds of smoke from cooking iil spilled through the doorway and drifted down the street.

"Look there's some empty tables," Alec said.

"We don't have time, . . . remember?" Mick said as hey hurried past a line of customers and crossed the street oward the throng forming at the station.

The onlookers, mostly blacks from the West Indies, nveloped the platform on three sides with a carnival itmosphere. Despite the heat some men wore neckties and ong-sleeve shirts and, as was the custom, almost everyone vore a hat to escape the relentless sun. Men sported brown edoras or white panamas and women wore wide-brimmed, ight-colored hats with colorful bands. Street vendors did a irisk business selling flavored shaved ice from brightly iainted, two-wheel carts.

"Not a cloud in sight," Alec shielded his eyes from the un and searched the dark blue sky over Limon Bay. "I vish it would rain."

"No you don't," Mick said. "It would only get more iumid and when it starts, it won't stop till Christmas."

The train's brakes squealed with a high pitched grinding noise until the cars clanked to an abrupt stop. A oud rush of air escaped when the brakes released.

Alec surveyed the passengers as they pushed into the irowd and began weaving their way toward the street. He glanced around the platform and pulled a large white handkerchief from his back pocket. Mopping his brow, he looked toward Mick and shook his head.

"Where the hell is he?"

"Maybe he missed the train in Panama City," Jacob said as the last of the stragglers gathered up their belongings and left the platform.

Alec used his handkerchief again, but it was of little use. Stinging perspiration was soon running into his eyes and dripping from the tip of his nose.

"Cor blimey, now what?"

After three deafening whistles, the locomotive started to move, blanketing the bystanders in a cloud of pungent diesel fumes. The corrugated metal roof above the waiting platform rumbled with the pulsations from the powerful twelve cylinder engine as it strained to leave the station.

Mick lit a cigarette and watched the train round the bend and pull up the hill toward Mount Hope. *How could we have missed him?*

The whistle sounded one last time as the train disappeared in the distance.

Jacob reached into his shirt pocket and pulled out a cigarette pack. He crumpled it into a tight ball and dropped it to the ground.

"Can I bum one of your fags?"

As Mick handed Jacob the Camels, he noticed a nun and priest standing in the shadows behind a wooden pillar at the far end of the platform.

The priest picked up two well-traveled, brown leather suitcases and, scowling at Mick, started to walk away.

Mick's eyes followed the priest. *Strike a light, it's Clive. What's he made up for?*

Clive Smith was perfectly suited for a job as an MI6 agent. He was completely forgettable.

Clive bent down and whispered something to the nun. When she turned toward Mick, a ray of sunlight highlighted her thin, upturned nose and delicate features.

Mick didn't expect to see Gwen Wells in Panama and was disappointed the veil and tunic of the traditional habit hid all but her face from view. Normally her vibrant auburn hair and stunning figure wouldn't go unnoticed, even in a crowded room.

"What are you doing here?" Clive demanded, glaring at Mick.

"We came to meet your train."

"That's obvious. Why?" Clive shook his head. "Never mind. Let's get out of here."

Alec and Jacob took the bags from Clive as Mick waved for a cab. A cream colored, 1936 DeSoto DeLuxe taxi pulled to the curb.

"Where to?" The cabby said as he finished loading the bags and slammed the trunk lid.

"Hotel Washington, por favor," Mick said as he turned toward Gwen and winked. "It's not far, but in this humidity, with your luggage, it's best to take a cab. We wouldn't want you to get all sweaty, now would we, sister?"

As usual, Gwen ignored Mick's innuendos. Her eyes momentarily met Clive's and rolled upward as she leaned through the back door and pulled the jump-seat down.

Mick slid into the front, next to the driver, and turned toward Clive.

"How was the trip from Panama City?"

"Scenic, but tiring," Gwen said.

Clive remained silent and stared through the side window while the cab jammed into traffic.

After a short ride, they turned down a palm-lined drive leading to the hotel's entrance. The lush green foliage and bright flowers in the expansive garden stood out against the stark white walls of the three storey mission style building. Lavender bougainvillea vines hung from the portico and hibiscus bushes regaled with giant red, orange, and yellow flowers dotted the walkways. A mild breeze from Manzanillo Bay carried the rich, sweet scent of guavas and tree ripened bananas through the cab's open windows.

"Crappers, what's this? Looks like the bloody Taj Mahal." Clive inspected the high arches and ornate double doorway leading to the main lobby.

"This is our hotel . . ." Mick's voice trailed off as Clive bounded from the cab, followed closely by Gwen.

"Leave the bags and follow me," Clive said, without waiting. He marched past a grouping of over-stuffed chairs and a large Red Fronted Macaw perched in a polished brass cage near the doorway to the main lobby. Gwen gazed up at a gleaming crystal chandelier centered in a soaring, domed skylight as they bypassed the startled clerk at the front desk.

"May I help you?"

"No," Clive said sharply as he continued toward the back of the lobby and through the open French doors eading into the courtyard. He stopped when they reached he seawall adjoining Manzanillo Bay and glanced around; he courtyard was empty. Clive spun on his heels and glaring at Mick, poked his finger against Mick's chest.

"Why did you book us at this damned mansion?"

"Pretty ritzy, huh?" Mick's chest puffed up as he brushed his pencil thin mustache with his index finger.

"Roosevelt and Taft stayed here . . ."

"Bloody hell, I don't care if Tutankhamen is buried where we're standing, we're not staying. Do you think we're on holiday?"

"Well . . ." Mick nervously pulled at his mustache as he remembered the snakes.

"We're trying to conduct a clandestine operation and you set us up to stand out like chorus girls with pasties in a Saturday night burlesque show. I want you three to split up and find rooms in separate, cheap hotels, somewhere in the main part of town. Meet me tomorrow morning at eight by the flagpole outside the Atlantic Terminal Office in Cristóbal. Don't be late and, for Christ's sake, stop strutting around town like horny sailors on boot liberty."

Clive and Gwen crossed back to the lobby, grabbed their bags, and headed down the driveway toward the center of town.

Alec pulled off his glasses and wiped the lenses with his handkerchief. His eyes narrowed as he focused on Mick. "Guess he still hasn't forgotten about New York."

"Kinda looks that way to me too," Jacob said with a grin.

Mick took a deep drag and flipped his cigarette over the seawall.

"Bugger off."